AMONGST

ISBN 978-1-957077-47-5

Illustrations by Julie Anne Franklin.

Publisher's Cataloging-in-Publication data

Names: Vanderleest, Robert E., author.
Title: Amongst / Robert E. Vanderleest.
Description: Littleton, CO: Robert E. Vanderleest, 2023. | Summary: Thirteen-year-old Enoch is not a hero. He simply wants to babysit his giant friend Kahdi. But one day, Enoch and his friends stumble upon a secret that could lead their people safely across the mountains. Proving their theory will either make them the unlikeliest of heroes...or dead.
Identifiers: ISBN: 978-1-957077-47-5
Subjects: LCSH Friendship--Juvenile fiction. | Survival--Juvenile fiction. | Adventure and adventurers--Juvenile fiction. | Fantasy fiction. | BISAC JUVENILE FICTION / Fantasy
Classification: LCC PZ7.1 .V36

Publishing assistance by BookCrafters, Parker, Colorado.
www.bookcrafters.net

To Jana, Mali, and Jacob,

Thank you for putting up with years of manuscript piles, forced chapter reading, and generally weird author behavior. Most of all, thank you for making our house a loving home.

Rob/Dad

OLIA
PROTEC
LEGEND
ORIGIN
Lake of the Depths
DARNOC
Darnoc River
The CLIFFS
EGG ISLAND
THE SEA
RUNAL QUARRY

HEALER
NORTH
UPPER RIVER
FARMING
Verandale
SASHA
WEST
EAST
FISHING VILLAGE
The MARSH
SALT RIVER
SOUTH
KAHDI'S BOAT
SCHOOL
The SEA
Village Square
ENOCH'S HOME
FALO
KAHDI'S FAMILY
RELA'S AND NELA'S PENINSULA
WATER GATHERING BASIN
SPIKE PRACTICE
SAP TREES
LOWER RIVER
KAHDI'S ADVENTURES

Decades ago...

Olia, a small but fiery girl, waited impatiently in the middle of the road, in the middle of winter.

Olia-protec leaned against Olia's right hip, hard enough to let her know he was there, soft enough so as not to topple her over. Large puffs of air billowed out from his nostrils and over iced fur before settling into the morning mist. His tusks curved out from under muscled jaws and narrowed into points sharp enough to pierce a snowflake.

Olia was mad at her little brother, Isaac, and his friend. Not just because they were annoying, but because they were carefree and kept lagging behind. Carefree didn't keep eyes on the trees; carefree didn't keep one person watching the road behind; carefree didn't keep you from becoming a morning meal.

They were only halfway to school and already running late when Isaac's friend stole his hat.

Isaac lunged.

Olia-protec growled.

"Isaac so help me," Olia scolded between clenched teeth while grabbing both sides of his head, "stop messing around and keep your eyes on the forest!"

Isaac's friend ran ahead, crunching through the morning snow and giggling with his new hat, to a towering pile of hay stacked beside the road. Seeing the promising gleam of a coin in the shadows, he knelt to pick it up.

As he reached out his hand, the shadows moved.

Part I

~

Surrounded by Trees

It is not impossible to leave this land. It is impossible to leave this land with your body still wrapped around your soul.
—Ibrakrim the librarian

1

Enoch knelt in the darkness and tried to quiet his breathing.

The first warm winds of the growing season carried the smells of the forest through the open shutters and into his room. He breathed the smells of sap flowing down massive tree trunks and the fragrant flowers of tlok vines spiraling up from the forest floor. The scents were as sweet as the night was dangerous.

He peered outside at the latest family guard; name not yet memorized. Though much of the day's heat remained, the muscled guard shivered beneath his tunic.

"Get away from the window," he snapped at Enoch.

The guard gripped a loaded spike and focused his eyes on the trees at the edge of the forest. He scanned for a mewing kitten, obviously denied its proper share of survival instinct. No matter how hard he tried, his body startled at every sound.

"I just wanted to see," Enoch grumbled, knowing he was wasting his breath.

"You need to get back into bed or you will distract

me," he said waving Enoch away. "Then all you will *see* is a Cof eating me for dinner. You can listen to that from your bed."

The Cofian music was unmistakable tonight. It came down off the mountainside and danced into the ears of Verandale's children, many of whom were not yet ready to embrace the innocence of sleep. Enoch's father said this sound was not really music, but the sound of horned Cof heads slicing the air as they bound through the forest.

Despite his father's teachings during much of his thirteen years, Enoch still envisioned the sound coming from an orchestrated Cof gathering, likely just before or after a kill. Like many other pre-pubescent boys, he had finally given in to temptation one day while in public and belted out his best rendition of the sound. This first and last rendition occurred in the village square, while walking with his mother and older sister, Sabri. Harsh retribution convinced Enoch he should practice his Cof impression only in the sanctum of the male refuse buildings at school…or not at all.

Enoch edged backwards until he felt a bedpost. He crawled into bed and pulled the covers over his face. He wanted to sleep, but this was the time of night ideas crept into his head. The ideas usually came from things his older brother, Berc, told him during the day. He tried to concentrate on something else, but he kept hearing Berc saying, "every time you sneeze, it means a Cof has just hopped over your future grave," and "you don't even exist, you are here as part of a Cof's dream." His thoughts slowly drowned out the sounds of night and he fell asleep.

As a younger child, he had wandered through many a dream, bravely protecting his village from hordes of attacking Cofs; now he simply dreamed of the day when he would no longer have a guard.

The tradition of the land had not changed for as far back as anyone could remember. The boys, except those first few weeks of life spent in a cradle by his parents' bed, would sleep in a room on the side of the house closest to the forest, and therefore closest to the Cofs. Each room would have one large wooden window surrounded by closable shutters made of fabled mander wood. A palace guard was stationed outside the window every night, until the boy came of age. At this point, when it was obvious the boy was developing muscles, was able to knee-wrestle his father, and towered over his mother, a Ceremony of the Door was planned.

Enoch witnessed his first Ceremony when he was five or six years old. He had stood open-mouthed, in awe and anticipation at every ceremony since.

The Ceremony of the Door began with the gathering of several hundred Verandalians along the road to the palace. It began at midday when the suns reached their apex in the sky. The boy's family would leave the house and gather outside his window, leaving him alone in his room. A horn would sound from outside the boy's window. Another horn would answer from the palace, marking the beginning of the proceedings.

After the boy climbed out through the window to join the throng, he would lead his family up the hill to the palace. The craftsmen, staying behind when the procession left, would carefully begin their task of dismantling the window. They would take apart the window and craft a door through which the new "young man" would enter and exit his parents' house, until the day when he would leave for good and begin a family of his own.

Depending on the location of his parents' house in the village, and his skill at the arduous mental and physical tests awaiting him at the palace, the Ceremony and travel time could last anywhere from the length of a meal to the rest of the daylight hours. The craftsmen of the door were some of the most skilled and well-paid workers in the land. Though the successes of subjects going through the Ceremony of the Door outnumbered the failures, many said the mark of a true craftsman was to make a window into a door, but be ready, as the shadows lengthened and no procession exited from the palace, to hurriedly make a man's door back into a boy's window.

With murmurs of failure hanging in the air, the crowds would walk away knowing there would be no celebration in the square that night. The boy would return to his room—and to his guard and window— pondering the increased training he would need to not embarrass his family even more the next year.

Berc had his Ceremony last year. Enoch would always remember that morning because it was the first time he had ever seen his father nervous. The relatives had gathered that morning to have the traditional family breakfast. Enoch's father, Egard, a stoutly muscled man with four confirmed Cof kills, spoke from his customary seat at the head of the table. He told the relatives—about two dozen of them crammed into the family dining pit—

how proud he was of Berc and how hard he had trained to represent his family.

Enoch saw Berc wince. Probably remembering—Enoch thought—all those days spent chasing Falo, the girl from down by the Sea. Enoch had even covered for him a few times when they were supposed to be practicing at the spike range or in the training pit, where Enoch was often delegated to the bruising role of "practice Cof." Even more concerning to Enoch were memories of study sessions in the palace library. Many times, they had found a dim corner, out of view of Ibrakrim and napped on top of the musty scrolls and books.

Their father finished his speech and stood. He pulled back his great chair, motioning a hand towards Berc. Enoch gulped. Was Berc going to sit in *that* chair, the one that had been off limits to them since they could crawl? Berc stood, a little too quickly, knocking over some of his breakfast. He looked clumsy—like the first time he had ever snuck some tlok-vine tea—tripping over imperfections in the stone floor as he shuffled to the chair. Once there, Enoch saw him sit—perhaps a little harder than intended—as all the relatives watched.

Orgard, family patriarch and Legion member, cleared his throat and spoke to the hushed audience.

"Berc, oldest son of Egard your father and Sune your mother, do you accept the challenge of the Ceremony of the Door? Will you stand vigilant by your door, protecting your family and your valor? Will you respond to the danger of the Cofs with each and every sounding of the tocsin? Will you represent our family before the Legion of Elders, as you are tested for fitness of both mind and body?"

"Yes," Berc's voice cracked as he stared straight ahead at his great grandfather, owner of nine confirmed kills—second most in all the land.

Everyone in the pit again focused upon Orgard, who had lost his own sons many years ago. This loss would one day force him to circumvent tradition by handing the family mantle directly to Egard, his grandson.

"Berc, you have passed your childhood days." Orgard's voice crackled with age but boomed with power. "You will walk to the testing today as a boy, surrounded by a nurturing family. You will return from the palace as a man and walk through the new door into your room and your parent's house. You will respond with spike and scythe whenever needed. Henceforth you will protect your family as they have protected you."

Orgard's ancient willful stare never wavered from Berc's at the other end of the long table.

Enoch looked at his mother, who was crying, and tried to imagine himself sitting in that same chair in two years. Goose bumps sprung up on his arms.

Berc arose and walked to his room. The family watched him leave, no doubt many of the older relatives remembering him as a baby and pondering the brevity of childhood. When he was out of sight, they arose as one and left the dining pit, exiting into the cool air of the early growing season.

Once outside Berc's window, Enoch found a vantage point between the elbows of an aunt and uncle. While awaiting his brother's climb through the window, he spied Falo straining to see Berc. She wore an all-white dress for the occasion and appeared more stunning than usual. He also saw the craftsmen hiding in the crowd and holding tool pouches behind their backs.

The suns reached their zenith, erasing shadows and signaling the middle of the day. A hornsman sounded his instrument from the middle of the crowd. Another answered from a spire of the palace, high upon the hill. His brother appeared in the window and dropped to the ground. He dusted himself off and began his march, leading the throng up to the red steps of the palace.

Much later in the day, Enoch saw him come out of the palace, bruised and exhausted from his testing. A Legion member raised his right hand triumphantly. Enoch trailed behind as Berc made his way back to his new door in a heavy downpour before dusk. The soaked crowd returned to their own homes for dry clothes, in preparation for the night's celebration.

Enoch pestered him for only a few moments, knowing no man was allowed to divulge secrets of the Ceremony to one who still looked upon the land from the comfort of a guarded bedroom window.

Enoch felt daunted by the thought of enduring the same tests his brother had just completed. He could not have predicted that he would never see his own Ceremony.

*A warrior palms his weapon at the first sign of trouble,
but a mother herds her children before the tocsin tolls.*
                                                    —Unknown

2

Enoch was in school, many days later, when he heard the loud warning wail of the tocsin reverberating through the village—a Cof had been sighted! He joined the stampede of students to the windows overlooking the village square below.

Though the village of Verandale was surrounded on three sides by steep cliffs and mountains containing the dense forests of the Cofs, the village and people's homes were nestled amongst crop lands and green rolling hills. The two tallest hills in the region were put to a specific use. Upon one was the palace, where the ruling Legion governed. The school was built nearby upon the other, with safety being the utmost concern for countless generations.

Enoch absorbed the jabbing and the pushing from late arrivers behind him. He saw the glint of drawn scythes, as men rushed through the receding crowd toward the dark forest.

Once the men were out of sight and the children back in their seats, the teacher regained control. With the quieting of the tocsin, Enoch realized Berc would have been one of the men to abandon any farm animals he was tending, or to drop any tools or plows from his hands, and listen for the complicated high and low notes rung by the guards to indicate the direction of the threat. Today would be the first time Berc would bring spike and scythe to anything more than a training bout.

The rest of the school day was endless. Biology lessons on the difference between the dolphins in the Sea and freshwater fish in the lakes, and grammar lessons based upon ancient Legion documents were unmerciful. History lessons on well-known attempts to traverse the forest and the mountains were slightly better, but Enoch still considered them unnecessary delays prior to hearing tales of danger from his big brother.

When the school day finally ended, Enoch raced out the door by the time the word "dismissed" was over. He sprinted through the streets, narrowly missing a couple of yoked oxen and their cart after turning a blind corner. He increased his speed through the openness of the square and was out of breath by the time he reached his house on the edge of the village.

Hunching over with hands on knees, he looked for signs of his brother. He found him in the field behind the house, shaving the coat of a yearling lamb. Berc smirked as he saw excitement mixed with exhaustion on Enoch's face.

"What happened?" The last syllable barely audible, followed by more sucking of air.

Berc righted the lamb back to its feet. He sauntered over to Enoch while pretending to brush loose wool off his garment.

"Oh, little one," he said grabbing Enoch's cheek and shaking his brother's head from side to side. "I cannot tell an out-of-breath little girl about a man's dangerous business."

Enoch took another big breath then dove at his brother's knees. They wrestled on the ground, scattering what had been a well-herded flock. After much grappling, Berc had a scrape and a small bruise on the side of his neck. But he had subdued Enoch, pinning his head against the green of the meadow.

He made him utter the most shameful boyhood acknowledgement known in the land: "I am now and have always been worthy to the Legion only as a few smelly pounds of Cof bait!" The last of Enoch's words came out grudgingly and snarled.

As Enoch lifted his head off the ground, the boys saw two of the sheep had wandered toward the trees.

"How is it that mutton can be counted on to do the dumbest and most dangerous thing whenever possible?" Berc said, running to the lost pair while cautiously scanning the treetops at the edge of the forest. "Father said the Cofs got another one last week. I can't imagine telling him two more were lost because I was wrestling my baby sister."

Once they retrieved the wandering sheep, and herded them back to the flock, the boys brushed themselves off and sat on a fallen log. They kept an eye on the forest. Berc retrieved his weapons bag—containing scythe, four or five spikes, and a club of hardened mander. He undid the cinching rope at the top and placed it between him and his brother. He began to tell Enoch of the day's events.

"Father asked me to go down to the square and check on the going prices for herky fish before we go out and follow the dolphins in a few days. So, I'm looking things over at the fish tables and right as I'm gnawing on a sample, I hear the tocsin go off. I did the usual looking around to see which direction the men were running. That's when I realize that *I'm* now one of the men who are supposed to be headed somewhere. So, I grab my weapons bag by the wrong end, and everything falls out after my first few steps. I nearly cut myself trying to pick it all up. Then I'm running as fast as I can, across the Lower River Bridge and toward a mass of people at the peninsula. I'm straining to see a cloud of dust or spraying blood and flying Cof heads or something. Then I realize nobody's really running anymore, and I've run right past it."

"A spiked Cof?" Enoch appealed, nearly more out of breath than his rambling brother.

"No, there wasn't any evidence of them anywhere," Berc said, pausing for dramatic effect. "Just the bloody remains of Rela the sap lady!"

"Rela, of Rela and Nela, the crazy old twins?"

"Yeah, it was so gross!" Berc paused as a shiver ran all the way to his toes and a little past. "I couldn't even recognize her at first 'cause it was such a mess. But that's when we find Nela over behind a bush at the water's edge. She was crying and huddled up, and out of it even more than usual. Some of the guys were able to coax her into going with them back to town."

"So, you went back with them for the interrogation?" Enoch was now convinced he would never, ever grow up fast enough.

"No, of course not, I had to stay and clean everything up with the other new grunts. I threw up twice and I can't get the smell off my hands. We did find a few parts though, like an arm, a leg," Berc pointed to his own limbs for instructional purposes," and most of her head. One of the Legion guys made us bury her out near the end of the peninsula. He said there was no use carrying parts off the peninsula since we'd have to carry all that bloody stuff right by the edge of the forest on our way back to the village. He said the only way you could more reliably attract Cofs would be to walk into the middle of the forest with an axe and start hacking into their trees. I guess they promised Nela they'd give her sister's body the proper death rites tomorrow."

Berc paused so he and Enoch could stand and count sheep.

"I didn't hear the rest until we got back to town, and I saw one of the guys coming out of the Healer's house. So, you know the twins are, or were I guess, barely normal when they were in the square selling their measures of sap. But people put up with them because, number one, you can't find too many other people volunteering to go pegging trees for sap when many of those very same trees have been stabbed just a little higher by the horn of a Cof. Number two, they lived kind of off by themselves on that peninsula and hardly anyone knew just how crazy they had become. Turns out, the interrogation she had with the big guys was the first long conversation she had had with anyone other than her sister in a long time."

Berc repositioned himself on the deadfall. He leaned forward with one elbow resting on each knee, as if he had to be super steady when telling the rest of the story.

"Well, so happens, even though the two of them had always been a few fruits short of a basket, Rela had recently started sinking deeper in her mental goings-on than Nela. Seems she had been getting overly protective of 'her trees,' and didn't think she should share her sap with those 'overgrown lizards!'"

Enoch's eyes opened wider.

"So, they were out today collecting some sap," Berc continued. "Up into the forest farther than a couple of old ladies should be. Rela spies a Cof sleeping in that curled-around-the-base-of-a-mander-tree-in-full-camouflage mode. The problem was, according to Nela, the tree was one Rela had spiked a few days before. So, she gets all offended, walks up and bonks the Cof on its big ol' head horn with her bucket of sap."

"No way!" Enoch screamed, horrified.

"Then, of course, all hell breaks loose. The bonked Cof actually swayed a little when trying to get up. Nela was able to get Rela at least headed toward the water, but one woke up deeper in the forest, a few more swooped down from the canopy, and the mauling was on. Nela finally saved herself by jumping into the Sea."

As Berc's story ended, the dinner bell rang. The boys and their flock began the trek home.

"Not even a bunch of protecs could have saved Rela from that kind of silliness," Enoch muttered, shaking his head from side to side.

Berc slapped his arm around Enoch's shoulder. "I gotta agree with ya, little brother. I gotta agree with ya."

Only a fool courts a lass without extolling her protec.
>—Jana, the Elder

3

Since the time when Enoch could walk and remember anything, he was drawn to the protecs. Actually, every young boy grew up fantasizing about the ferocity and endless strength reserves of the protecs. Many had memorized details of legendary Cof vs. protec battles including location, weather conditions, ages of participants, and of course, injuries and outcomes. At the same time, most were respectful, if not fearful, of protecs they encountered throughout the village, the school, and even in their own homes.

Enoch was different. From a young age, they were his main source of fascination. As a toddler, he would wander toward one any chance he could get, usually slobbering the word "kitty" en route. His mother and sister were on constant lookout, but he had still suffered a few "nips" on his hands and bore one large scar over his right eyebrow.

The ways of the protecs were mysterious to say the least. There were many theories regarding their origins, and their motives. By now, the number of theories exceeded the declining number of people in the land.

Ideas on the subject ranged from the simple; they like to impale things with their tusks and eat them, to the ridiculous; they are baby Cofs, to the complex; they are sent by a great savior on the other side of the high mountains. What was actually known about the protecs had not changed for generations.

When a young girl began the changes marking her passage into womanhood, her protec would arrive. There was no formal ceremony akin to the boys' Ceremony of the Door. But the excitement of seeing a lone protec leave the forest and wander into countryside or village could inspire reverence in even the crustiest old villager.

The protec's pace would slow considerably after sprinting through the trees. He would then sniff the air and go directly toward his "assignment"—a girl whom he had never seen before, and a girl at whose side he would stay for the last dozen or so years of his life or until he gave his life to protect her. The faithfulness of a protec to its girl was unparalleled by any duo of best friends, spouses, or even family.

Enoch was nine and Sabri was thirteen when her protec arrived some four growing seasons ago. The family was eating breakfast in the dining pit of their home when Enoch—who had been discussing and looking for the yet unseen Sabri-protec throughout the winter—heard a sound not recognized by any of the rest of the family. He splashed his wooden soup spoon back into his bowl and tripped over his chair scrambling to the front of the house, ignoring parental demands to sit back down. Whipping open the front door, Enoch looked down upon a tattered and panting animal, Sabri-protec. It had fragments of leaves and pine needles caked to its dark fur and was covered in the fine dew of the forest. A small amount of blood dripped from its underbelly. Enoch's eyes fixed upon the tusks, marked by scratches and mud. They began at opposite sides of the protec's throat, protruded forward as curved knives turned on edge, and ended at two iridescent sharp points below the animal's muscled lower jaw.

All sense and early training left Enoch's head and he lurched forward to hug the animal. Only the protec's exhaustion after an unimaginable journey saved Enoch from suffering another injury. Sabri-protec uttered a weak growl before shedding Enoch and traveling down the dark hallway to the dining pit. It sniffed a shocked Sabri then laid across her feet.

Sabri was overjoyed of course, and a procession of friends and family arrived throughout the morning to view her protec. None was more joyful than Enoch, however. After two days of staring at the animal, refusing to sleep, and trying to go with his older sister everywhere including the refuse building, Enoch's father finally told him he would have to give his sister and her protec some space, or he would be sent out on the fishing boat for a week. Enoch relented, but not before he named the animal "Dew." His parents explained to him that protecs did not receive names, but he insisted and, after a short while, Sabri-protec was known as Dew to Enoch, his extended family, and friends.

As with all her girlfriends, the arrival of Sabri's protec marked the time in her life of rapid change. She was transforming from the little tomboy always sent to accompany her unappreciative little brothers to the spike-throwing fields.

As a young woman now capable of preening for half the morning before a trip to the square, she could use her accoutrements to catch a boy's eye then stomp on his lustful stare with a twirl back toward her mother that she combined with feigned indifference. She refined this to a science with the arrival of Dew. Now, all she had to whisper to Dew was, "What's that boy doing?" The hair on his back would stand up while he growled and thrust his head between land and suns in a threatening pantomime.

Becoming the object of a protec's focus could disrupt the thoughts of any boy, man, or Cof. Covered with a sheen of mixed black and russet fur, the protecs musculature flexed with every step and expanded with every breath. Standing at a height well above an adult knee, most would walk in step next to their lifelong charge, then lean against her mid-thigh whenever she stopped. Dew performed this task with one noticeable variation; walking on one side of Sabri—with head and ears alert—then ducking and lurching behind her to walk on the other side after every few steps.

Dew's gait and name were peculiar, but Sabri and Dew were unlikely to become the most famous duo of girl and protec. This designation belonged to the late Olia and Olia-protec.

Olia-protec had emerged, not near the Salt River at the eastern edge of the Sea as had all other protecs in memory. Instead, it was first seen some seventy harvests ago charging out of the trees at the southern edge of the Lake of the Depths. It dove into the revered lake "a few hairs ahead of a whole mess of Cofs." This, according to the only witnesses, three fishermen.

The stunned men stood up in their boat. The protec was just keeping its nose and tusks above the darkness of the cold lake waters. Fearful of the water, the Cofs bounded back into the forest and out of sight. The cautious fishermen coiled up their nets and rowed toward the animal, one of them having now sworn off tlok-vine tea forever. They struggled to hoist the heavy protec over the bow. It was the largest and most spectacular protec they had ever seen.

They rowed as fast as they could as the protec's chest heaved with labored breathing. The hide of a rear leg bled around a spicule of exposed bone. One eye remained open on its oversized head. A large grayish-white stripe ran down the back of the drenched animal, ending above its tail.

Upon docking the boat, one of the men ran up the hill to find a few of the sparse inhabitants of Darnoc. They ran down to help lift the dying animal out of the boat and placed it upon a blanket at the dock's edge. There was no Healer in Darnoc, a two-day journey from Verandale, but there was Urgoh.

Urgoh was a sail-mender who once worked with the Healer before being banished to Darnoc several seasons before. His crime was selling meat from oswatts, little rodent-like creatures that roamed the farmlands, as venison. His sentence was to work in Darnoc, the most dangerous unforested place in all the land.

Urgoh was proud, though already intoxicated in the early morning, to have been considered the obvious candidate to save the protec. The other Darnocians were amazed to not only see a protec—the first in a while since there were only two older women living there—but realized this protec was different. Maybe even another breed altogether.

Urgoh fed the protec "remedy soups made from my memory" and fashioned a brace that he strapped to the broken leg. The animal slowly gained strength and after a fortnight, was able to stand and walk on its own. The once dying protec became a living legend. Urgoh basked in his new fame and gave daily medical updates to all who would listen.

The inevitable had been discussed amongst the daily cluster of onlookers before it finally happened. It had chewed off its leg brace and was now stronger than its handler.

Urgoh was answering questions from the crowd about the protec's origins. "Since it came from the mountains of the northwest forest, doesn't that mean it came from a different land than the other protecs?" An inquisitive young boy of likely less than nine harvests wanted to know.

"Certainly, the mother lands that nest these beastlings…," the last word slurred as Urgoh's arthritic hand was caught in a knot of the animal's tether. "…has always been presumed to be over the eastern forest wall since most first show themselves near the palace or the village square."

"So, he is from a different land altogether?" asked another from the back of the crowd.

"Neither you nor I can know the true origins of this little pup. We also cannot know of his predestined future except that he would not have one, if not for me." Urgoh paused for effect and the animal lunged toward a guard standing in the throng. The tether tightened, cutting off blood flow to Urgoh's hand. A unified gasp arose from the crowd as the protec broke free, its tether dragging behind as it split the crowd and loped down the long and always perilous Darnoc trail, toward Verandale. A couple of the faster boys ran after it but dared not continue the chase much farther.

The confusion and wonder of Darnocians was matched only by that of the citizens of Verandale late the next evening when the animal arrived at the eastern end of the trail with the tattered remnants of a rope around its neck. It traveled to the room of a farm girl who lived down by the mollusk fields. It would be known forever more as Olia-protec. No Darnocian would know of the fate of the striped protec and no Verandalian would know the origin of Olia-protec's tether until the next winter when the annual caravan traveled from Verandale to Darnoc, uniting the two stories.

Olia was a small, meekish girl who had no qualities worthy of fame before her protec arrived. This changed suddenly, as one would imagine. All the inhabitants of Verandale, many of whom barely knew Olia's name, came to see the unlikely pair during the next few days. Olia-protec's incessant growling and occasional snarling and lunging were initially attributed to the strain and exhaustion of the animal's travel into the land. After many days however, it was clear this extraordinary protec was extraordinarily protective.

Olia's parents could no longer discipline her. Her desk at school had to be set aside from the other students. She could no longer join the family business of diving for mollusks in the marsh because her protec would not stay on shore. Instead, he would jump into the Sea and noisily muddy the waters, while trying to swim behind her.

It was two growing seasons later when the legend of Olia-protec became immortal.

On the infamous morning when Isaac's friend, Alexander, stole his hat and ran past hay stacked on the side of the road, he could not believe his luck when he squinted a look into the shadows. He spied a too-shiny coin and reached for it. He realized, too late, he had fallen for one of the oldest Cof tricks as one lunged out of the darkness.

Before he could utter any sound, the Cof was on top of him, and the head horn had ripped into the flesh of his right shoulder. Before Olia and Isaac could reach him, a second Cof was in a full dive from the nearby treetops.

But a sprinting Olia-protec made it to the tumbling masses on the ground first. The Cof's left wing was nearly torn off by the charge and when it turned to fight, Olia-protec impaled it in the mid-chest, leaving the Cof lifeless. Olia-protec shook his head violently back and forth trying to free his tusks from the body and turn to the battle behind him.

This delay gave the diving Cof ample time to land on top of the protec. Still unable to dislodge its tusks or turn its head, Olia-protec's only defense was to roll backwards under the dead Cof. As Alexander lay bleeding, Olia and Isaac plunged their scythes into the Cof's flank.

The tocsins were now deafening. Villagers rushed down the road as Olia-protec finally freed his tusks from the first Cof and clamped his jaws upon the second Cof's head. The combination of flank and head injuries proved fatal to the Cof by the time any adults had arrived.

But Olia-protec would not relinquish its lifeless head.

They rushed Alexander to the Healer. He eventually

lost his entire right arm. He also went on, however, not only to lead a full life but also served as leader of the Legion of Elders for many seasons.

Throughout the course of the day, Olia-protec would turn to observe, or snarl at bystanders. He would not let go of the Cof head, despite Olia's pleadings. When she began to walk away, his eyes grew large. He would growl and whimper while trying to drag the entire carcass down the road, after Olia. Olia finally gave up and sat down by his side. As the suns set, the protec was able to gnaw the head horn off the rest of the body. Only then, was Olia able to coax him to run back with her to her parent's house. While Olia slept a restless sleep that night filled with violent nightmares, Olia-protec gnawed incessantly on the horn beneath her bed.

Over the next several days, Olia went to and from school and the village square with her striped protec. All the while he carried his trophy in his mouth—a shrinking Cof horn of increasing mushiness. It would not be the last Cof horn he would ever carry, as he saved many lives in the coming seasons.

Olia grew into her role as partner to the most famous protec ever known. She married and tried to live a normal life while raising her children—the youngest of which she named Ibrakrim.

Many years later, Olia-protec turned gray and died of old age. She followed him just a short while later.

Sasha

The future, by definition, is premonition.
—Historical Professor

4

Enoch awoke with an unpleasant sensation in his left ear. He batted at the object but could not dislodge it. He opened one groggy eye enough to see Berc standing next to his bed, smirking. Berc's index finger, wet with saliva, was lodged in Enoch's ear. Enoch swung a fist as hard as he could into Berc's forearm.

"Oooow!" Berc said, rubbing his arm and grinning. "That is definitely the hardest I have ever been hit by a girl!"

Enoch ripped back his covers to lunge at his brother, but found an ankle tied to the bedpost. His eyes grew wide with rage.

"You look like you've seen a ghost!" Berc was now laughing so hard he crashed against the doorway leaving Enoch's room.

"And don't forget, today is the last day of school. Maybe *next* year will be the year when you finally get a girlfriend." Berc yelled down the hallway.

Enoch's mood improved with his mom's breakfast of eggs and ani deer sausage. He was able to slip some meat under the table to Dew, lying against Sabri's chair. He smiled at Dew's newfound skill of eating quietly to avoid detection.

After breakfast, he walked to school with Berc, Sabri, and Dew. They talked about Sabri's last day of school as she was now eighteen and would be "turned-out." Sabri talked about how much she was going to miss her classes. Berc mentioned she might have to go back for another year because the only way she would ever get married would be to meet a younger man. Enoch found himself unable to take part in the banter due to his sadness—which he would never admit around Berc—at the thought of Sabri and Dew ever leaving the house.

Once at school, the day became more fun and chaotic. Enoch received high marks in most subjects. One of his teachers mentioned if he kept this up, he might be able to have his testing and his Door Ceremony a year early.

To most of the children of the school, however, the grades and morning goodbyes served as simple preamble to the mid-day banquet marking the last event of the school year. This always meant two big happenings. One: manko fish soup, the rarest and richest food, would be served—the only day it was ever served at school. Two: the closing speech given by Professor Andrew, Legion member and headmaster of the school.

The speech marking the official end was the same every year. The kids knew he would remind them of the dangers around them and how to be safe during the growing season. Though the speech was always the same—in fact, some of the older kids insisted even the words never changed—they cherished the delivery by

Professor Andrew. Like the man himself, it was short, derogatory, and delivered in a pool of sarcasm that only he could pull off.

Enoch searched for his assigned seat in the dining hall of the school. He found the tables covered with a fine cloth and name cards behind each bowl. He found his nametag at one of the tables near the front of the hall. The nametag next to his read "Sasha."

Enoch's heart raced.

Sasha was a year younger than him. They had similar schedules last year and Sasha tended to follow him around a lot at school. She was fond of pointing out the fact that they used to play together often as infants before her parents had moved to the farms down by the docks. Enoch had thought of her as nothing more than a walking annoyance at the time.

Last winter though, her family had volunteered for the winter caravan to Darnoc. She had not only safely returned but, by the next time Enoch saw her, was a little taller and could now look down upon Enoch ever so slightly. She had also learned to bat her eyes and cause a type of paralysis to descend upon Enoch and his friends whenever she walked by.

"Hi, Enoch," said Sasha, smiling and bumping her shoulder into his.

"Hi…uhm…Ba!" Enoch turned to see her in a white dress with a pinkish shawl covering the changing outline of her body.

"Who is Ba? Enoch, are you going to tell me that you've forgotten my name?"

"No, I was saying 'Hi…because,' Sasha, I meant…you came to say hi to me."

"Well Enoch, you sure can confuse a girl. I don't remember you being this confusing when we were in the same pen, crawling all over each other."

"I was two then."

"That means that you were dating a woman half your age. Shame on you!" She leaned over and whispered into Enoch's ear. "But if you're nice to me during the banquet, I'll consider us even."

Enoch pulled her chair out. He felt a strange sensation in his stomach as she glanced over her shoulder to whisper him a thank you.

A low drumbeat signaled the start of the banquet. The curtain parted at the front of the hall. A procession of well-dressed teachers, guards, and parents passed through in single file. Each carried two large bowls of soup. Four adults appeared at Enoch's table and placed a bowl in front of each student.

Enoch gazed into the fluid and saw the reddish-brown puffed manko meat dumplings, prepared using the same recipe for generations. He leaned over the bowl and inhaled. The aroma was warm and meaty rich, flooding his sinuses and bringing a deep serenity into the back of his head. He looked over to Sasha. She tucked her dark brown hair behind her ears and closed her eyes as she also inhaled the soup's fragrance.

The drumbeat ended, and the hall became quiet. Students began to fill and empty their spoons, careful not to let a single drop fall upon table or clothing. Enoch savored each spoonful. He remembered his father saying next winter might be their family's turn to volunteer for the caravan to Darnoc. At this moment, Enoch believed the extra meat allotted to each traveling family from the manko fishing grounds, would be worth any amount of danger.

After they drained their bowls, first by spoon then by tilting and slurping, the students leaned back in their chairs, sated and happy. Professor Andrew was introduced. Everybody cheered. The school year was moments from its end, and the professor would now bask in his short-lived annual glory.

"Thank you, teachers and parents." He bowed to the adults at the front and edges of the hall, then sneered while looking straight ahead at the seated students. "Now listen up, Rodentia. As we end another year in which we have attempted to inject brilliant wisdom into middling minds, I am reminded of the infinite importance of my annual oration to a group of beings who will leave this hall today and will be unlikely to form thoughts between now and their return to school in the fall.

"I will now tell you all you need to know about Cofs in both a short version and a long version since many of you have the attention span of an oswatt, taking a nap." Jeers and scattered clapping erupted from students as the professor had thrown in a brand-new insult this year.

"The short version: Cofs live in the forest. They are *noc-tur-nal*. Have your mothers explain it to you when you get home. If you are in the forest or out after dark, you might be dismembered and eaten. If, despite our best efforts here at school, your intracranial faculties are deficient to such an extent that you send yourself into the dark *and* into the forest...you will not survive to pass your faulty genetic code onto future innocent generations." More cheers. Enoch briefly considered his impression of the Cofian whistle but decided against it.

"The long version: In the recorded history of the land, there has never been a time when we existed and Cofs did not. There is no part of our land that is not surrounded by enormous mountains containing thick forests of evergreen and mander trees. There is no part of the forest that is not haunted by the omnipresent evil of the Cofs. Herein lays the puzzle that has plagued our forefathers and their forefathers.

"One of you seemingly mindless youngsters in this very room may be the future leader of the Legion of Elders who is able to breach the Cofian forest and introduce the whole of our people to the wonders of the mapless lands beyond the mountains."

"He left out the part about how we want to get out of this land and not be dead," Enoch whispered a little too loud.

"As you work hard in the fields and fishing boats of your fathers and mothers during this growing season, be safe. Stay out of the forest and come back next school year as an annoying little person and not as a statistic. This school year is now over. You are dismissed!"

Thunderous applause erupted as the students rose to their feet. The girls exchanged hugs and tears, the boys, slaps upon the back and headlocks.

Sasha turned to Enoch. "So, what scares you, Enoch?"

"Uh, well nothing right now, I suppose." Enoch was a little scared at the stirring sensation in his stomach but decided to leave that out.

"Good then," Sasha said. "So, if you're not scared of the Salt River Bridge then how about you cross it and come see me a couple of times this growing season? Mother says I'll surely be getting my protec very soon. So, you should get to know him, so he doesn't want to eat your foot or something later."

"Ok…I'll plan on it."

Sasha hugged him. Enoch realized there actually was something better than manko soup. He smiled as he watched her leave. This surely was the best day of his life. A day so great that it could not be ruined.

Enoch pushed his chair back from the table. As he turned to leave, he sensed a towering presence behind him.

"Soooo!" Berc had the widest grin possible on a human.

Please, oh please, tell me he was not standing there long enough to see anything, Enoch pleaded to himself.

"Soooo…" Enoch remained silent while Berc went on—there was no way he was volunteering any info to Berc, no matter how many annoying sounds his brother made. "…I'm thinking 'Enashchaos' would be perfect."

"What are you talking about?" Enoch gained hope that this was just standard Bercian nonsense and his brother had not actually overheard any of his conversation with Sasha.

"Enashchaos. You and Sasha can name your first kid Enashchaos, thereby using all the letters from your two perfectly combined names." Enoch's heart sank. "I shall pen a notice and paste it to the front of the palace so all of Verandale can share in your wedded bliss!"

This was bad, Enoch thought. *No, this was worse than bad.* He would have to come up with a bribe, a bribe so spectacular that Berc would actually…

"Sashaaaaaa…!" Berc was yelling and running out of the dining hall and into the revealing light of the outdoors. "Sashaaaaaa, my lovvvvvvve!"

Enoch took off in pursuit of his brother, the fastest he had ever run.

A Cof in hand is worth two graves.

—Berc

5

The small, shimmering, red sun chased the yellow sun through the late morning sky. The growing season was now nine days old and Berc and Enoch were at the spike fields. Enoch slumped with exhaustion. One day remained on his bribe to do all Berc's chores. Berc had kept his end of the bargain also, as far as Enoch knew.

Each morning, they would train together, then Berc would wander off to the village, free for the day. Enoch did not know where he went or what he did. He did know that Berc was incredibly happy. During the day, Enoch would run from the mutton fields, to the stables and the family orchard. He was even forced to attend Berc's supposed summer apprenticeship at the livery. Every night, after Enoch said goodnight to his guard and laid down in bed, Berc would wander by his door. He would look around to ensure no other ears were present and whisper "Enashchaos," then giggle all the way back to his own room.

Enoch now stretched his right arm, sore from the

combination of chores and spike-throwing. Berc tossed an unloaded spike at him, and Enoch snatched it in midair to avoid a welt on the side of his head.

Spikes were invented around the time Runal was discovered. A spike was a heavy ball of forged metal, made to fit into a man's hand. It was made up of two equal hemispheres. Between the hemispheres was a row of embedded spikes that lay down to form the weapon's incomplete equator. The spikes could be transported this way, in a safe or "unloaded" manner.

To load a spike, the thrower would place their hands on both sides of the weapon. A quick twist in opposite directions made the sharpened spikes pop up and lock into place. The thrower would then carefully place it between their middle and fourth fingers with the spike-free part against their palm. Though an accomplished thrower could hurl a loaded spike safely, most had cut into, if not removed, the web space between their third and fourth fingers long before adulthood. Berc and Enoch had both acquired this "mark of the land" many years ago, as it took only one errant grip or errant throw to cause this injury.

The practice field was in a large vacant expanse of land near the Lower River. Heavy use rendered the area free of vegetation except for one mander tree at the target end. The enormous tree had succumbed to numerous spike wounds long ago as it was used to simulate the most difficult of all spike throws.

Berc and Enoch had already completed their requisite throws—beginning at ten paces and ending at thirty—at the heavy hide-covered wooden Cof simulators. Enoch had done well, with more than half his throws ending with a spike embedded into the target area—the softer skin of a Cof neck.

Berc dragged the largest of the wooden Cofs over to the tree. A large branch was on the ground to help in the setup of this specific target scenario. Berc placed the body of the Cof behind the tree and leaned it against the branch. From Enoch's vantage point, twenty paces away, this simulated one of the most feared sights in the land—a Cof, barely visible, preparing its ambush from behind a tree.

Berc stopped to admire his propping skills, then ran back to Enoch.

"Alright little brother, you've just returned from a day of drinking at the tavern. The suns are setting. The sky is darkening and ominousing."

"That is definitely not a word," Enoch interrupted.

"Your physique is being admired by a gathering of young, recently protec'd ladies near the edge of the village square. They are giggling and braiding each other's hair. Oh wait, that's my story…

"Ok, you are returning from a day at school where you learned to tie your footwear. You see a herd of ponies with braided manes and you long to pet them. But all of a sudden," Berc paused to make a deep, guttural, drumming sound, "you realize there is a Cof, the largest Cof ever seen. He is crouching and ready to pounce, behind that tree, right over there." Berc thrust both hands dramatically toward the practice tree. "You know his buddy is perched high in the forest nearby, neither of them has tasted meat in at least four days. Your only chance to save the ponies is to kill the first Cof with one throw and hope you can reload another spike in time to prepare for the onslaught from above. All of Pony Land is depending on you!"

Enoch rolled his eyes and grabbed a spike from his brother's hand. He twisted it with sore hands until the teeth popped up with a loud twang. He rotated it carefully, placing the spikes between his fingers, the smooth surface against his palm.

As he had done a thousand times before, he squeezed the weapon while planning the arc and speed of his throw. He paused as an idea came to him.

"Berc, you know how our little agreement made at the banquet is over after today?"

"Yes." Berc placed his hands on his hips, growing impatient.

"How about we make a little bet? If I nail this Cof where it counts—a real kill shot right to the neck—I am done with this dumb bribe and therefore all your chores. If I miss, I'll finish the last day of your chores today and add an extra day of chores tomorrow."

Berc paused a moment. His eyes lit up under raised eyebrows. "You got yourself a deal, but you don't just have to hit the Cof, you gotta land a solid shot that sticks. The kind of shot that will drop the Cof right where he stands on his single leg. The kind of shot," Berc shouted, "that will make it so he never eats another deer, oswatt, pony, or Enoch ever again."

Enoch nodded in agreement. His heartbeat and his breathing pounded, but he had made this throw before, and it was time to shut Berc up for a while. He held the spike above his right shoulder. He eyed the target one last time and drew back his hand. He exhaled all his air, twisted, and lurched violently forward. The spike flew out of his hand, making a low whooshing sound as it sliced the morning air. It traveled in a perfect path toward the tree. Enoch waited for the slight curve and dip that would carry it, on target, to the neck of the wood Cof.

Enoch was already pumping his fist as the spike curved, but then it curved a little more. It sailed past, managing only to tick the front edge of the Cof horn before landing in a puff of dust beyond the target.

Berc flashed Enoch a huge smile and slapped him on the back. "You had me worried there at first. By the way, Father says I have to help train Kahdi here tomorrow. This, of course, now means that you will be training Kahdi in the ways of the spike, since *you*, congratulations, are now me for one more day. Good luck. I'll see you at dinner." Berc gathered up his bag. He sang with the birds and danced with the butterflies on his way to who knows where.

Enoch leaned over, hands on his knees, and muttered a few "unbelievables."

Bad enough to do all these chores that are going to make my hands fall off, he thought. *Now I have to train Kahdi, the untrainable kid.*

Enoch walked toward the spike in the distance. He pulled it out of the dirt, wondering if there was some way Berc could have planned this all along. He unloaded the spike and dropped it into his bag, kicking the wood Cof over on his way back.

Kahdi was a few years older and twice the size of Enoch, but a year behind him in school. He had probably learned all he was ever going to learn, but his parents had worked out some sort of deal with the Legion. He attended school half the time, hopefully staying out of trouble while within the walls of the building. The rest of the time, he spent with various others to see if he could acquire a skill to make him useful.

There were calamities along the way as Kahdi failed at one potential avocation after another. Much of the trouble started with the Kahdi version of communication. As Kahdi was, by far, the largest person in Verandale, he looked down upon anyone who tried to speak to him. He spoke only in one- or two-word sentences if he spoke at all. More often he would just cock his head to one side or the other when confused. This was if things were going well. An increasingly more common scenario was the large, but docile Kahdi could turn into an out-of-control, raging, spitting, and tumbling-to-the-ground Kahdi. This version, difficult to control even with the help of two or three palace guards, could show up at any time, and for any reason…or no reason at all.

The most oft talked about Kahdi episode happened during the early winter a couple of years before. It was the middle of the school day. Kahdi's parents were manning the family fruit stand in the village square. His parents tried to keep him away from the market because he often interpreted the bartering between the fruit sellers and buyers as a conflict needing violent resolution.

He was assigned, on that fateful day, to one of the old fishermen down at the docks. Many of those who lived in the fishing village had a reputation for being experts in the ways of following the dolphins and throwing their nets to haul in boat loads of herky fish—one of the main staples of Verandale.

But the harsh, shortened days of winter were dark

times the seafarers often filled with the intoxicating delusions of tlok-vine tea.

The old fisherman assigned to watch Kahdi had started imbibing from his flask rather early. He gave Kahdi what he thought would be a perfect task for a boy of simple notions. He had shown his new protégé a collection of polished and coarse stones used to smooth the roughness of the inner hull of a fishing boat. This would enable the later application of resin to protect the boat while stored on land during the Sea's winter ice floes.

Kahdi was on the boat and off to a good start. He was seemingly a quick study in the ways of rock sanding, humming while rubbing rocks against wood. The old fisherman watched him work for a while. After a fair amount of supervising, the contents of his flask were discovered to be unacceptably low, and the seafarer began a short trek back to the house for a refill.

Kahdi continued his task until a small splinter became imbedded in his forearm. He grunted and stood up, presumably looking for help nearby. Seeing none, he attempted to punish the imbedded splinter by bashing it with his sanding stone. This caused a surprising pain to travel up his arm. He struck again at the pain and then started a high-pitched wail. He hit the bottom of the boat with his fist, then with a rock. By the time the fisherman and many villagers heard the commotion, Kahdi had fractured the ship's hull and lost the rocks to the Sea bottom. As water seeped in through the sinking vessel and around his ankles, he grabbed an oar handle and began pulverizing the boat's remains.

The boat was half sunk by the time the speediest of

the villagers made it to the dock. Despite the water level now at his chest and pleas from those onshore to save himself, Kahdi would not leave the sinking boat. Several frantic villagers finally jumped into the icy waters and, with great effort, wrestled him onto shore.

Kahdi's days as an unsupervised boat winterizer had come to an end.

Enoch was moping as he polished his practice spikes at the field the next morning. A few others, two of them training young boys, were there as well. Enoch had already set up a pile of rocks, to serve as "safe spikes" for his student.

Enoch heard a disturbance at the far end of the field as a petite woman, Kahdi's mother, coaxed and pushed a life form—larger than the training Cofs themselves—into the throwing area. All trainees stopped what they were doing and looked at the sight. The fathers and their trainees left shortly thereafter. Kahdi's mother pantomimed a quick "thank you" to Enoch and was on her way.

Enoch walked up to the giant. He offered his hand as a form of greeting.

"Mirk!" Kahdi responded as he leaned backward and shied from Enoch's hand.

Enoch pondered for a moment but was then able to lead him toward the sunsbaked rock pile. "OK, um, you sit here," pointing to a large boulder. Enoch was leery of turning his back on a standing Kahdi.

"Here's what we need to know." Enoch picked up a

spike-sized stone, still unsure if he should show Kahdi a real spike. *Maybe he already knows about spikes*, Enoch thought, *from one of his many apprenticeship days over the last couple of years.*

"You pick up the spike, I mean the stone, and you throw it to protect your girl…or like your mother, from one of the bad Cofs. I mean, not that there are any good Cofs."

Kahdi stared at Enoch.

Enoch decided to give up explaining and just demonstrate. They were only at the twenty-pace line, but Enoch's rock sailed well over its target as his arm had become accustomed to the heavier throwing weight of a real spike.

Kahdi leaned to the side, looking around Enoch to peer at the sailing stone. Enoch took this as a sign that Kahdi was at least interested. Enoch demonstrated once more, this time striking the target, though a tad below the neck.

"OK, now you try." Kahdi looked at him blankly at first and then rose to his feet. Enoch put a rock into Kahdi's palm and took a step back. Kahdi stared at the target. "Go ahead Kahdi, just aim and throw."

Kahdi backed up a few paces, almost stepping on Enoch's feet. He ran forward, stopping before the line, and flung his rock over his head in a vicious and clumsy downward motion. The rock sailed at greater speed than Enoch thought possible. It struck the wood Cof in the upper neck. A loud crack rang out and wood fragments flew. The wood Cof was decapitated.

"Hit," mumbled Kahdi.

"Hit! Just hit?" Enoch looked down the line to see

the other throwers' reactions, before remembering they had left. "Kahdi, that was so not even possible! Here, try another one."

Kahdi looked at the target and said, "No head."

"I know Kahdi, like aim a little lower."

Kahdi did his confused, tilt-the-head thing for a moment then repeated his violent wind-up and throw. This rock flew with similar velocity and lack of an arc. It struck the target at the top of its now exposed neck, knocking the wooden creature to the ground.

"What in the name of the other side of the mountains? Oh Kahdi, I would have said there is no way you could… or anyone could ever do that, especially twice in a row! You've done this before, right? 'Cause there is just no way. I mean no way! Does the Legion know about this? You realize this is the best throwing I have ever seen, right?"

Kahdi looked straight ahead with no words and no facial expression.

"Here is what we gotta do. You wait right here. I'm going to go prop up another target right behind that tree, then we are going to back up a little, okay?" Enoch backed quickly away, keeping an eye on Kahdi at first, not wanting to be confused in the least little bit with a target. He dragged one of the other targets over to the tree, while looking at the headless, downed Cof once more in disbelief. He then ran back to Kahdi and convinced him to help carry the pile of rocks and back-up to the forty paces line.

He explained the whole Cof, tree, ambush idea but couldn't tell if Kahdi was listening. After urging Kahdi to put down all the rocks but one, he told him it was again time to throw. Kahdi looked at the target, said "far," and then released the rock with a loud grunt. This rock appeared to be off target to Enoch and, sure enough, struck the tree instead. It then bounced off the tree, striking the Cof neck with a heavy thud.

Enoch looked at Kahdi, laughing. "There is just no way Berc is ever going to believe this. You are something, Kahdi!" Enoch started to do a gentle punch to the shoulder, but then thought it would be better not to.

They threw until the rock pile was gone. Enoch decided against letting Kahdi throw or even look at a real spike lest the spikes cut into his hand and cause one of his tantrums.

Kahdi was staring into the dirt where the rock pile used to be.

"Hey Kahdi, how 'bout we call it a day and I'll walk you back home?"

"More," was Kahdi's response.

"Well okay, but we gotta set up some more targets, then you gotta help me bring the rocks back up here."

"No, old."

It took Enoch a second to process this. "Are you saying the rocks are old? Because that is not a thing, I mean they don't get hurt or nothing. Well, I guess maybe yours do. Come on, you come with me and help."

"No, old." Kahdi whispered. He turned and ran toward the Lower River.

"Wait Kahdi, no!" Enoch watched him briefly while not believing what he was seeing. It looked like he really was going to the river which ran high this time of year, still bulging at the banks with the melted remnants of winter snows. Enoch took off after Kahdi, not wanting to be the protagonist in another "guess-what-somebody-let-Kahdi-do-near-the-water" story.

Enoch sprinted and quickly caught up with the clumsy, tottering mound of flesh that was the running version of Kahdi. Enoch pulled on his arm. Kahdi turned his head and said "mirk" before driving his forearm back and striking Enoch to the ground.

Pain pounded in Enoch's chest. He brushed himself off, realizing all he could do now was watch.

Kahdi reached the river but did not slow down. The water caused his legs to slow but his massive upper body continued forward until he somersaulted face-first into the raging waters.

Enoch made it to the water's edge and again looked behind him for someone, anyone who could help. His screams for help were drowned out by the river's white-capped rushing currents.

Looking to the middle of the river and seeing no human sign, Enoch thought for the first time that Kahdi could be dead. Then he heard a noise farther downstream. Kahdi was struggling and bobbing above and below the surface of the raging river. But he was also using a wild version of a protec-paddle to approach the other bank.

Enoch ran downstream, trying to yell across the river. Kahdi ignored him. After his feet were swept out from under him on the first two attempts, Kahdi made it out of the water and onto the far riverbank. He clawed at the rocks and shrubs at the river's edge but was then able to stand and look back in the general direction of Enoch, who exhaled a sigh of relief.

Kahdi breathed heavily. He looked down at his torn

and dripping clothes. He straightened his shirt and ran into the vaporous forest.

Enoch stood open-mouthed with disbelief across the river into the thick trees marking the southern edge of Verandale. He saw Kahdi run for only a few steps before he blended into the green darkness. After waiting a while for Kahdi's hopeful return, he ran, with cautious glances back over his shoulder, back to the village for help.

Knowing it would be impossible to find Berc, Enoch ran behind their house. He found Sabri sleeping in a bright sunlit portion of grass. Her head was resting on Dew's chest. The protec was lying on his side, also asleep, one visible tusk reflecting the suns.

Enoch backed slowly away. He'd made the mistake before of startling a sleeping Dew and had promised himself he would never do that again. He continued his slow backward steps until he was back outside the front door. Enoch then shuffled his feet noisily on the gravel of the path before slamming the front door and walking through the house, back to the same place he had just been. Dew was crouching in front of Sabri. His front legs were spread apart, ready to lunge.

"You scared me to death, Enoch!" Sabri exclaimed as Dew's barking deflated to a growl.

"Sorry but this is huge, I mean hugely bad. Kahdi's dead, he ran into the forest!"

"Enoch, wait." Sabri paused to put her hand on Enoch's shoulder. "Did you see Kahdi's body?"

"No, but he swam across the Lower River for no reason after shouting something about an old rock. Then, he just looked at me like I wasn't even there and ran straight into the forest. I can't believe I killed Kahdi!"

"Enoch look, Kahdi runs into the forest all the time. Sasha saw him run in the day after school ended." Sabri stopped to get Dew to sit down. "And remember last year when I was supposed to supervise him as a seamstress for a day? Well, right near the end of the day, I'm worried he is getting all enamored with me or something. I tell him we are going to end a little early. He gives me this sad face and mumbles something that I swear sounds like 'co frist.' Then he runs straight into the forest. He comes back before I can even run to get help. When he does, he brought me an apple, the first one I had tasted that year. So, I gave him a little hug, and he just walked away." Sabri shrugged her shoulders at the end of her story.

Enoch looked at her and tried to imagine Kahdi—or anyone else for that matter— regularly venturing into the forest and returning unscathed.

"I'll tell you what, little brother. You don't tell Father I was sleeping on the job today and I'll take you to Kahdi's parents' fruit stand, right after we get some food. Then you can see that everything is going to be okay."

A short time later; Enoch, Sabri, and Dew traveled to the square, finding the stand mixed in with others, around the perimeter. Enoch recognized the petite woman, washing some fruit and putting it away for the day. Sitting on the ground, hiding as much as he could behind the table, was a wet and muddy Kahdi. He remained quiet, but upon seeing Enoch, reached between his crossed legs, and held out a rock, roughly the size of a spike. He silently repeated the same motion but reached from a different pile to give Sabri an apple.

"Thanks, Kahdi, you are so sweet." Sabri bit into the fruit as Enoch looked aghast at her and Kahdi.

Kahdi noticed the third party in the group and offered a damp rock to Dew. Dew took a step backwards and leaned against Sabri's thigh.

"Thank you Kahdi, but Dew doesn't need a rock right now," his mother said, pulling her son's forearm back from the confused animal.

Sabri laughed between bites of her apple, cupping her hand below her mouth so as not to lose any of the juices. Enoch looked from Kahdi to his mother, unable to speak. Kahdi's mother answered anyway.

"Enoch, my son tells me that the two of you had quite an adventure today." She paused to wipe some dust from the side of a peach with her apron. She held it up for inspection before placing it in the storage bin below. "Apparently, he had quite a grand time at those throwing games of yours, but then you asked him to throw a broken rock or something."

Enoch could not understand how any information could pass from son to mother using only grunts, made-up words like "mirk," and two-word sentences.

She continued. "There's something about rocks, or broken rocks, that really sets him off ever since that horrible misunderstanding down at the boat docks."

Enoch interrupted her to add the part—the most important part—about Khadi's run across the river and into the forest.

"Oh sweetie, he does that all the time. At first his father and I tried to stop him but…," she stopped to playfully ruffle her son's hair, "as you know, that is not an easy thing to do. So, I always tell people, whatever you do, just let him go into the forest. Somebody could really get hurt trying to stop him, you know."

Enoch winced as he ran a hand over his bruised chest.

"We used to worry terribly, but he always comes back. And the last few times, he came back with fruit. Now, we call him our best little fruitier. I told your brother Berc all these things a couple of days ago when I heard he would be training Kahdi. Didn't he tell you?"

Enoch stopped to bring a halt to his breathing and to grit his teeth. Sabri laughed. The family dinner was going to be more than interesting tonight.

It was possible that even Dew laughed, just a little.

*A pretty girl can bestow more danger than
the grumpiest of guards, the crankiest of Cofs.*
—Egard

6

Early morning. Enoch was happy. Maybe even deliriously happy, though he tried hard not to let it show. Having left his house moments before, he approached the village square where merchants were setting up their tables under a canopy of fog and smattering rain. Enoch stopped at the blacksmith's table to view the various cookware and, the way more interesting, weapons. The aged man spied Enoch and interrupted his preparations, to demonstrate his new creation and practice his sales pitch.

"Young man, this here is the newest, the latest, and the best way to defend your life." He brought out a short, gleaming piece of metal anchored in a bone handle and sheathed in deer skin. "Son, you ever tried to spike a Cof from two paces away? Of course not! But I have." He lifted his tunic to reveal an ugly scar, covering his elderly, emaciated left flank. Enoch made a face and took a step backward.

"I was a young lad once, just a wee bit uglier than yourself. 'Twas many seasons ago. A wet and quarrelsome morning, much like this one. I was on my way to the orphanage, traveling down the very road that just carried your own two feet. Just minding my own business I was when these two Cofs jumped me...for no reason! You think my spikes could help me? No!" The old man's voice crackled louder, while shouting, spitting, and flinging his damp wisps of gray hair to and fro.

"You think my scythe could save me? No! Luckily, I was blessed with bigger than normal brains for my age. I quickly snapped the handle off my scythe with my bare hands. After striking several blows and spewing Cof blood, the Cofs bounded back to their Cof-mommies in the forest where, no doubt, they refused to prey upon humans for the rest of their miserable lives. And now, I have created the instrument to save anyone, anywhere," he paused to drink from a flask pulled from beneath the table, "from any threat emanating from the dark and biting evil of the forest."

"Oh, well…actually I was just walking by because I'm going to see my girl. Well, not my girl, just more of a girl that is mine to know." Enoch backed away, blushing. "Just one who will see me when I get there. So, well… thanks."

Enoch turned to complete his retreat as the old man yelled after him, "But can you protect her, my boy? Can you duly protect her?"

Leaving the village square behind him, Enoch resolved to talk to no other peddlers. He walked first in one wagon track and then the other, avoiding puddles on the worn road to the Salt River Bridge. Looking over the dense forest, he compared the fluttering spring green of the fruit trees and giant mander trees with the dark needles of the evergreens. The views on a windy and dark day such as this were vastly different from that of a sunny day in which Enoch could see clear to the Darnoc Range in the distant northwest. It was this view that caused Enoch to be distracted by the calculation that had occupied his thoughts for many seasons: How many unseen Cofs lived in the forest, and why was it that no human had ever found a way to successfully breach the forest?

He approached the Salt River Bridge for the first time this growing season. The salty sting of the mist from below lashed at his nose as he stepped up to the wooden rails. Seeing no horse or oxen-drawn carts approaching, Enoch walked to the middle of the bridge, enjoying the brief vertigo that came from looking through the slats at the tumultuous waters far below.

Enoch remembered the ancient story about the bridge's construction. Before the bridge was built, the people of Verandale could only cross by first hiking down to the Sea where one could usually find a sober ferryman. Coins would exchange hands and the ferryman would take people from either the village side or the farm side by sailing out a short distance into the estuary.

The ice floes of the winter months made this sort of transport impossible. So, shortly after the first frost, all practical traffic and communication between the two populations ceased. Heartier and braver souls, however, could climb the palace steps that formed an arch over the river's source.

The Salt River began, not as the tributaries and creeks that formed the freshwater rivers of the rest of the land, but at a sudden giant gaping maw along the steepest edge of the mountains to the northeast. The torrent of saltwater blasting forth from this cavity was about the size of a large house, and according to written records, had never perceptibly changed.

Many generations ago, the Legion of Elders had decided the water was a gift from a higher power from the other side of the mountains. To honor this gift, the Legion proposed a great temple, honoring the deity, to be built around the origin of the Salt River.

All agreed, the only acceptable building material for this mighty structure was the recently discovered Runal rocks found at the southwestern edge of the Sea. The giant stones of this region were unlike any other. During the day they appeared dusty, with an unremarkable pinkish hue. Unbeknownst to the casual daytime observer however, the rock surfaces collected the light and heat from the suns. Seen at night, they gave off a mesmerizing red luminescence. If one were surrounded by enough Runal rocks, the light given off made torches unnecessary.

The builders drew plans and constructed boat docks during the daytime at the Runal quarry site. They debated a security plan and assigned guards. Ferrying workers across the Sea, to and from the quarry, was difficult at best. Thus, they decided to build the town of Runal. But when work began on the excavation, countless lives were lost in battles with the Cofs. This continued over the many years it took to construct the temple. The people tried many different approaches to make Runal safer. The initial town—constructed between docks and quarry—was eventually moved to an area between the quarry and the adjoining red sand dunes when workers discovered that the one-legged Cofs had trouble hopping through the sand. This provided little deterrence to attacks by air, however. The Runal Quarry assignment became even more dangerous than the winter caravan.

Those that survived the quarrying were then exposed to a long, slow trip back to Verandale in transport ships unsteadied by their heavy loads. It was said, even now, on clear windless nights, when the Sea is calm, one can see a haunting red glow from skeletons of submerged shipwrecks near the Sea's southern shore.

When the temple was finally completed, there was no doubt it was the finest structure ever built. Four towering spires with deep, vertical windows anchored a faultless dome that loomed over the massive front entrance. Legion members and visitors entered via one of two walkways. Each was fifty paces across and flanked the Salt River as it crashed out the back wall of the cavernous foyer. At night, the glow of the temple illuminated the waters and the Salt River ran red as it roared and sparkled from mountain to Sea.

The Runal quarry would be mined only one more time—many years later for construction of the Darnoc Bridge. The magnificence of the bridge could not approach that of the temple. The cost in lives however, proved just as great. Therefore, with the completion of the bridge, the Legion of Elders handed down the Runal Law: No person shall ever again mine rock from, or even set foot in Runal.

The magnificence of the two structures was increased by the knowledge that Runal rock would never be used again. Enoch had never seen the Darnoc Bridge, but he felt it impossible for any construction to rival that of the palace—the temple having been renamed when the Legion began ruling from the building.

Looking up at the massive crimson of the palace in the misty light of the day, Enoch marveled at the four spires, stretching skyward high enough to stab the clouds. It was said—though no living person knew for sure—that the spires, one for each compass direction, were built with the goal of providing a human view over the tops of the mountains. The planners and craftsmen failed only when gravity and constrictions of weather prevented further ascent.

From Enoch's vantage point at the center of the bridge, he could look straight up at the massive geyser shooting out of the mountainside and through the front of the palace. At close to a thousand paces, he could just make out the silhouette of the stairs carved above the mouth of the river and into the massive back foyer wall. Egard had once taken his three children on an expedition, up one side of the now defunct steps and down the other. There were two hundred and thirty-four steps in all. The stairs had always been perilous, but the passage of time and corrosive effects of the brackish water had caused the frightening trip to become so dangerous that many years ago, the Elders had commissioned the building of the Salt River Bridge upon which Enoch now stood.

His awe came to a quick end with the approach of two horse-drawn carts. Enoch hurried off the remaining rails of the bridge, not wanting to be caught in the tight space between the bridge's edge and the nervous horses who disliked the height of the bridge and the sounds of the raging water below.

Leaving the bridge, Enoch kicked at a small puddle

and sent water spraying into the air before him. He walked around a bend in the road that led to one of the best views in all the land. Stretched out before him, the Upper River Valley was filled with the sounds of lowing cattle and the aromas of a sprawling patchwork of farms and orchards fed by crystalline flows of meandering canals.

As Enoch traveled down the road, the rain softened. The suns started a slow burn through the remaining clouds. He looked down upon the fishing boats of many shapes and sizes moored at the docks or drifting over the mollusk fields. After a short detour to drink from the water of a small canal, Enoch arrived at his destination. He brushed off his clothes, patted down his hair, and knocked on the door.

Sasha's mother and little brother answered the door.

"Oh my," she cried while giving him a hug. "Little Enoch is turning into a young man, and a muscled one at that!"

He noted a flash of human activity in the background, realizing he may have arrived too early for much of the family to be dressed for visitors.

The little brother tired of the scene and ran off. Sasha's mother escorted Enoch down the hall where he met Sasha's father and her other twin little brother.

Sasha came down the stairs as her mother began round two of the look-how-big-Enoch-has-become speech. Enoch concentrated on not blushing. Sasha had become quite tan in the near fortnight since the end of school. She was wearing a short dress, was smiling, and was prettier than Enoch had ever remembered.

"Why Enoch, I certainly am surprised to see you here."

"Nonsense girl," her mother chimed in mockingly. "Sune told us that Enoch would be over the very first instant he had no chores!" Now both blushed as she gave them instructions to care for the horses and ushered them out the back door.

Enoch's thoughts churned, trying to think of a way to break the silence without sounding like a true dotard, the way he had at the banquet.

When they were a safe distance from the house, Sasha thankfully spoke first, "So, you've had a lot of chores, huh?"

Enoch explained losing a bet to his brother, dancing around the role Sasha had unknowingly played. He explained the Kahdi story—which Sasha found incredibly funny—and how Berc had "forgotten" to pass along the essential warnings from Kahdi's parents.

"Then last night," Enoch went on. "Berc is late for dinner as usual, and Sabri and I have told our parents the whole story. I mean we spill our guts so there is no way Berc can worm his way out of this one. Sure enough, Berc comes in all happy with his I-am-so-good-for-the-land grin plastered all the way across his face. He kisses mother on the cheek and greets the rest of us. But I'm thinking he is starting to figure out something is wrong.

"Before his backside even hits the chair, my father asks him 'so how did chores go today?' Berc pauses, says 'they went just fine, thanks for asking,' and takes a bite of dinner. The silence is starting to bear down on him by this point. Then he asks Sabri 'so how is Dew doing?' This has to be the worst try at changing the subject ever. I put my fork down so I don't miss one single syllable. My father almost broke a smile, but then his deeper voice comes out and he tells Berc that he has one—and only one—chance to explain the truth.

"Now he's scared, as he should be, and the whole story comes out, making it like…the greatest moment of my life! Turns out, he would leave the house in the morning and hide behind some bushes where he could watch the road connecting Falo's house to the village square. He would sit there quiet as a rabbit, until Falo's mother would ride by, on her way to work. Then he would run down the road and hang out at Falo's house all day while I did all his stinking chores."

"Wow," Sasha exclaimed, "and her mother is a widow, right?"

"Yeah, ever since the sixth forest breach," Enoch continued, enjoying his audience and basking in the telling of a good story. "Now today, he gets to do my chores, which include going to the docks and preparing our boat to go out tomorrow. That is a lot of work when there are three of us. But now it will be just him and father, all day long. Oh, and the best part, on the way home from the docks, they're stopping by to tell the whole story to Falo's mother. I would give anything to see that!"

Sasha giggled. "And what if they find *her* chores unfinished?"

"And maybe the tlok-vine tea supplies just a little low." Enoch laughed and leaned back against the side of the barn. "Now my brother is doing double chores today and all is right in the land, the end."

Sasha looked at him and smiled. "Now you're here to tell me Berc will do your chores for the rest of the growing season, and you can spend it here?" She handed him a brush and pointed to a white mare. Enoch stared at the brush while holding it upside down. Sasha grabbed his hand to turn it over.

"Well, I wish, but father says the official punishment is 'to be determined.' I guess it depends on how the meeting goes at Falo's house and our fishing trip and stuff. But I do know he gets my next couple of Kahdi assignments. I'm not going to miss those. That guy could get you killed or something!"

The two of them spent the rest of the morning brushing, feeding, and turning the horses out to pasture. Sasha filled him in on the trip she had seen Kahdi take up into the forest. She also told Enoch that her family would likely go on the winter caravan again this year, how they were attacked on the Darnoc Trail last year, and about the man who was injured and later died. She also swore there was nothing better than manko meat and that she would volunteer for the caravan every year even though she had never been colder, or more scared. They also discussed birthdays and realized Sasha would turn thirteen, and Enoch fourteen, all in the next few days.

They had lunch back at the house. Sasha's mother asked Enoch about his ceremony and the rumor she heard about him having it a year early. Enoch wondered if there was anything that happened in the land that wasn't known instantly by everyone's parents. Sasha had to go with her mother to the orchards for the rest of the day. She walked Enoch out the front door to say goodbye.

"You stay safe out on that boat tomorrow, Enoch.

You've got to come back from your trip because I've never had a fourteen-year-old boy as a friend before."

Enoch promised, and Sasha hugged him goodbye. Enoch began the long walk home with one eye on the treetops, one eye on the boats bobbing in the Sea below, and that feeling back in his stomach.

That night, a companion arrived at the house that would be with Sasha for many seasons. One of the twin's guards had startled and raised a loaded spike, but then nodded knowingly, smiled at him, and opened the front door. He climbed up the stairs, sniffed, and turned into Sasha's room.

Sasha-protec had arrived.

He lay down on his side, between bed and door, with one paw tucked under his left tusk. It was probably the deepest sleep he would ever have. The kind of sleep a protec can have only after he has traversed the endless forest and found his girl.

Fate, chosen or not, will be your third shadow.
—Olia

7

Enoch awoke early the next morning for their trip to the Sea. Egard had made them load and recheck their backpacks late the night before, checking for water, food, weapons bags, and layers of dry clothes. Enoch was tired, and Berc was grumpy, but excitement reigned for their first trip on the Sea this season.

The three of them retraced many of Enoch's steps from the previous day. It was still early enough for the roads to be empty and their watch to be vigilant. Each knew his assignment, having traveled this route many times before. Berc traveled in the right wagon track, with spike in hand and eyes on the forest. Enoch walked in the left track, watchful for any movement or potential ambush site ahead. Egard was several steps behind, looking over his boys and to the sky, with frequent glances behind.

They crossed the Salt River Bridge and traveled through the farmlands. A startled ani deer sprang from the underbrush at one point. Enoch yelped and hoped no one had heard the sound.

"Father," Berc questioned "historically, has one ever successfully traded in a little brother for a protec?"

They arrived at the docks without further incident and approached *The Indomitable*, the old vessel that had navigated the Sea for the last thirty or so growing seasons. Enoch threw his backpack aboard and laid the weapons bag on the deck, feeling the boat's undulation as it danced beside the dock. He noted the careful detail with which the cloths of the mainsail and the jib were folded. He resolved not to bring the subject up, knowing that Berc was likely still fuming about doing all the tasks by himself the day before.

The boys tightened their tunics against the pre-dawn chill. Egard nodded to Berc, and he untied the ropes attached to the dock posts. The boat made a deep wrenching sound as the boys pushed off from the dock—first with their hands and then with their oars.

Enoch braced himself against the mast and awaited the signal from his father. Enoch took one last glance at the dock, chiding himself for imagining a Cof running down the dock, leaping over the water and into the boat.

Egard guided the tiller and nodded to the boys to raise the mainsail and the jib. The precisely carved angles of the vessel lurched and groaned as the wind flicked the sails open and the hull cut through the water.

Enoch surveyed the shore, now rushing past, and noted with amusement, one empty dock, adorned with strips of red cloth, warning potential dockers of the barely submerged mast of a boat that would never again sail. It stretched toward the water's surface, longing for the lost companionship of Sea air and serving as a permanent reminder of Kahdi's most infamous escapade.

Enoch left the mast and moved to the bow. From this position he surveyed the Sea's surface, scanning between the occasional pelicans for dolphins and the possibility of a school of herky fish.

The eastern shore had receded from view by the time Enoch spied the dorsal fins of a pod of hunting dolphins. Berc took down the mainsail and moved toward the nets. Egard stood at the rudder, steering in the direction of the dolphins and their prey.

The first dolphins appeared to be just frolicking in the ship's pre-wake, but soon broke off from the boat and encircled the frantic rippling of thousands of herky fish. All three turned in the direction of the disturbance. Berc hoisted the net to his right shoulder. Enoch quickly took down the last sail as Berc hurled the weight of the net forward. But Berc caught the front of the net on a lifeline and the rest of the net slithered down the side of the boat.

Egard adjusted the ship's direction to turn and retrieve the net—now soaked with Sea water. Berc uttered profanities. He was reprimanded as they hauled the net back on board. Enoch snickered to himself as he tried to keep his focus on the moving fish. With the now much heavier netting on board, they raised the mainsail in pursuit and steadied their feet on the deck of the lurching boat. Berc hoisted the net up above his head again and was covered this time with saltwater and the aroma of last year's marine catches. For a moment, Enoch pondered the thought of offering to take over Berc's job as smelly net thrower if he would tell him every detail of yesterday's meeting with Falo's mother.

This time, the combination of Enoch's keen eyes and

Berc and Egard's aim paid off. The weighted circular net landed in the middle of the boil of frantic herky fish. The dolphins drew down—as they always did when the weights smacked the water. Berc counted, then jerked the draw line.

Enoch strained to see the bulging net as it was pulled from the water. He almost forgot his scorned duty at this point—to provide ballast at the other side of the boat—until a sharp glance from Egard reminded him. Enoch traipsed port side and knelt, placing his chest against the hull, and leaning his arms over and into the water. He despised this job, each and every time, staring dumbly into the water on the actionless side of the boat while his brother and father worked to haul up the net and reveal its bounty.

After an inordinate amount of grunting behind him, Enoch was finally given permission to un-ballast. He turned to find the net alive with hundreds of fish, most about the size of his forearm. Some had escaped the net and were skittering across the deck and back into the Sea.

Enoch scrambled to lift the lid off the live well. They hoisted the heavy, squirming net on the side of the well and released the drawstring. Hundreds of fish plummeted into the water of the container. The satisfied fishermen sat down to catch their breath.

Egard turned to his boys and rustled their wet heads. "What do you think, boys? Not bad for the first dance on the Sea this season, eh? If it wasn't for Berc here trying to net our ship with the first throw, I'd say we were darn near perfect."

Enoch giggled. Berc lunged for a headlock but was

stopped by a stern warning from Egard before he caused the boat to rock to one side.

"Come on boys. We've got a lot more work to do so that we are back in our beds before the dark. Also, look what is headed our way." Egard pointed a steady hand toward the rim of the high western mountains. "We shall soon have banks of clouds hiding the water's surface from the suns and inviting the herky fish up to feed. A couple more hauls like the last one and we can sell our take in the village square and still be home in time for the evening meal."

They raised the sails. Enoch began his watch anew, thinking that fishing was a whole lot easier than he remembered from previous seasons.

By midday, Enoch's mind had changed. The clouds covered the entire land, followed, in short order, by fog and incessant drizzle. They started a fire in the small stove at the stern, so they could take turns warming themselves and drying their gloves while operating the rudder. They had only seen one dolphin since their big catch. It played in the wake of the boat, jumping and spinning but not leading them to fish, or even to other dolphins. Eventually, Berc declared the dolphin was "obviously stupid," and they let their sails down to rest. They huddled shivering around the stove to eat their lunch.

They were drifting and discussing their late day strategy when Egard stood and pointed, through the rain, to a site neither of the boys had ever seen. In the distance to the far west of their location, was the misty and barely visible outline of an island; Egg Island, nesting ground of the Cofs.

Enoch and Berc had read about this island in school

and how there once was a man, named Orem, if Enoch remembered correctly, who decided he would save all of humanity by sailing to the island and smashing all the Cof eggs. He did not fare well, but achieved posthumous fame, nonetheless.

Even Egard, who had sailed the waters ever since his youth, had never sailed this far west on the open Sea.

"Boys," he said with alarm, "I'm afraid my Sea-faring skills are suspect in this early season. We will have to forego further fishing in favor of a sensible and quick route back to the safety of the docks.

With nervous backward glances at the island, the three took bearings and decided on a quick initial northward route that would make their return trip slightly longer. This would enable them, however, to then follow the northern shore, sailing in shallower waters but using the down sloping winds, rolling off the mountains, to their advantage.

Enoch was in charge of storing the nets and operating the sails. Berc watched for rock outcroppings.

The rain continued to soak their clothes and the return trip felt three times longer than the morning trip. Vigilance and cold led to boredom and discomfort. The suns, hardly visible through the fog, drew closer to the rims of the mountain tops that would soon turn their light into only shadows.

With all pretense of fishing now abandoned, Egard changed the assignments on the boat. Two would operate the rudder at the back of the boat, and warm themselves near the stove. Rotating watches at the bow would track the shore and the water ahead. Egard used hand signals to trim sails or alter the ship's course.

Each had completed one watch and Egard was into his second. Three herky fish fillets were cooking and the smoke from the stove rose from their boat to mix with the fog above. Enoch and Berc were discussing Kahdi to pass the time. It began with an unanswerable question: "What will the Legion do about Kahdi?" It then waxed philosophical and waned ridiculous.

"Do you think he is trying to kill himself with his water adventures and his trips into the forest?" Berc questioned. "Or do you think he is trying to kill the poor mutton-brain who goes after him?"

"Maybe we could get him a girlfriend," Enoch added before realizing the insult.

"How 'bout this? We announce there is to be a drawing," Berc said. "Someone has to take one for the good of the land and be Kahdi's girlfriend forever!"

"A forever-girlfriend is called a wife, you pea-brained big brother."

"Okay, we announce we are going to put the names of all the marrying-age girls in a hat and draw one out." Berc stopped a moment to flip the herky meat over on the stove. "We put Sabri's name on a few dozen pieces of paper, throw them in a hat, wal-lah, she's his forever girlfriend and can now watch him forever and keep him out of trouble."

The boys were so consumed with laughter that they almost missed Egard's silent hand signals.

Enoch reached for the rudder, but then recognized the stop signal instead. He arose to move forward and take down a sail.

"What the...?" Berc paused with more frantic hand waving from Egard, including a hand-over-mouth to signal silence. With the sails down and Egard stepping gently toward them, the boys scanned the shore in the direction of their father's pointing.

Neither saw anything through the mist other than a quiet cove surrounded by a rocky shore and trees dripping with moisture. Still unable to get his point across, Egard positioned the boys in front of him. He pointed an outstretched arm between their heads, in the direction of the shoreline.

Berc was the first one to utter a gasp, prompting Egard to throw a hand over his mouth, reinstating a silence in the cove broken only by pellets of rain and gentle waves lapping at the shore.

Enoch looked desperately but could see nothing except rocks and trees. Then, his focus was shattered by the thick, perfectly camouflaged hide of an enormous Cof—in the forest, but only a few paces up from the water's edge.

It lay in the position typical for sleeping Cofs—draped over the gnarled roots of a young mander tree and curled around the trunk. Its back protruded out in the direction of the water.

Enoch could make out the left wing tucked beneath the animal. He hoped it was a carcass. But the body expanded with a slow, giant breath, causing the right wing to lift upwards and then fall back slowly as it exhaled.

Egard motioned Berc and Enoch up to the bow. He leaned over and carefully grabbed a weapons bag, pulling out a spike. He loaded it while pressing it against his side to muffle the click of the spikes. He handed it to Berc, whose pupils were wide and black. He loaded a second spike for Enoch, then whispered the plan to his sons as heartbeats pounded in everyone's ears.

"Berc, I am going to take us a little closer. From there, we can hopefully spy its neck on that side of the tree. If we can't, you need to aim for the middle of its back. If you spike it there with enough force, you can at least paralyze it…or so they say."

Berc looked confused at first, but then nodded his understanding. Egard caught his breath and turned to his youngest child, "You must keep your eyes on the sky and the forest canopy."

Enoch flashed back to the favorite saying of one of his teachers, "Wherever there is a Cof on the ground, there are two in the trees."

Egard continued, "Do not avert your eyes to watch your brother's throw. I'll stand and load a third spike when we hear impact. Only at that point can you throw if you see another target. Everybody got it?"

Both nodded while keeping their frightened gaze on their assignments.

Egard stepped across the deck and fixed the oars into the oar locks without creating a sound. He knifed the oars slowly into the water before turning the blades and pushing the boat forward.

Two more rows with the oars. Enoch was terrified to be this close to a Cof. It was now clear they could not see the animal's neck unless they were to land the boat, in which case it might be the last thing they ever did.

Egard gave the signal for Enoch to watch high and left, and the all clear for Berc to throw. Berc looked one last time at the spike in his hand. He replanted his left foot beneath him. He took one final look at the target and inhaled a large, quiet breath.

Berc put his left forearm before his face, then threw

his body and wind-milled his right hand forward, releasing the weapon as hard as possible. They heard the projectile leave Berc's hand and slice the air with the whistling sound of a well-thrown spike. The Cof startled and lifted its body just before impact.

The spike tore into the left wing of the creature, missing its back and torso.

"Enoch, now!" Egard shouted and dropped the oars. He turned the bag upside down and released all the weapons crashing onto the deck.

As Egard loaded the next spikes, Enoch turned away from the treetops. He looked at the injured Cof which had righted itself and was bounding furiously away. It was holding a dripping left wing out awkwardly while sending rocks screeing down the mountain. Enoch locked his aim into the back of its neck, but while drawing his arm backwards, he saw a form descending upon them from the treetops—Enoch's previously assigned vantage to his left.

The second Cof was in full dive. Its shadow was cast over the boat when it likely realized the closeness of the water and drew up, exposing its full silhouette. Enoch wheeled on instinct and threw without even aiming. The spike left his hand and traveled far enough to reach full speed before Enoch heard and felt the impact. The spike lodged thickly into the Cof's neck. Its upward momentum stopped, and its wings flailed roughly as it somersaulted past the front of the boat. It smashed into the water's surface, sending Sea spray in all directions, and rocking the boat. Enoch opened a scythe as his brother and father rushed to the front of the boat with their spikes.

Enoch grabbed his weapon and turned back to the

water, but the flailing had already stopped. The Cof's head and neck, losing blood and weighted down with the embedded spike, turned silently toward the depths. It sank, leaving only gentle blood-tinged rings of water expanding quietly outward toward the shoreline.

All three turned their heads to the forest and the sky. Seeing no other predators, they showered Enoch with congratulatory hits about his back and head. The exultation and hollering of all three was now heard by many ears in the northern forest, none of them human.

After a short time, Egard stopped the celebration to man the oars and orient the boat back out of the cove. The boys hoisted the sails. The normally long trip home passed in an instant.

As the boat pulled into the fishing village, the first sun was dropping behind the mountains. The second bathed Verandale in a reddish hue. Enoch was beaming as he helped unload the live well.

Egard and Berc recounted the story for all that would listen.

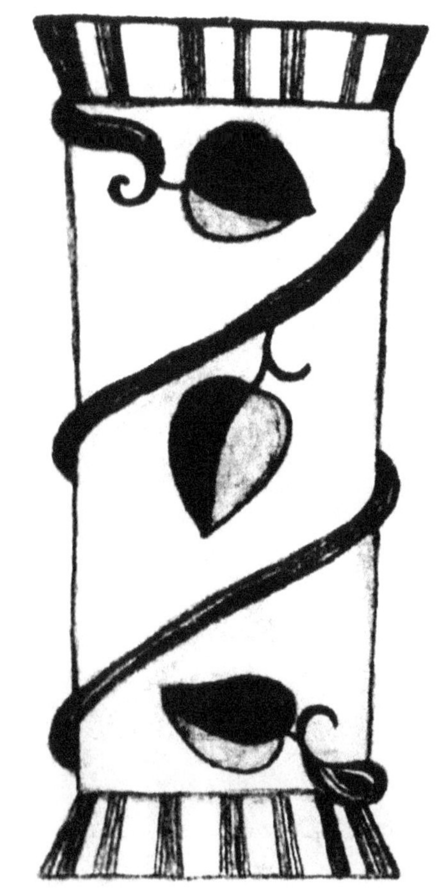

In your life, you will travel down both right and wrong paths. Travel both with excellence.

—Egard

By the time he awoke the next morning, weary and sore, every Verandalian had heard the story of Enoch's first Cof kill.

"Come on honey, you must get up," said his mom shaking his shoulder. "Everybody is going to be here soon, and you need to have a little breakfast in your belly." Enoch was still too groggy to hear all his mother was saying, "…or you're going to throw up when you get your mark."

Enoch's eyes flew open and his memory scurried. He threw off his covers as his mother left the room. "And don't forget dear, you can invite whomever else you would like to come see you get your mark this morning."

Enoch immediately pictured Sasha, but then tried to get her image out of his head. He had heard from many before him, that the mark—administered by the Healer and his armory of notorious needles—was one of the most painful things a person could endure. There was no way he was going to invite Sasha to see him do anything looking like a whimper. He finished dressing and walked the hallway to the dining pit.

Aunts and Uncles and hugs were everywhere. Egard walked up to Enoch and the family. He looked like he was going to say something, but Enoch noted a glint of hesitation welling in his father's eyes. Egard slapped him on the back instead—before walking back to tend the food over the fire.

Enoch sat down in his usual chair, relieved that at least he didn't have to do that sit-at-the-head-of-the-table thing. His mother served him first, setting down a steaming plate of one of Enoch's favorite dishes—a mutton and kale omelet. The smell was unbelievable, and Enoch thought he might be able to eat despite his nerves after all.

Sabri came in and sat down in Berc's seat, right next to Enoch. Dew laid his head on her thigh before turning his eyes to Enoch and opening his mouth.

"Don't think I'm going to be able to sneak you anything today, boy. Not with all these people…" Enoch stopped in mid-sentence upon processing Sabri's empty chair and her current occupation of Berc's chair.

"Where is Berc?" Enoch grimaced, already guessing the answer.

"He went to get your young friend, dear," Sune said as she set more steaming, laden plates onto the table. "Just like you asked him, he is a very special brother, that Berc."

Sabri tried to hide a grin as she lifted her plate to her face to take in the aroma.

Enoch whispered to her between clinched teeth, trying to act normal. "Don't tell me."

Sabri put down her plate. "Enoch, Berc told us how you begged him, while hiking up from the docks last night, to get up early this morning and go get Sasha." She stopped as Enoch looked aghast. He faked smiles as he continued to receive congratulatory hugs.

"What were we supposed to do?" Sabri continued, "go wake you up to make sure he wasn't telling us a tall tale?"

"But what if…" Enoch's desperate plea was interrupted by Sune telling him to hurry and eat, followed by Sabri finishing his sentence.

"What if she sees you cry?" Sabri blurted out. Enoch started to protest, but she continued, "You know I'll always be ready to protect my little brother's manhood. If I see a little tear crawling down your face, I'll just tell Dew to a-t-t-a-c-k somebody and cause a distraction." Dew rolled his eyes in her direction. "Sasha will never know."

Enoch took a deep breath, realizing he would be powerless to stop any of this. He brought the first bite up to his lips. As he did, the front door opened to reveal Berc, Sasha, Sasha-protec, Orgard, the Healer, and the Apprentice.

He tried to quiet his nerves. He tried not to look at Sasha. The Healer, on the other hand, was a sight impossible to avoid.

Enoch had not seen him since last year. He appeared more chiseled than Runal rock itself. There were so many deep wrinkles covering his face, it was difficult to discern which crevices contained his eyes. He walked with a large and colorfully stained walking stick in his right hand. His hair bounced in haphazard bundles that mirrored the colors of his staff. His skin was darker than any in the land and contrasted with the cloudy robe that hung over his thin frame.

Enoch spied the gnarled hands of the Healer. They did not appear capable of handling sharp instruments. He wished he could just go back to his room, lie down for a while, and come back out to an empty house.

Sasha's mother helped the Healer over to the upper edge of the dining pit. The Apprentice, whose real name Enoch had not heard for several years, produced two tall stools. He then brought out a large satchel, undoing strings and flaps until all instruments were shining in the open air.

He then led Enoch to a stool as two men helped the Healer up to the other stool on his left. The Apprentice produced a knife and grabbed the left sleeve of Enoch's tunic. He began to cut. Enoch startled and his eyes grew wide.

"The Healer says you will not want a sleeve on this arm for the next couple of days." The Healer's lips had a slight tremble, but Enoch had not heard him speak a word to himself or anyone else. "Besides," the Apprentice continued, "I think you are going to want to show off your mark to that little girl in the yellow dress over there." He pointed in the general direction of Sasha and the growing throng of people around her.

"I'm not going to look at her, if that is okay," Enoch whispered, drawing a hearty laugh from The Apprentice.

"Of course, the Healer says he understands your feelings very well, indeed."

Enoch again looked at the Healer, neither seeing nor hearing anything from his mouth. He was about to ask the Apprentice how he discerned these words from his boss when he felt a cold, damp cloth against his exposed shoulder. A cup made of a heavy stone was placed in his right hand. The crowd quieted.

Whispered into his right ear, "Healer says drink this to make the pain."

"You mean to make the pain go away?"

The Apprentice answered by pushing underneath the cup to bring it up to Enoch's lips.

Enoch drank the contents of the cup in two quick gulps. A strange spicy aroma filled his nostrils. He felt a burn starting in his stomach then spreading up to his chest like a burning pyre.

"Guuk," Enoch exclaimed and looked to the Apprentice—who returned only a smile before nodding his head. He heard a tap at his left shoulder, followed by a sharpness that penetrated his skin and lanced pain down to his fingers, then back up to his neck.

Resisting the urge to howl, Enoch looked to his shoulder and tried to steady himself. The Healer was holding a small metal rod in his right hand. On the end of the rod was a misshapen forged metal ball, with sharpened points of different sizes, protruding outward in all directions. With his left hand he pounded a small club rhythmically against the ball, causing the rotating points to pierce Enoch's bleeding skin.

The Apprentice again whispered into his ear and through the pain, "You will need to be opening your eyelids wider. This will bring to your eyes more air and dry out those wannabe tears that are trying to stay in your eyes."

Enoch followed his directions, willing to try anything

to get through this. As the tapping—and the pain—continued, Enoch felt a second, and more soothing, warmth starting to rise from his torso. He began to feel that he might be able to tolerate the pain, might even be able to get through this process. He risked a look to the audience. The first person he saw was Berc, grinning and giving him an enthusiastic thumbs-up sign from the back of the crowd. Enoch thought back to how the first Cof raised up just a moment too soon, otherwise Berc would be on a stool also, and likely, due to seniority, be undergoing this torture before Enoch. At least, he thought, he would be able to hold his mark over Berc's head, once the pain went away.

Enoch focused his concentration on an imperfection in the stone floor, unwilling to chance another look up. Soon after, the tapping stopped, and the lancing pain became a dull throbbing. Enoch had survived his first mark! He looked to the crowd, and then to the Healer, who was placing instruments back in the satchel. Enoch wondered when the applause would start. He looked to the Apprentice.

"I did it, right?"

The Apprentice placed a hand on his back. "Enoch, the mark has been put into your brave Cof-killing skin." Enoch smiled for just an instant. "Now it will be cured."

Enoch's mind was still contemplating as the Healer pulled out some black steaming thing out of a pouch. The Healer continued to mumble. He closed his eyes, and then opened them as wide as Enoch had ever seen. He picked up the steaming, palm-sized patch—with a now gloved hand—and slapped it onto the marked skin.

It sizzled, and Enoch absorbed a pain, far surpassing

that of the metal points. The Healer was up and off his stool and putting all his weight behind his hands, holding the substance against his patient. The Apprentice, pushing from the other side, kept Enoch on the stool. After an unclear amount of time, the pressure at Enoch's shoulder ceased.

The crowd erupted into a loud and prolonged applause as Enoch's head dropped forward. He felt grayness come over him but was pretty sure he did not pass out. Upon opening his eyes, he focused on a small drop on the ground beneath him. Realizing he could not lean down close enough to identify the fluid as tears or other, Enoch lifted up—bravely, he hoped—and looked out to the crowd, still boisterous with applause.

Sasha was clapping, but also leaning close and talking into Sabri's ear. He noted her yellow dress and thought there was no way that she put it on for a day of doing chores around the farm. He also knew there was no way he could talk to her right now. He avoided her until the crowd filed out of the house.

Egard came over to Enoch and placed a hand on his unmarked shoulder. "I'm quite proud of you, son. You know, this likely makes your Ceremony a certainty for next year. With your manhood so quickly approaching, there is one other thing you will need to see."

Egard turned Enoch around and marched him down the darkened corridor and into Enoch's room. With one more glance backwards, he led him to the window.

"I thought we would leave out the back. This way, we will avoid any unnecessary socializing in front of the house, and you can blow air on your shoulder anytime you want."

They crawled through the window and Enoch winced. He stole a quick look for bystanders, then blew the first soothing breath onto his angry red shoulder.

He had to admit, it looked great. The center of the mark was a bluish pillar. This represented the surrounding area—in this case water—that Enoch was on when the attack occurred. The pillar was encircled by a climbing vine with three large leaves for the three members of the party present for the kill. He wondered how much labor he would have to do in the fields of the growing season, to make his muscles a little bit bigger. Then he could show off his mark all the better—at least for the first days of the next school year, before the cold weather set in.

Egard announced they were going to the palace but would take a quick detour behind the hills of the school. Once there, Egard bent down to a very young evergreen sapling. While Enoch kept a close eye on its bigger arborous relatives growing at edges of the forest, Egard ground some of the youngest and softest of the pine needles between two rocks. He told Enoch to hold out his two hands, cupped together, and placed the gooey poultice into them. To this he added some flour from a small pouch in his trousers, and cool water from a tiny rivulet flowing nearby. He stirred this with a finger and then tilted the entire concoction into Enoch's right hand.

"Alright, I don't need to tell you to do this gently, but just hold your right hand above your mark and let the mixture drip onto the sore spots. At first, it will only feel sticky, but by the time we get there, the soothing will begin to take effect.

"Um, you haven't told me where we are going."

Egard remained silent a moment longer until Enoch did as he was told, and greenish semi-liquid streaks covered his mark and burn.

"Son, we are going to the palace to meet with Ibrakrim, the librarian and the possessor of more marks than any other human in the land."

Enoch held his arm out to the side—trying to keep the clammy substance from contacting his armpit and chest. He thought about their destination and all the events of the last two days as they started again to walk along the warmed earth of the road.

*The forces of good and evil, when poured together, can make a
bitter stew. Two forces of good, can sometimes make the same.*
                                                    —Unknown

9

Enoch hiked, with his father, through the fields along
the eastern border of Verandale. His awareness
instinctively heightened as the sound of the river pouring
through the palace drowned out one of his protective
senses.

They approached the stones of the rightward path,
smoothed by the many thousands of people who had
trod this way going to ceremonies, weddings, death
rights, and judicial matters over the many years since
the palace's construction. Many passersby stopped to
congratulate him and look upon his new mark. He felt
like they might never make it to the library at this rate. But
as the path brought them closer to the source of the Salt
River, the deafening sound made small talk impossible.
The saline veil of mist around them also made it easier
for Enoch and Egard to walk in anonymity, though the
salty air stung Enoch's shoulder.

They continued through the grand foyer until they
reached the rightmost of the two large doors flanking
the river's mouth at the back wall. Enoch reached the

door ahead of his father. He momentarily forgot his pain and reached for the forged iron handle of the door but cringed and stepped aside to let his father brace his feet on the damp floor and pull the massive door open. He motioned for Enoch to enter.

Egard pushed the door closed behind them. The reverberation pounded against their feet. The silence that followed was profound as the door returned to its frame and blocked nearly all sound from the foyer.

Enoch took a moment to run his hand along the stone walls built with stones twice the size of a grown man. Though lit with many torches, the hallway was dreary with decades of soot coating the Runal rock.

They passed doors leading to the quarters of guards and other workers. At the end of the hall, they stopped before the ancient wood of a larger door carved to represent hundreds of books. Some were merely etched into the wood while others were colored with dyes. Most of the books were closed, with delicately chiseled titles visible on the front. Others were held open by hands, freed from the restraints of the rest of the body.

Egard knocked four quick raps against the door and waited. Enoch was about ask about the librarian's whereabouts when he heard a slow and gentle shuffle from behind the door. A latch turned, and another interminable wait ensued before the door began to move inward.

The light inside the door was even dimmer than in the passage. It took Enoch a moment before he could make out the tall form and mythical broad shoulders of Ibrakrim. The librarian looked down at Enoch. A frown began to cross his face until he was able to also make out the shape of Enoch's father. He smiled and grabbed Egard, pulling his head playfully downward.

"Egard, you old oswatt-eater, what brings you deep into the palace on such a fine day?"

"I wanted to show my son what can happen to a man who breathes dust all the time and never sees the light of day," Egard jousted back as the two men laughed.

"Well come on in and let me get you some of the finest aged tlok-vine tea you will ever come across. I am assuming none for the boy due to his sleeping problem."

Egard shot a glance at Enoch, who winced.

"Indeed," as he popped the wooden plug off a jug and broke out two cups. "I was considerably worried when your boys would come here to study. I would see them looking around for the darkest corner. To be fair, I suppose I could have reminded them that I have eyes not only in my head, but also amongst the shelves... like any respectable old librarian. So, did your brother Berc pass his ceremony or did he sleep through that, too?"

Enoch wanted to shrink beneath a table, but his father rescued him.

"Well, Enoch and I will have some talking to do on our way home. But Ibrakrim, there is starting to be a little more man than boy in Enoch. Show him, son." Egard turned him so his mark was visible in the light of the library's flickering flames.

Ibrakrim leaned forward and squinted his eyes a short distance from Enoch's shoulder.

"Hmmm, I would say either someone spilled blue on your shoulder, or you actually have the mark of a genuine Cof kill. And to think I always considered you two boys about as useful as the cats that nap all day on the rocks, out behind the palace."

Enoch smiled as the librarian leaned closer to read the details within his mark. "Killed a Cof with the help of your brother and father, I am guessing. It appears you were on the water. You do not see marks like this very often. Good work, Enoch. I say they will make a man out of you yet."

Egard made Enoch recite the whole story, even though Enoch figured Ibrakrim had already heard the story and even anticipated their visit. He listened patiently and again offered his congratulations to Enoch while refilling his and Egard's cups and producing a third, which he filled with water and gave to Enoch.

The three of them drank in the next few moments of silence. Ibrakrim stood and unfastened the front of his cloak as Enoch put down his cup and stared ahead breathlessly. He had heard of Ibrakrim's eleven kills—tales told at school and around the family table—but neither he nor any of his friends had ever seen his marks.

Ibrakrim draped his cloak over the back of a wooden chair. He rolled up the sleeve of his undershirt, walked around the table to Enoch, and bared his arm. Three marks— somewhat faded with time—stretched across the top of his shoulder. Below these, other marks were placed more haphazardly as someone—likely the Healer, Enoch supposed—had been forced to cram more and more marks into the finite space between shoulder and elbow.

Ibrakrim nodded to Enoch, then stood still as Enoch

ran his fingers over the marks. Each mark told a tale and was laid down according to strict rules, paying homage to the traditions of the land.

Most of the pillars were covered with multiple leaves of the encircling vine, for all the people involved in, or at least present for, each of the kills. Two had only one leaf on the vine, to show that Ibrakrim was alone when he killed a Cof. The pillars were one of the three colors Enoch had learned about in the classroom. Green for a Cof killed in the forest, yellow if killed in the fields or rows of crops, and blue like Enoch's mark, if killed in or at the edge of water.

One mark on Ibrakrim's skin stood out from the rest. It was the first mark, a pillar covered by a vine and two leaves. Unlike the marks that followed it—and all the other marks that Enoch had ever seen—the pillar was a deep dark brown. Enoch looked at the mark and wondered if it represented dirt. He paused with his finger below this first mark and stared at Ibrakrim, then to his father who only nodded back at the librarian. He felt stumped and inadequate before realizing this was likely the reason he had been brought here.

After a short pause, Ibrakrim turned his sleeve back down and pulled out a chair to sit directly in front of Enoch.

"Enoch, the reason I showed you my marks—and, I'm assuming, the reason your father brought you here today—is because life is conquered not only with power and intelligence, but also with luck and fate. I will tell you the story of my first mark so I can share with you the ways in which a person can prepare not only for the killing of one of the vile menaces who threaten our people, but also for the unexpected challenges that will be set before you in this land and in this life.

"I was a happy young boy who had seen only seven growing seasons in a land I considered to be magical and beautiful. I had learned the most rudimentary of reading skills and would eagerly try to read anything I could find at home or school. I did not yet understand the difference between a true story and one fashioned solely in the mind of the writer. I believed all tales were created for my amusement.

"My parents often told my siblings and me about the dangers of the Cofs. They would tell us how our people could become extinct if we did not find a way out through the high forests. But I filed this in my kitten-sized brain in the same manner as stories of fairies, gods, and talking animals. I was a walking example of happy stupidity.

"It was a cold day in the midst of winter. My aunt had reached a milestone birthday—her thirtieth—and scores of people were packed into our home for the occasion. As part of the celebration, my mother brought a crate of fruit up from the cellar. It had been carefully dried and wrapped in storage skins along with a special blend of sap and Sea salt.

"As was so often the case, our palettes craved this taste, having been deprived since autumn. Each of us received an appropriate child-sized portion of the fruit as a reward for finishing our meals. We inhaled the fruit, and then ran and played happily with full bellies and with fragments of sweetness still coating the insides of our mouths.

"Later, with the nighttime merriment wearing on

and adult supervision waning, we found the old crate sitting near the other foodstuffs in the kitchen. We looked inside at our new treasure. This was a great find. My sister and I, as well as a couple of other playmates, stole the box away to the darkness of a back room and filled our gullets as we giggled long into the night. We singlehandedly finished off all the fruit—except for a portion that spilled on our way out of the kitchen and was gulped up by someone's protec.

"I don't know if the guilt itself would have ever been sufficient to release my confession. In the middle of the night, however, both my sister and I awoke with cramping pains in our midsections and fruity explosions waiting to be released from our hind quarters. I do not remember vomiting, but it would have been preferable to our many trips out to the flimsy outbuilding that bordered our field of corn.

"Our parents took turns bundling us up and walking us the short distance to relieve ourselves. As it turned out, this distance exactly matched the time it took for one scathing parental lecture."

Ibrakrim paused to pour some more tea.

"Later in the night, we felt the worst was over and the whole household fell asleep, exhausted. Unfortunately, my digestive system was not quite done yet. I awoke one last time before daybreak. I called for my father, but he was deep asleep. Also, I was not quite sure I could take yet another verbal lashing. I walked over to my window and gently scratched on the shutters before opening them, having learned not to open them suddenly or loudly next to a cold and nervous night guard. The guard, a tall, gentle man named Indell, turned his ear toward me while keeping his eyes on the surrounding night. I asked if he could take me out to relieve myself this time so I would not have to wake my parents. He smiled nervously and ruffled my hair, saying he thought that would be fine.

"I grabbed my fleece, and he helped me through the window. I asked him if I could have a 'horse ride.' It was a frequent morning tradition where he would load me onto his shoulders and gallop around the dirt road beside our house before his shift ended. He explained how this would not be a safe option in the dead of night. He checked his weapons bag and removed the glove from his right hand to better grip his scythe. He led me a couple of steps before him, and we headed down the path.

"I heard no sounds except for a gentle wind. A couple of times, Indell stopped me with a hand on my shoulder. I turned to see his eyes focused on a distant point, heavy condensation rhythmically leaving his nostrils. He assured me all was well, and we continued to the malodorous shack.

"He stopped me so he could open the creaky door and peer inside. Having been given the all clear, I stepped in and struck a flint for light before closing the door behind me. My trousers on the floor, I began my noisy and embarrassing elimination.

"After a few quieter moments had passed, Indell whispered through the crack to ask if I was okay. Before I could answer, I heard a shrill whistling sound followed by a thunderous crash against the front door. The whole outbuilding rocked, nearly off its foundation, and I heard Indell scream. I tried to stand and grab my pants, but in my terror, I managed only to fall against the flame, extinguishing my only source of light. I heard a ferocious battle move to the side and then behind me. I cowered on the floor and prayed out loud for the first time in my life.

"I'm not sure how long the battle went on. It was probably very brief, but it felt like a lifetime. I was hearing fewer expletives and more groans from Indell when suddenly the back of the outbuilding was torn from the ground. It tipped onto its front with a crash, violently throwing me down against the door.

"The sounds of battle suddenly ceased. I could hear troubled breathing as well as a sound like scratching on the other side of the wood beneath me and I realized a life was trapped by the toppled building. I tried to feel all the surfaces around me in an attempt to get my bearings. There was the tiniest amount of pre-dawn light coming through the hole that I had been sitting over just moments before. I instinctively backed away from it and leaned against the other end, which used to be the roof of the structure.

"A form suddenly blocked the light over the seat hole. I gasped. I tried to be as quiet as possible—holding my breath or at least my crying sounds. A loud gurgling sound came from the form. It sounded like attempted words, and I realized it was Indell.

"'Ibrak, I've…was gored. I can…not get you through the 'ole. Tha Cof under you… 'sal most dead. Do not move, will get hel…help.'

"I could see Indell twist upwards, trying to stand. He took two steps, then toppled backwards with a thud, never to move again.

"I tried to sit as far away as possible from the still breathing form trapped beneath me. I eventually found my pants in the increasing daylight and tied them around the door handle, hoping this would make it more secure. The movement beneath me slowed then stopped. I sat looking out the hole at Indell's lifeless form. As the first sun rose, I sat covered in my own excrement and shivered and cried until I heard the voices of my panicked family running down the path.

"I yelled out to them until they came running to right the outbuilding. My father carried me over the dead Cof and past the body of Indell. After reaching our house, my mother bathed me and dressed my wounds. I stayed in my parents' bed for the rest of that day and the day after. Though I had no interest whatsoever in receiving my first mark, tradition superseded my wishes, and the mark still took place the next day. I have never felt that it was deserved, but to my knowledge I am the youngest person to ever receive a mark.

"I do not know if it was a strict interpretation of the rules or the Healer's own long dormant sense of humor, but he colored the mark with either the brown of the outbuilding's wood, or the brown of human waste; perhaps both.

"I vowed to never forget this lesson I learned too harshly and too young. With each additional mark to my shoulder, I thought of Indell's bravery. He was killed by a vile being, but also by bad fortune. Had he not saved my life, my skin would have decayed along with the rest of my body, long before it ever saw one mark, let alone eleven.

"I tell you this because many a man has been buried

in the cemeteries of Verandale with one mark on their shoulder. They became too assured and too brave to ever gain another. I can teach you many things young Enoch, but the most important is this: always remain humble while seizing those times when fate is good to you, always endure those times when fate is cruel."

*No children, oswatts, protecs (if the protec's girl
is mad at you), Kahdi, or exceptions!*
—Sign at entrance of The Drunken Oswatt

10

A farmer's hog was on the loose and only one person could save him.

The days became shorter as the growing season neared its end. The children were racing home against the setting of the suns. Sune had sent the three of them, and Dew, to the village to buy wheat and corn. They were hurrying back home when Dew stopped in mid-stride and began a rumbling growl. The fur rose up on his back, like quills on a porcupine, while his unwavering attention focused on the tree line. Berc and Sabri stiffened and began to push Enoch behind them. Enoch was about to protest and give them a healthy dose of "I have a Cof kill and you don't" when they heard a rustling coming from the long shadows of the forest.

The boys tore open their weapons bags. But Sabri nudged them to stop when she recognized the source of the sound—a large hog from the farm down the road, burrowing its snout into the undergrowth of the forest. Once satisfied there was no sign of Cofs, they ran the short distance over to the farmer's house. They told him the fretful news and led him back to the hog.

The gruff farmer, having taken in the scene, explained there was no way to retrieve a wayward hog from the forest. He turned to leave.

"Wait, we know someone who can get him out of the forest," Enoch pleaded.

"Son," the farmer started, taking a piece of hay from his mouth, "there is a not a person alive that can safely traipse into the forest after a noisy hog that has probably already alerted every hungry Cof this side of Darnoc. My best suggestion for you kids is to put some distance between you and the trees. Then avert your eyes from the impending carnage."

"But mister," Sabri added, holding back a still growling Dew. "Kahdi's house is right down the lane. He goes into the forest all the time."

This was all the encouragement Berc needed to run off, yelling for Kahdi.

The farmer turned away, grumpier than before, muttering about how "kids in my day at least had some sense."

Berc left the main road and ran down the lane leading to Kahdi's home. He rounded a corner and stopped when he found Kahdi sitting outside his house, talking to some birds nested in the thatch over his parents' front doorway.

"Kahdi, you have to come quick," he panted.

Kahdi ignored him and Berc moved closer, remembering to stay out of striking distance.

"Kahdi," Berc yelled, with his hands cupped on either side of his mouth, slowly pronouncing each syllable. "Is anyone home inside your big head?"

The mountain of flesh in front of Berc failed to move or in any way acknowledge his presence. But, when one of the birds chirped, Kahdi tilted his head in the direction of the tiny creature and chirped back.

"Hey, Kahdi," Berc stopped to roll his eyes upward, "do you want to play with a pig?"

Kahdi turned to face Berc.

"That's right Kahdi, if you help us bring the pig back to the farm, the nice farmer will let you play with all of his pigs." Berc said, happy to finally get Kahdi's attention but not knowing how he would ever make good on his promise.

Kahdi took off and ran to the other side of the house. Berc paused an instant, trying to understand the actions of a non-understandable human. He shrugged his shoulders and ran after Kahdi. Upon reaching the other side, he saw the back end of Kahdi, circling the house. He chased him back to the site of their original, one-sided conversation. Kahdi had simply run one lap around the house. He now headed to the road, in the direction of the gathering hog watchers, most of whom cheered upon seeing Kahdi and the trailing Berc.

Sasha and Sasha-protec were now in the growing crowd of people who had responded to the ruckus. When Kahdi and Berc arrived, Enoch decided to take charge, all the while knowing there was no way he would try this if Sasha wasn't there.

"All right, everybody," Enoch began, "here is what I want you to do." The farmer raised his bushy eyebrows in Enoch's direction, and Sabri giggled.

"Kahdi," Enoch put his hand up on Kahdi's shoulder, "I want you to run in the forest and bring that piggy back. The rest of us will, will…"

"Watch you." Berc finished his sentence and stood smiling next to his stammering brother.

Many laughs from the crowd, then some started chanting Kahdi's name. Kahdi turned away from Enoch and leaned over a few people to look into the forest before taking off to rescue the hog.

Except he didn't rescue the hog, or even take a step in the direction of the forest. Instead, he mumbled something—possibly a "mirk" variant—and turned back to the road, quietly walking back to his house.

"Kahdi, what are you doing?" Enoch ran up to him. "You have to go get this guy. I mean this pig. You're the only one who can go into the forest like that. Come on, we are all depending on you." Enoch pleaded while Kahdi kept walking. He struggled to catch up with him and turn him carefully around on the road.

Enoch now stood up on his toes and whispered so that his words only made it to the ears of Kahdi.

"Alright, Kahdi, I'll tell you what. See that girl over there?" he said tilting his head in the direction of Sasha, now leaning over her protec, and stroking his fur while glancing up at the two of them. "See, she likes me. The problem is that her protec doesn't like me quite as much. But I am thinking if she sees both of us working together to get that pig, she will like me even more, and then I will take you wherever you want. I can take you to the spike-throwing range every day. Or, you know what, we can go tomorrow, and I'll even give you the real spikes and we can throw until our arms fall off." Kahdi stared at Enoch. "Or I will take you out on the boat...anything you want. Just help me get him out of the forest. I mean, I can't go into the forest. But I know you can. You can do this for me, right?"

Kahdi started toward the trees as Enoch stopped and held his breath. Kahdi lumbered to the edge of the forest. He ducked his head a little from side to side before digging through his pockets. He pulled out a clump of meat that looked like a meal remnant…from several days ago. He straightened his arm out in front of him, in the hog's direction. All behind him were quiet.

He made no sound. The problem was the hog was at least fifty paces into the forest and did not even raise its head to acknowledge Kahdi's silent offering. It continued digging with snout and hooves, occasionally stopping to chew a newfound root.

"This is unbelievable," Berc shouted, throwing his arms up in the air. "We are standing at the edge of the forest, it will be dark soon, and our parents are going to kill us even if a Cof doesn't. Meanwhile, brainchild here usually runs into the forest to get rocks or who knows what, but today has decided to only go to the edge and offer a pig his last week's breakfast!"

"Berc, you have to settle down," Sabri said. "I'll go get Kahdi, so we can go home."

Sabri walked up to Kahdi and put a hand on his arm. "Come on Kahdi, let's get you home."

Kahdi stood motionless, giant arm still extended. Sabri tugged at his arm to try and turn him away from the trees.

"Kahdi, this is serious. Look at the suns, we have to get going," Sabri pleaded. She finally put enough force into Kahdi that he began to twist to the side.

Kahdi began to frown.

When Sabri pushed harder, he yelled "Mirk" and threw her to the ground. She hit the ground with an audible thump.

And that is when Dew bit Kahdi.

It wasn't a nip. It was a ferocious bark followed by a lunge that impaled Dew's tusks into Kahdi's calf. This was followed by top and bottom jaws extending to clamp onto his leg while growling and thrashing his head from side to side.

The ground shook beneath Enoch's feet as Kahdi toppled over and brought forth a primal scream that some would say they had only heard once before… during the Kahdi boat-sinking.

Villagers ran to the melee. Some were trying to get Sabri out from under Kahdi. Others were frantically trying to pull Dew away. Still others, like Sasha, were trying to keep their own protecs out of the pile of bodies. All were screaming, but one scream rose above all others to echo off the high mountain walls. The sound came from Berc as Kahdi bit him in the leg.

The chaos increased until Sabri got free and was able to call Dew off Kahdi's leg. Dew backed away, still growling, and Kahdi ran bleeding and limping along the road back to his house.

Just as all parties were off the dusty ground and away from the trees, Egard and Sune came running up the road. Sasha said a quick goodbye and sprinted off in the opposite direction with her protec, knowing she did not want to have any part of the upcoming discussion.

As the darkness grew outside, six chairs were positioned around the family table; one for each member of the family and one for Berc's bandaged leg. Dew sat next to Sabri's chair, traces of blood still drying on his tusks.

Egard stood up. He looked at each of his children before starting to pace around the table.

"I need to make sure I have understood today's events correctly. The three of you put together have less than one brain's worth of common sense. And the only being I thought capable of keeping you out of trouble," he looked at Dew, who hid his head under Sabri's elbow, "responded to today's crisis by biting your simple friend in the leg."

"I guess the most amazing thing to me right now, is that Kahdi seems to be the only one today who made a rational choice—not to go into the forest."

"But Dad, he goes in all the ti…"

Egard stopped Enoch's protest with a glance. His lecture proceeded on through the time normally set aside for the family meal. The hungry siblings went to their rooms without a chance for rebuttal, not that they could have come up with one.

THE
CHIMERA

*Repercussions can follow percussions if
you are not careful…or even if you are.*
—Someone's grandmother

11

The draft horses stomped their tracks through the early-morning condensation on the road. They paused often enough for Egard to reach for the whip at his side but not long enough for him to use it. Behind him, the open wagon was weighed down, but not with animals, grains, or tools. In the back, leaning with their backs against the driver's bench and facing the road behind them, sat Berc and Kahdi. Each wore an unhappy look on his face. A wooden trunk lay turned on its side near the back of the wagon. On top of this was an old blanket, folded neatly to cushion Kahdi's left leg, and Berc's right.

Enoch, Sabri, and Dew walked behind the wagon. They stayed back to avoid the wet spray coming off the wagon wheels. They stayed a little farther back to hide their snickers from the unpleasant trio ahead of them.

"I haven't seen Kahdi this banged up since last year when he got into a fight with that family of beavers," Enoch said.

"You know, it is common knowledge the beavers

started it," replied Sabri as she turned her head and tried to cover her laugh.

Egard had spoken sternly to the siblings as they finally filled their growling bellies with the morning meal. To make amends for their transgression of the previous day, he declared they would spend the next two days at the vacant schoolhouse. They were each to write a paper about one aspect of Verandale's history. While researching and writing, they would be responsible for Kahdi—the woodworker to whom he was previously assigned was more than happy to give up his assignment—from the time their father dropped them off, until the time of the evening meal when Egard would come back to take them home.

Egard reined the horses in front of the building that remained quiet since the end-of-school banquet. Egard spoke with the palace guard posted at the front. The four of them helped Berc and Kahdi from the wagon, through the school doors, and up the creaking wooden steps. Egard opened the door to a room reserved for the smaller children during the school year. Enoch figured his father had probably picked this room, on purpose, above the larger and more age-appropriate rooms.

Enoch saw three small desks facing each other. On each was paper and writing quills placed besides imposing stacks of documents and scrolls. In the center of the room was a larger desk. Normally unseen particles danced in the sunlight above it. Upon this desk, was a ball of sewn leather, colored drawing sticks, and some old papers deemed worthy of reusing to help hold Kahdi's attention.

Egard left after wishing his children a good day "filled with the wonders of learning and the greater wonders of responsibility." He closed the door behind him. They listened to his footsteps grow softer while looking at each other in the silence of the vacant building.

"Well, me and my leg need to rest," Berc announced while leaning against the wall and sliding downward, barely stifling a yawn.

Enoch glared at his brother, but it was Sabri who started in on him first.

"Listen up, Mister Brother with the always bad ideas. If you think you are going to take a nap while we work our tails off for punishment, your brain really does work slower than a hibernating oswatt's!"

"Besides…" Enoch started but was immediately cut off by the force of his sister's continued argument.

"I don't even need to mention that it was your idea to go get him in the first place."

"Hey, I'm not the one that got him all riled up to start with by tugging at his arm or sweetly murmuring in his ear…whatever you were doing to him at the edge of the forest to turn him into a rampaging ox, not to mention a rampaging, biting ox," Berc finished while grimacing and repositioning his leg.

Enoch began his second try at interrupting his sister until Kahdi, temporarily ignored, caught his eye. He had sat himself down at the large desk and was looking sideways at the arguing kids. He was also well into eating his first drawing stick.

Enoch lunged at the stick and pulled it carefully from Kahdi's mouth.

"Whoa big fellow, we packed you some food. Let me

get you a biscuit or something, but these you use to draw stuff. Like this…"

Enoch curled his upper lip up ever so slightly as he wiped the moisture off the chewed end onto Kahdi's sleeve and began to draw.

"See, look. I'm using the stick to draw some ears, then I draw fur, and look, I made a kitty and you…can make a kitty, too. In fact, you might want to draw a bunch of kitties, or maybe draw every animal you have ever seen. As long as you are drawing for a really long time, because we have all this work we are going to be doing or our father is going to kill us."

Kahdi picked up the stick and began making indistinguishable marks in front of him, some on the paper, some on the desk. Enoch slowly backed away to Sabri, who was propping Berc up and helping him into a desk. The three of them hatched a plan whereby Enoch and Sabri would take turns accompanying Kahdi on any necessary trips outside. Berc, being less mobile, would oversee any issues arising from within the room.

Enoch sat down at his too-small desk with the scrolls and writing quills before him. On one paper was a short note describing his assignment. He recognized the handwriting of Ibrakrim.

> To Sir Enoch, second son of Egard:
> Beneath this paper lies one of the most
> precious and most fragile of all the writings
> known to exist in our land. It is believed to
> have been written by Yilsad, who was my
> grandfather's great grandfather. It is the oldest
> writing known to exist under the two suns.

In this writing you will find a tale that will sometimes suffer from a poor understanding of a language more commonly passed from generation to generation by spoken tale rather than written word. Some words and even large portions of whole pages have been soiled or even lost over the many generations since it was first discovered. But the remaining words tell a tale that has been repeated, in one fashion or another, by many teachers, mothers, and fathers. It is the tale of the first attempt of our people to breach the forest that surrounds us; to breach the forest that provides nourishment and shelter to the Cofs who prey upon us.

In you, I see great promise. In you, I believe we can place great trust. It is my hope this will serve to guide your mind and body so one day you may help lead our people on a journey that will be remembered and recorded as the first successful journey out of our land; a journey to discover the world that lies beyond the mountains.

With deference to your future, I. t. L.

Enoch breathed a silent "whoa." He started to describe the incredible contents in front of him but stopped after eyeing the others in the room. Berc and Sabri were intently focused on their own documents. Kahdi was quietly drawing with one stick while nibbling on another. Lying over Sabri's right foot, Dew worked a lamb's bone, pausing only occasionally to sneer at Kahdi.

Enoch could wait no longer. He carefully untied the ribbon and uncurled the aged scrolls before him.

My name was Yilsad, writing this now to tell and war..ng of our time tha..... were once only foods for the Cofs. My great hope is for my son and his............for them to be reading this one day, having left this land and de feate...............so that we can grow our crops and tend our livestock without the always threat of deat... our persons and harm to our greater village.

Myself and my family have many times heard the tales of those who left to travel the forest, yet no one has ever seen a person come bak, nor have they spoke to person who has ever seen a person come bak. For this reason, I believed that we would and should be the first to try this travelling, and to do this for the sake of our land, sake of our people.

The day of making my decision has been the utmost hurt of finding my brother, Yhaim, his friend, my cousen and her protector all dead and savagely torn apart mostly for........eating...that we wold bury them by the sturdy timbers of their home that they had helped to build, but wold also honor their livings memories by forging plan and forging sturdy bodies or sols that wold leave our land by travelling the forest, surviving the Cofs.

I have elected my own self to be master and owner of this plan and to take full responsibility for the plan and my own life and any other willing human lifes who are to be risked to this plan.

Many of our wisest have said for generations that cutting the trees of the forest would be the one and only way to have a path that leads through the steepness of the mountains while offering sitel ines to any Cofs coming to kill and feed................have approached the temple elders to inquire about the taking down of mander trees though this is forbidden by the teachings of our Creator.

We have spent long days discussing the trees and their importance to us as well as to ours enemi. For long as I remember, I have never seen a person cut down an evergreen tree without suffering the wrath of flocks of Cofs. I have never seen a person who has cut down a mander tree because we all know this would likely result in the wrath of the Legion as well as youe neighbors, that is if you even survived the Cof attack that surely follow. We have been debating this for so long but have made no progress toward a solution or even a possible solution that most can be agreed.

After working the Legion members long into night however, we forged our plan. After a drawing of names, half of the eight members would be part of expedition and would appoint a member of their family to serve on the legion if they die or not return, other four would appoint a member of their family to go on the expedition while they stay behind. Eight peoples making up this party would necessarily include two women or girls and their protecs. The four of us whose names were drawn, had much simpler task of notifying our loved ones. Those that had to pick a member of their family, I cannot envy or possibly imagine their pain.......to comfort them is all I could try.

We assembled our force and rehearsed for many days. Our eight person grouping would travel in a line of six people, with two going 20 paces ahead and then turning to face down the mountain to monitor the progress of the other six, four looking ahead, monitoring the backs of the preceding two, and the person on each end spying the group's flank during the progression up through the trees...

....

....

....

....

....

....

....

....

....

was obviously the first sign that the journey would be as dangerous as we had all unfortunately predicted. Much of the townspeople wer assembled at dawn to see our party off at the village square. As the expedition members wer exchanging embraces and shedding tears with their family members, a gasp was heard near the forest edge and those that turned their heads quick enough witnessed a larger Cof flying down from its perch and landing, looking quickly at us before bounding away into the receding shadows.

I could not properly talk to my offspring for I would have to lie to them in order to give them any hope of my returning. With the first light, we knew we had to start, the Legion had, as its best try at an estimate, 2-3 days to reach the summit of the eastern wall. We wanted to use every bit of our daylight so as to try for our hope of spending only 2 nights in the forest.

It will always be one of my most profound sadness that we never made it even to the first night. We waited briefly while our families and seeers off receded to the village square. We stepped forward into the obscured light beneth the trees. My station was in the middle 4, next to Evter, son of my fellow legion member. He was just a fortnight after his Door Ceremony and owned no marks. We stayed in our practiced formation, so that no attack could be unseen. All had weapons drawn and at the ready, but when the attackers came, they outnumbered even our most horrific estimates and soon overwhelmed our practiced strategies.

After only a very short while, our journey was interrupted when we heard a stiiring to our left and a Cof bounded clearly out to within just a few paces from our flank. I lunged with my scythe a.......ew past my head, the one from Evter connecting and quickly felling the beast. I drew back my weapon and allowed within myself a nervous exhalation as did the remainder of the eight. It was at this moment that a many Cofs attacked form our right. The first ones we saw were diving from heights impossibly near the forest canopy, others appeared seeming to form out of the trees themselves. Most attacked the protecs first and the next moments were filled with more death than I can ever..
....
....
there was only myself, one oth legion member and a daughter of another. How we escaped the forest I will never know. When the girl also died two days later, I knew that I would not be able toevr live with our naïve approach to finding

a way out or even the guilt of my survival. I lived maybe for one reason and I will heal and stay with my duty as Legion member for.........urpose of advising and voting against all further expeditions into the forest. At least that will be my cause – to honor the loss of six lives by trying to prevent this kind of evil from taking its toll in this manner again, with only one other human and my honor as my witness,

Yilsad

Enoch unwound over the last page of the scroll, feeling empty. He looked for writing on the back, or even a second part to Ibrakrim's letter. Seeing none, he let out a big breath and looked at Sabri and Berc. They looked up and the three of them began to tell each other about their reading all at once. They finally settled on going from oldest to youngest.

Sabri had a document, which was much more Legion theory than actual history. It discussed Darnoc and how it once may have been a separate population, not just a place to send the misfits and criminals of Verandale. She also read a section on the prized manko fish of The Lake of the Depths. According to historians, people had attempted to capture these fish by multiple failed methods. Then someone had finally tried to hook a fish during the winter months, through the ice. This method evolved until it became the grand production and pilgrimage it is today.

Berc was assigned the most studied and researched papers of the three of them. Topics included the current makeup of the Sea, including the different freshwater tributaries and the lone Salt River source. Before the palace was built, he said, the population generally regarded the giant maw at the river's mouth as an unstable and dangerous area. Parents told their children to avoid the area as much as possible.

It was designated, with the advancement of religion in the land, a sacred ground.

One year, the Legion of Elders meeting became more contentious and more dramatic than usual. Verandale's sole priest had lobbied to build a great palace. He had discovered, he said, a smattering of ancient writings. He concluded the people were errant and disrespectful in not honoring the Salt River and its obviously celestial origin.

"We are not honoring our God. Almost every week, we lose a life to the hands, the wings, and the horns of evil patrolling the forest." The priest stopped to catch his breath and dab a cloth across his brow.

"If we do not undertake this task, the population of the land will continue to decline. A few generations from now there will be only one human left. He or she will then spend each day, not only awaiting their own death but mourning the death of our species. With the construction of a palace, we will finally show the deference our Maker deserves."

The priest stood—shaking and sweating—before the quieted Legion. Most of the eight members of the Legion stared at him with some disbelief. But they were shaken by recent losses of livestock, humans, and even protecs. They spoke and argued long into a night filled with harsh words and many fists pounded onto tables. At the end of the meeting, they made their decision. They would quarry and cut the hallowed, glowing, giant stones of Runal. They would haul and load them onto great ships that had yet to be built. They would build a great palace, larger and grander than any structure, around the giant maw of the Salt River. It would honor the being or beings who gave the rivers, the Sea, the protecs, the suns, and all that was good in the land. In short, it would honor all, but the Cofs.

They went on reading and sharing stories. Many, they had heard at least once before. While Kahdi continued, thankfully, with his drawings, the three absorbed as many stories as they could. They read about the four ships lost to the Sea while laden down with Runal rock. Three of these were found over the years and plotted on most current maps. A few people even claimed to have seen the glowing red skeletal outlines of sunken ships on the Sea's darkest and stillest nights.

The fourth ship was the biggest of all, the largest ever built in the land. It met its fate many years after the others, while carrying the stones destined for the bridge at Darnoc. Though no one was thought to have survived this last voyage, the stories—despite their questionable origins—persisted. The story was not required reading before a boy's Ceremony. In fact, it was not taught in any school room nor written in any official text. It was recited by unattended children in refuse buildings, by orators sitting on stools at The Drunken Oswatt, or whispered by big brothers to wide-eyed younger siblings who should have fallen asleep.

Believing the story was unofficially banned, no one in the room would have ever guessed it existed in written form. Berc held up the papers proving otherwise. Enoch and Sabri, even Kahdi, pulled their desks closer to Berc. He handed the faded papers to his sister, possibly thinking the story too important to be read by anyone other than the oldest sibling. Sabri cleared her throat before reading the words in front of her. It was one of the scariest stories in a land of scary stories. It was the tale of *The Chimera*.

Many men worked to mine and extract boulders from the Runal Quarry to build the Darnocian Bridge. A few of these men had been in the original work detail to extract the stones for the palace. They were a cynical, hardened bunch. Their eyes had seen more than they could ever tell their loved ones when they returned home.

It had been three days since they had lost a man to an attack emanating from the surrounding forest. Because of this—and the fact that they could see the tops of the massive, billowing sails of *The Chimera* at the dock below them—the morale of the twenty-man crew was slowly improving.

The construction of the ship had taken over three years. The Legion had poured over many boat designs to try and avoid a repeat of the shipping disasters of the palace-building era. All official accounts of the ships that went down were taken into consideration. The one variable common to each of the tragedies was the weight and volume of Runal rocks loaded onto each ship. Due to the danger incurred by any ship docked at Runal for any length of time and the slow, heavy trip to Darnoc, the past seafarers had obviously wanted to make as few trips as possible. In studying these plans, after the fact, it seemed the ships had taken on too much quarried weight and suffered from great instability during the voyages.

They decided to build a larger ship. In fact, they

decided to build the largest ship ever in order to decrease the number of trips and make it a safer journey for all those who had endured the dangers of Runal. The woodworkers and the shipbuilders of the time drafted a grandiose plan. In a rare display of agreement, everyone supported the project.

The problem was obtaining the shipbuilding materials. Mander wood was preferable to evergreens due to its strength and smooth texture that cut the water well. But mander trees were never cut down. By decree of the Priest, the wood was used only if the tree had fallen due to natural circumstances. Mander was therefore always in short supply. The evergreens of the forest were much more plentiful and could be cut down—albeit at great risk of attracting Cofs.

The Legion tallied the wood stored at the woodworkers' shops as well as abandoned houses at the edge of Verandale. There was not nearly enough to build a sizable ship.

Thoughts then turned to ships in the harbor that could be converted, but none were large enough. Finally, someone had an idea that showed some promise. The official ship used by the Priest was the largest seaworthy vessel currently in existence. He used it mostly for funeral ceremonies of the populace who had requested a water burial. Though seldom used, it was a solid vessel made entirely of mander. Its crew was well-trained and accustomed to the staunch demands of ceremonies conducted by the priest himself.

The other ship was a large fishing vessel. It was older, creakier, and more difficult to navigate. It was made of evergreen wood, but it had also been built with an expansive deck specifically for hauling large harvests from the Sea. It was not long before someone suggested the idea of combining the best parts of both vessels—the sturdiness of the priest's mander ship fore to split the waters and the expanse of the evergreen wood aft to carry the bulk of the precious cargo.

The entire Legion left the temple to go and visit the priest at his home. He was not the least bit enthralled with the complicated plans that would cannibalize his ship. In the end, however, they reminded him how many lives they had lost to carry out the plans for the palace. The Legion members convinced him to give to the cause to build the magnificent ship to carry stones to Darnoc.

It took a whole growing season to expand the dry docks overlooking the mollusk fields and bring the two giant boats out of the Sea. They spent the colder months aligning the two hulls end-to-end. Workers dismantled small portions of the back of the Priest's boat along with the front of the evergreen boat. Most of each ship remained intact. As the days passed and they connected the two hulls, the site became a great curiosity for all Verandale.

The darker, more solid mander wood swept backwards to join the lighter evergreen wood. The wooden remnants of each ship were eventually joined together by thousands of forged nails and held together by a dark resin. The result was such a bizarre combination of shapes and colors that numerous bets were placed on its future seaworthiness. All the residents of Verandale were on hand with the thaw of the next year to christen the ship. As part of the christening process, they named the ship born of two naval parents. They named it *The Chimera*.

The townspeople, who bet against the seaworthiness

of *The Chimera*, lost their money. Not immediately, however, as the size and shape of the boat made steering out of port hard for even the most experienced captain—a grizzled widower of a man, named Acetr.

Acetr was eventually able to gain a sailing mastery of the great vessel and command a crew to do the same. He worked hard to train two first mates so they could captain the ship—between Runal and Darnoc—even if he, himself were not to survive the quarrying process. By the time of the first voyage to re-open Runal, the crew was trustworthy, and the miners were able to sail with the belief that the voyage would not be the most dangerous part of their journey.

To ensure the ship's seaworthiness, the hunchbacked Acetr went through one last step. He painstakingly carved instructions for piloting the ship into the rails near the ship's main wheel, lest command of the ship should fall to someone possessing lesser skills than him or the first mates.

The Chimera sailed without incident from Verandale to Runal, but the men suffered many wounds during the first days at the quarry. The Cofs launched a well-coordinated attack right after the men had set foot onto the land, their stomachs still queasy and their legs still shaking from the voyage. Many weapons were spent. There were wounded to tend to. Morale was low, and the task seemed impossible into the second day. On the third day, however, there were no attacks, and the men were able to rest and better establish the logistics of the camp. The veterans also taught the newer members of the party to watch and trust the peacocks roaming Runal. The men learned to watch for "the warning stop."

This was the moment when the iridescent green animals froze in place. Once the crew learned to watch for this, they realized it came before the warnings of the peacocks themselves and before the guards could sense something was wrong. It became the most reliable sign for the men to put down tools, grab weapons, and watch the treetops.

"Wait, just a moment," Enoch interrupted his sister. "What in the world is a peacock?"

"I learned about them in school," Berc jumped in. "They're like shiny green cows or something or I'm not really sure, but they are pretty and… I've never seen one."

"How do the headmasters pass you on from one school year to the next," Sabri laughed. "I am just going to keep reading."

Though the attacks continued, they loaded the first quarried stones onto mule-teamed carts and then onto *The Chimera* only a day behind schedule.

Acetr and his men worked tirelessly. After twenty days, they had caught up and Acetr ordered a day of rest. They brought feast and beverage onto shore and celebrated. At dusk, they boarded amidst the red glow of *The Chimera*'s cargo. They awaited the rise of the suns and the trip to Darnoc.

The Chimera made it to Darnoc, not just once but twice. The crew arrived back at the quarry the second time with reinforcements, including the Priest.

After loading the ship, a third and final time, the remaining crew set off to deliver their precious cargo to Darnoc; then finally travel back to their home port at Verandale. The priest conducted a brief memorial service for the two men killed during the quarrying.

They hoisted the cargo ramp into place with pullies. Acetr checked all the men into their assigned positions. He gave the order to raise sails and guide the ship into the open waters. With the decks and cargo holds full, *The Chimera* was slow and the long trip to Darnoc—giving wide berth to Egg Island along the way—could not be completed during the span of one day. Acetr solved this by anchoring offshore, signaling the crew stationed at the docks, and waiting until dawn for the lengthy unloading process.

The shore guards lit torches at the landing and prepared to man their stations until morning. *The Chimera*'s crew took the sails down. A single torch illuminated the ship's bow, bobbing up and down in the rhythmic darkness of the nighttime waters.

Sometime deep into the night, the shore guards heard angry shouts, along with sounds of battle from the ship. Shielding their eyes from the flames on the well-lit shore, they could make out shadows of frantic, scurrying men and unbelievably…Cofs.

The men on shore ran for their rowboats and fishing vessels as fast as they could, grabbing weapons along the way. The men in the rowboats—facing toward the shore to row backwards—could not see the besieged ship. They could only hear human screams and Cofian whistles.

Three of the men jumped into an old fishing vessel with tattered sails and lines. Two of them were sober. They were able to catch the cold, night winds coming down off the northwest range and orient their boat in the direction of the battle. The legend of *The Chimera* was woven together piecemeal from their harried accounts.

The men rowed as fast as possible. One of the men, Ulta, was beneath the sails of the fishing vessel. He had been sent to Darnoc four winters ago as punishment for falling asleep as a night guard outside a young lad's window. The legion sentenced him to one year in the wasteland of a village that surrounded the Lake of the Depths. Unlike just about everybody else ever sent to Darnoc, he decided to stay, enjoying the solitude, lack of a ruling Legion, the lake, and the manko.

He recalled later how he looked over at the three row boats and saw men rowing desperately. He noticed they were pulling ahead of his own boat and would likely reach *The Chimera* ahead of them. He wondered if they would have enough strength left to climb up into and fight upon *The Chimera*.

Ulta and the others were about halfway to the ship when they began to recognize details from the battle. First, there were now more Cofs on the boat than men. The discouraging sounds of battle and the cries of the wounded became louder. They saw men falling from the ship's sides and splashing into the water far below. It also seemed to Ulta that they were now losing ground on the ship. He then noted with horror that the sturdy anchor rope usually drawing down tautly into the water had been cut, hanging from the bow, and twirling in the wind as if being stirred by an invisible hand.

Also, within the most vicious part of the battle near the center of the ship, the main sail had been partly hoisted but was stuck halfway up, blowing awkwardly but catching enough wind to move *The Chimera* away from the other boats. One of the other men handed Ulta the single oar they found in the fishing boat. He took his turn at the bow and began to row as fast as he could, trying to muscle and will his way to help those dying in front of them.

Ulta took his eyes off the vessel to get a few last strokes into the water before giving in to exhaustion and dropping his paddle. The man behind him was pounding on his shoulder and yelling words he could not understand. He stopped for a moment to look at the target ahead of him. *The Chimera* was now much easier to see in the darkness of the night because the central mast was on fire. The ship was turning in the water and he could see flames extending down the side of the vessel, as the black resin that connected the two formerly separate boats was also ablaze.

The men in the other boats also stopped rowing as the sounds of battle stopped. All became eerily quiet before them. Many men stood balancing on the tips of their toes against the rocking of their boats. They strained to see over the sides of the cargo ship, looking for any signs of human life. They saw another sail near the bow raising up and breathed sighs of relief.

Ulta's sigh was cut short when he saw a single horned head above the ship's rails. It fell and rose up, again and again, moving toward the front of *The Chimera*. As it reached the bow, the beak and eyes were now clear to the men below. Many men in the row boats began to scream and rowed even harder than before. But Ulta stood frozen.

The bloodied head of the Cof turned downward toward the water below and focused onto Ulta's eyes. The creature's left eye, behind a sharpened beak, then looked briefly back at the captain's wheel, one wing resting on a top steering peg while the creature leaned forward and bent its head down closer to the rail.

Ulta tried to understand the Cof's actions as he saw another one fly down from the tops of the Runal rocks stacked at the back and around the central, flaming pillars of the vessel. The second Cof landed next to the first and they both looked at something in front of them.

Ulta thought back to his long periods of time spent on the ship during the first two unloadings. The next part of Ulta's story never once changed or wavered for the rest of his life spent in Darnoc. Despite many different questioners and more than a few skeptics, Ulta claimed both Cofs moved their heads slowly from left to right as they read together the sailing instructions, meant for his fellow man, and carved by Acetr into the polished rails of *The Chimera*.

The Chimera completed its turn, and the men now faced the nameplate on the stern of the boat as it sailed away from them. It was clear that, even with the fire on board, the remaining sails of *The Chimera* would carry it, at least for a time, much faster than any boat full of men could ever row. But after a brief assemblage of the smaller boats, they decided to load six of the men, each with two oars, into the sturdiest of the rowboats along with the only jug of water they could find. Their hope was to reach the boat and any possible survivors, assuming *The Chimera*'s seaworthiness might be short-lived.

Ulta tied the remaining boats to his own. They watched the massive stern of *The Chimera*, carrying its glowing rocks and glowing fires away from them. It was followed by a tiny boat loaded with men rowing the hardest they had ever rowed in their lives. Both vessels receded farther and farther from Ulta until *The Chimera* was barely visible, its chasing speck of a rowboat, not visible at all.

Neither of the vessels were ever seen again.

In the coming days, an emergency meeting of the Legion convened. While meeting below clouds of grief, they decided to close Runal, once and for all. They modified plans for the Darnoc Bridge, using non-Runal stones to complete the project.

"Wait, wait a moment," Berc finally spoke up, no longer able to just listen. "Are you trying to tell me that a bunch of smelly Cofs flew onto the ship, killed the miners, and sailed it away?"

"I'm not telling you anything, I'm reading the official documents put on your desk as part of your assignment," Sabri retorted.

Enoch added, "I could almost believe that they might be able to hoist a sail and turn the captain's wheel with the little handie things under their wings, but actually reading instructions with their tiny reptile brains…I don't know."

"Yes, oh wise little brother, this seems much more make-believe than real. Next thing you know," Berc painfully stood, pointing to Kahdi and then to Dew, "Kahdi will compose a great musical piece of art and Dew will hop on his hind feet while dancing to the tune!"

Dew opened his eyes to look up at Berc.

Sabri ignored her brother's antics and read the rest of the remaining page.

The official Legion conclusion was that the Cofs had flown onto *The Chimera* when it sailed too close to Egg

Island. Others thought the attackers may have stowed away on top of the massive cargo while the ship was still docked at Runal. No case had been documented, before or since, of a Cof ever setting its leg-pod-extremity onto a Sea-going vessel.

The fallout from the disasters at Runal and the surrounding waters was immense. Within the next few seasons, they decided to close Runal once and for all, and the Priest's job was left unfilled.

Kahdi, who may or may not have been listening, stood up and stretched before starting for the door. Enoch followed him out, walking with him to the school refuse building, noting that Kahdi's leg—though still swollen—appeared to be working much better. Kahdi said nothing during the walk to or from the building, despite Enoch's efforts. Upon returning to the classroom, they found Berc and Sabri hunched over Kahdi's desk.

Sabri looked up at the two of them. "Enoch, you have got to see this," she said, waving him over.

She had been holding Kahdi's coloring page but put it carefully back on the desk. She and Berc moved aside so Enoch could see. He saw the entire piece of scrap paper covered with a picture of the edge of the forest, complete with detailed leaves and needles on every tree. Sitting with their backs to the observer were eight kittens. They were looking into the forest at a single cat, to their right, playing amongst the trees. No other beings were visible. The picture spilled past the edges of the paper and onto the wood of the desk. Once Sabri had repositioned the paper, the edges lined up exactly.

"Wow," Enoch exclaimed under his breath.

"Oh, but that is not even the best part." Sabri picked

up the page and flipped it over, again aligning the edges with parts drawn on the desk. On the back was a forest picture as elaborate as the drawing on the front. This perspective was from inside the forest. The back of a single cat was visible. It was looking out of the forest and into a wide-open space illuminated by the suns and backed by distant representations of the palace and the school. Eight kittens—their big eyes looking into the forest—sat before the trees.

Enoch stared at Kahdi. Nobody said a word.

"Well, makes perfect sense to me," Berc said, exasperated, throwing his hands up into the air. "He can nail a practice Cof, dead on, from farther than we can even throw; draws better than anyone we have ever seen; and can go into the forest anytime he wants and not be eaten." Berc continued, his volume getting louder, "But slap us upside our heads if we should ever ask him to speak in sentences or to stop biting people!"

"Berc, you have got to settle down," Sabri said, putting a hand on his shoulder. "Kahdi, what Berc means is that you have many talents inside of you. We just need you to help us understand what they are. Do you think you could draw another picture that would explain everything to us?"

Kahdi turned his head sideways at her, but again spoke no words. Enoch grabbed a blank paper from his own desk and put it on Kahdi's desk, to no avail. But Kahdi continued to do nothing purposeful during the short remaining time until the kids heard the horses of their father's wagon in front of the school. Enoch and Sabri ran down the dark stairway to get their father and bring him up to see the picture.

Egard picked up the paper, turned it over while raising his eyebrows, then put the pictures back down again.

"You know children, Kahdi is very special." He slapped a hand onto Kahdi's back. "But I am going to tell you the same thing the Healer told his parents when Kahdi was only about this high," holding his hand palm down at waist level, "and tried to ride an ani deer. That is, do not try to figure him out, or you will go mad. Try to keep him out of situations that are bad or don't seem at all bad, or you think Kahdi could make them bad."

Egard asked everybody if they were ready to go. Kahdi lined up the drawing sticks he had not eaten. He handed the picture to Sabri before going to stand by the door. She looked at the picture, then got an idea.

"Father, how about if Berc, Enoch, and I stay here tonight?" She held her hands together in front of Egard. "We won't leave the building and we will have the guard out front. That way we can work on our projects until late. We know where the extra stores of food are. We won't get into trouble, we promise, and our reports will be better than ever, when we finish tomorrow… please?"

Egard paused long enough for his sons to join in the pleading, before he gave in. He reiterated the night's strict ground rules before helping Kahdi limp down the stairs. He spoke with the guard out front, promising to bring him extra coins upon their return in the morning. He loaded Kahdi into the back of the wagon and started the horses down the road to deliver the boy back to his parents.

The kids ran back to their desks to pour over documents and discuss their report. Shortly, they remembered to eat and use the refuse buildings before dark.

Then they set about their task. They wondered aloud how much Kahdi heard and processed from their conversations. They wondered if they could ask Kahdi a question such as "where can we go into the forest?" then give him paper and drawing sticks and see if they could decipher an answer. They poured over his pictures again but could find no hidden clues.

"It seems to me that if we ask him to throw a stone at a fake Cof, then he throws a stone at a fake Cof. If we ask him to draw kitties, then he draws eighteen kitties." Enoch put his quill down on the desk for emphasis and crossed his arms.

"Well then explain to me what happened to the 'go get the piggy, and he doesn't go get the piggy' part of your explanation?" Berc smiled, before crossing his own arms.

"No, I think Enoch is onto something," Sabri interrupted. "Why don't we start working on our reports, describing what we have learned today, but come up with some questions to write down and ask Kahdi tomorrow. We might learn nothing, or we might learn something that could save all of Verandale, but we will never know unless we ask."

"I am going to ask him to draw a peacock," Enoch said while starting to move his own quill along the parchment.

The kids worked deep into the night. They read and wrote diligently except for one point when Berc announced he had come up with his first question. He held up a paper for them to see. Written across the top was:

1. What exactly is your problem?

Berc erased his contribution. Together they debated and agreed upon more serious questions. They retrieved mats and blankets from other rooms in the school, dimmed their torches, and lay down on makeshift beds. Sleep came fitfully as they contemplated Kahdi, his pending morning arrival, and the meaning of it all.

The path to greatness will sometimes be weedy.
—Enoch's last year's term paper

12

They were still sleeping the next morning when the guard entered their classroom. He knocked over desks, propped against the door for extra protection, and tensed at the noise.

"It was for my sister. She gets scared a lot," Berc said sheepishly.

Enoch and Sabri rolled their eyes and scoffed at their brother as they threw off piles of blankets from their sleeping areas.

Enoch thought the guard was paying a little too much attention to his sister. His thoughts were interrupted with the sound of their father's wagon coming up the hill. They quickly dressed and were waiting outside by the time their father and Kahdi stepped onto the well-worn path leading up to the school.

"Well, it certainly looks like you have had a full night of it," Egard's voice remained stern, but Enoch caught an underlying tone of relief and pride. He checked on their supply of food and asked about their plans for the day. Sabri gave him a filtered version, keeping in mind Kahdi's proximity.

Egard made room for the tired guard on the wagon's front bench. He waved to his children before starting the horses into a quick trot. The kids watched the wagon's trailing dust cloud before turning back to their desks.

"Well, Kahdi old boy," Berc began, "we have the biggest of all days planned for you. You are going to hear things and share things…"

Kahdi made a noise.

Sabri started to reinforce her brother's encouragement when Kahdi crowded past them. He broke into a run. They had learned from their previous run-ins and simply stepped aside, even Dew.

Kahdi did not look back. He ran straight ahead and between the trees, jumping over bushes and fallen trees despite his injured leg. He took only a few more steps before he was swallowed by the long morning shadows. A few steps after that, the forest produced no Kahdi sounds at all.

"Well, I guess I'll just have to stick with my original question," Berc said, exasperated.

"This is way too weird for me," Enoch sighed before sitting on the ground.

The three of them sat and stared at the edge of the forest for a while. It was clear, however, that Dew would not be able to relax this close to the trees. They agreed on a plan where Berc would stand watch while the other two dragged a few desks outside. They figured they could at least start writing their reports while waiting for Kahdi to come back.

They set the desks far enough back so they could see the tree line but also not be obstructed from seeing around the side of the school. They organized each of their work areas quietly until Sabri broke the silence.

"Well, at least if we are questioned, we could enlist the help of all the people Kahdi has injured, or whose boats or stuff he destroyed. That must include half the population by now, right?"

"How about if we recruit a whole lot of people; like a bunch of guards and protecs and smart people. We'll get the whole troupe to just follow Kahdi around all day, every day until he runs into the forest. Especially now with the gimpy leg, it is not like he is going to outrun any of us. All we have to do is stay out of mirk-clubbing range and be bored for a while, but then we may find out all we need to know." Enoch paused long enough for Sabri to interrupt.

"One of the keys to the plan will be to bring along Berc." This caused her brother to look up, half surprised but half puffing out his chest.

"Yes, you will be a vital asset, a key to the survival of the rest of us," she paused, reveling in the closing of the verbal trap set for Berc. "That is if we assume a Cofian strategy of first culling either the lamest or the dumbest from the pack."

The banter kept up for a brief time before they turned back to the more serious topic of Kahdi.

"I've noticed," said Enoch, "that he usually turns his head to the side a little when he is looking into the forest. Do you think he is looking for a clue, listening for a clue, or has some sense that the rest of us do not?"

"I don't think he has a clue," Berc added, in a rare tone of seriousness. "No, really, think about it. I've seen that very same confused look on his face before he drinks water from a goblet. I think he is confused or baffled by much more than we are. The reason he runs into the forest could just be that he is missing the part of the brain that tells people not to run into the forest."

"You know what the ultimate combination would be?" Sabri asked them, while keeping both eyes on the tree line. "If and when we follow him into the forest, we load him up with a bag full of spikes. Can you imagine, with his aim and range, we go tromping into the trees in the middle of the day and look for a bunch of sleeping Cofs, hanging out on the forest floor?"

"The best part would be," Enoch said, motioning with his hands, "the poor Healer when he learns that he has to take out his bag of ink and torture and apply a whole bunch of marks to the biggest and most dangerous arm he has ever seen."

The kids savored this vision then gathered their writing tools and parchments. They set about finishing their reports while keeping hopeful ears trained against the looming mountain.

They finished writing their reports, entitled "What we learned from our two days of punishment." By the middle of the day, Berc and Sabri were ready to eat from their loaded packs and again raid the school's food stores. Enoch had other ideas, having planned for this moment. He briefly bargained with his older siblings. He left them at the school and went to see Sasha for the first time since the disastrous hog incident.

Enoch chewed on a piece of jerky. He peered from behind the tall corner of the house next to Sasha's. He told himself he really didn't want to sneak up on or deceive her parents. But he was worried his own father might find out he had skipped out on the last day of his punishment.

He waited as long as he could—until he ran out of food. He walked up close enough to see the closed front door to her house. He began to walk around the side of the house, spying the pastures beyond. He saw horses in their stalls, as well as cattle and sheep grazing in the lush grass fields. A barn stood in the distance. He kept searching for any sign of Sasha or her family.

A few moments later he turned a corner while approaching the barn and stopped. Before him stood Sasha-protec without Sasha. The animal looked nervous.

Enoch trembled.

He tried to remember a time when he had ever seen a protec without its owner. He could remember none. He chided himself for not bringing his weapons bag and, for that matter, ever doing anything in this land while not being prepared for the worst.

He was within a few paces of the animal when he heard a noise behind him. He turned quickly, preparing to drop and launch a leg wrestle onto the attacking Cof.

He must have looked quite humorous. Sasha was holding her hand over her mouth, trying to stifle her laughter. He started to be mad at her as Sasha-protec rushed past him and his mind whirled.

She knelt by her protec and ruffled his neck and hugged his body.

"Who's a good boy?" she exclaimed.

She looked up at Enoch, gleeful. "Do you know how many days it took me to train him to stand clear over there and pretend like he had lost me?"

Enoch just stared at her, his heart still pounding.

"I'm sorry," she said, stepping forward to embrace him. "I couldn't resist. Sabri told me about the whole family-getting-in-trouble thing. I kind of figured you would get all your chores or whatever done and then you would be heading this way, sooner or later."

Sasha had remnants of hay in her long hair, was sweating, and looked completely amazing to Enoch.

"Me and S.P. here, we have been working on this for quite some time. You should have seen him the first few times that I tried to get him to stay in one spot while I went to another. You would have thought he was going to growl for the whole rest of the day. He was cracking me up so bad. Here, we can take a walk," she told Enoch, whose heart was still beating way too fast.

She released her protec to resume his usual guardianship against her thigh. "Just so you know, my parents think you are a big deal. They say you will have your ceremony at least one year early and that you might one day figure out what Kahdi knows, and it could one day lead to us getting over the mountains or saving our whole population or something." Sasha paused to take a breath and look at Enoch.

"Um, well, I just wanted to get out of trouble. I thought I could get Kahdi to stop destroying things, or to stop traipsing into the forest and everything, but we've been reading all these official documents yesterday and today. They are about some of the attempted breaches of the forest and how people built the palace and the Darnoc Bridge. Berc, Sabri, and I have been talking about Kahdi and trying to figure out how he goes into the forest—he ran in again this morning."

Sasha stopped him by putting her hand up in front of Enoch while they walked.

"I want to try something. Will you try it with me? "

Enoch stopped in the path along the edge of the newly planted field of winter wheat.

Sasha stepped between Enoch and her protec. She held out her left hand, grasped Enoch's right, and began to walk. She acted as if nothing had changed, but Sasha-protec, already on edge after her earlier stunt, growled at them both. He stopped in front of them and blocked their path, tusks pointed up to the sky.

Sasha dropped Enoch's hand and motioned for him to cross behind her, now holding her right hand within his left. This placed her protec between the two of them. Though still on edge, the animal let out only a small growl and hint of displeasure before resuming at a pace designed to match their own.

"Well, this might work out just fine then," Sasha said while looking down at her protec, then smiling up at Enoch as they continued.

"So, are you going to be ready when school starts up again, in a few days?" Enoch asked.

"I think so, but I can't help being sad about the growing season coming to an end. You know school, it is always exciting for the first few days and then the days start crawling by way too slow when the snow starts falling and we're waiting for the winter caravan." Sasha veered slightly to kick a rock up the path ahead of them. "By the way, my father says your family was planning on going this year also."

"Interesting that," Enoch stopped mid-sentence, thinking how going on the winter caravan, seeing Darnoc and the manko, and doing all of this with Sasha would be a dream come true. "Um, I mean interesting that he hasn't told that to any of us yet."

"Maybe he's been just kind of busy with disciplining you, Berc, and Sabri. I mean, with the hog and all kinds of people biting each other. And now you've even lost Kahdi again," Sasha was swinging her hand and Enoch's more excitedly with each remembered event. "Then, in your most dangerous and irresponsible move yet— you have escaped your detention and run off into the fields with a strange girl!"

Enoch stopped to face Sasha who was now using a finger of her free hand to mockingly point at him. "You know, I have half a mind to turn you in. You know, maybe see if there is any reward money."

He grabbed her hand from in front of him so that he was now holding both of hers within his own. Sasha kissed him over the faintest protesting growl of a protec.

Part II

~

Darnoc

Never steal food from a protec.
—Schoolyard legend of the One-handed Man

13

Outside the school, leaves were breaking from their branches to take their first and last flight. Inside, there was spelling, math, and history. Between classes, there was teasing, wrestling, gossip, and seeing Sasha in the hallways.

Kahdi had returned to his house a little after dark the day he had run from the kids. Luckily, Sabri's prediction—that adults would understand their failures with Kahdi—turned out to be true. They explained the story to their parents and Kahdi's parents the following day. Though he was the source of most good stories in both school and tavern, there wasn't much Kahdi could do now to surprise anyone.

It took a while for Berc and Enoch to adjust to walking to and from school without their big sister, though they would never admit it. It also took Sabri a while to adjust to more work around the house and more days in charge of Kahdi.

Upon returning home one night, Enoch's parents sat the three down to tell them that, indeed, they had requested and been approved to travel in the winter caravan. They would be traveling with four other families.

Enoch was bursting at the seams but was unwilling to inquire out loud about any more details.

"Enoch wants to know if Sasha and her family will also be going," Sabri blurted out.

Berc thought this was funny and Enoch tried to elbow his sister in the ribs, but everyone in the room knew what Enoch was thinking. Egard added that yes, Sasha and her family would be traveling with them. Sabri, Berc, and Enoch would be seeing Darnoc for the first time. They would take part in one of the most storied and prized activities in all the land—the hunt for the great manko fish.

Their father continued, adding the usual warnings about great danger and greater responsibility. They would have extra materials to study, detailing the trip along the Darnoc Trail, the accommodations, the people of Darnoc, and the skills needed for the great hunt.

Berc wanted to know if Kahdi was coming along. Enoch thought this was a good question. But when Sune stated that no, he would not be in the caravan, and the reason was Darnoc might not survive his visit, Enoch joined Sabri in ridiculing their brother for asking such a stupid question.

After the kids had asked the rest of their questions, they were excused to bed. Enoch's father grabbed his arm before he could leave. He closed the door and motioned for Enoch to sit down.

"Enoch," his father said seriously while Enoch pounded his memory, trying to think of anything he had recently done wrong, "I was called to a meeting today with your great grandfather, as well as Ibrakrim and the other members of the Legion. They told me what I already know—that you show great potential, backed by a strong heart and a strong mind. They have asked for you to be prepared for your Ceremony at the start of the next growing season. I don't think you need me to tell you how infrequently someone is given this early opportunity."

Enoch sat still, not moving and not talking. In truth, he felt a little dizzy.

"I agreed with them and said you were ready for this task and bigger tasks that lie waiting for you in the future. We will prepare you well, and we will expect much of you. We will not ask more from you than you can accomplish," Egard said.

Enoch figured the very first task expected of him—rising to walk down the hall and into his room—might prove to be his first failure. But he was able to get out of his chair, thank his father, and put his hand upon the door handle.

"Oh son, one more thing you need to know as a young man of great promise. The Legion will now think of you not only as bright, but also as an investment in the future hopes of our land and our people. You will be watched more closely from this point onward."

"Alright, Father," Enoch stumbled, failing to realize the inner message in these words. "What does that mean I should do?"

"I am not telling you what you should and should not do." Egard lowered his voice to a whisper, audible only within the room, "I am telling you that all your actions whether they seem important—such as letting Kahdi run into the forest—or unimportant, such as shirking your assigned punishment to hold hands with a pretty girl in a field, will be witnessed and recorded so that the Legion may properly assess you and your future."

Enoch's face flushed.

"But I assure you, that judgment will start now. I promise all judgments up to this point will be kept within the family and will not affect your Ceremony, your standing with the Legion, or future burdens placed upon your shoulders."

Egard took in a deep breath, "Sleep well my son, I am proud to be your father."

They say you are not really a person until you've traveled the road to Darnoc. The problem is…some become not-a-person because they traveled the road to Darnoc.

—Professor Andrew

14

Enoch could not remember being this cold in a long time. He tried to quell his uncontrollable shivering and remain motionless behind the boulder. His eyes scanned the road. It was hard to see anything past the huge snowflakes, racing each other to the ground as if pushed by thousands of tiny hands. He gripped and ungripped the weapon in his right hand, making himself that much colder.

It was moments before dawn, and Enoch's years of training were about to pay off as the target made its way down the road, looking nervously from side to side.

Enoch estimated the distance before the being would be within range. He spied the exposed soft flesh of the neck—knowing an impact there would have the maximum effect. He followed the natural up and down undulations of the target as it approached.

He rose up, giving away his position, and cartwheeled his hand forward. The projectile screamed away from him on a near perfect trajectory. The target turned its head—too late—in Enoch's direction. The timing was as perfect as it had been in Enoch's imagination the night before.

The snowball hit hard against Berc's upper neck. Shards of snow and ice exploded up into the air and down beneath his collar.

Berc yowled as Enoch sprinted onto the road. The race was on. Enoch hoped he was as fast as his older brother. Now he would find out.

Back when Enoch chased his brother out of the end-of-school banquet, he had to give up, realizing defeat while only a few paces into the sunslight. If his speed hadn't improved, Enoch would soon find his face forced into the packed snow of the road. He was able to see torches up ahead, still shimmering in the dawn's light. He tried to pump his legs harder with every step toward the adults carrying out the final preparations at the wagons.

He was able to make out the people, appearing in slow-motion through the thick snow at the back end of the caravan. He yelled for his mother but tried to act normal, knowing she represented the only person likely to save him from Berc's revenge.

He reached her barely ahead of his brother. He tried to speak in a calm voice, but it came out in a desperate wheeze of a sentence. "Hi mother, have you seen my beloved brother...Berc?"

He fell against the back wheel of the last wagon as Sabri and Dew came around the corner. Even as Berc came skidding to a stop behind him, he felt safe and wondered if this would be the last time he would feel this way in the upcoming days.

His mother looked up at him and smiled, but he could sense the strain as she prepared to take her family, for the first time ever, on the trip considered to be the most dangerous in all the land.

The caravan consisted of four families and four guards, twenty-three people in all. They would drive six wagons—two of them full of empty crates, hopefully soon to be filled with manko meat. Enoch couldn't believe it was really going to happen, but he had been through every practiced attack scenario so many times, he felt like he could be a wagon leader himself.

Enoch would be in the second wagon. For the first day, his assigned position was on the front driving bench with his mother. His father and a palace guard were on the back, along with a large weapons cache. Berc was in the lead wagon; Sabri, riding with much of Sasha's family, was two wagons back. Enoch and Sasha had wrangled a promise from the parents so they could ride together on the return trip.

With the glowing rim of the first sun peaking over the tops of the eastern mountains, the caravan began. Sune tussled the reins and started the horses.

Enoch marveled at the wagon in front of them, traveling over ground untouched by any human since last winter's caravan. Unlike the roads and paths throughout Verandale, the ruts for the wagon wheels were much rougher. The brown grass and brush poked up through snow and whipped against the front bench and the bottoms of their boots.

The schedule for the caravan had been the same since

Enoch's parents were children. They would leave after the second heavy snow. This would ensure the people of Darnoc—being a much colder and more inhospitable place—were now able to travel across the solid ice of The Lake of the Depths and begin preparations for the year's hunt. It also meant the Cofs would be entering their winter state.

No one knew for sure how the Cofs approached the freezing cold of winter. Some theorized they were either awake for a lesser amount of time each day or just ate less. Others thought they might take turns hibernating for unspecified lengths of time. At least the attacks on the people and animals of the land were less in the winter, but they were never zero.

The time taken to travel to Darnoc varied, depending on weather and problems, but generally took two whole days separated by one frigid night of non-stop travel.

Enoch sat with his mother for much of the morning, occasionally leaving to look out the back or talk to his father. With any big bends in the road, he would try to look back past a couple of wagons to catch a glance of Sasha.

Enoch checked the spikes cradled in a small compartment next to him. He picked each one up, twisted the halves until the piercing points popped up, then untwisted and set it down.

The morning was almost gone when he saw a guard in front of him jump from the still moving wagon, yelling to stop the caravan. Enoch grabbed two spikes, ducked under the reins now held taut by his mother, and jumped down to the ground. His father and the guard were already running past him to the lead wagon.

Upon turning the corner, he saw one horse—from the lead team of four—bleeding on the ground. A Cof perched over it, thrashing its head from side to side. The closest man immediately dove feet first at the Cof's leg to try and leg wrestle it to its side. Egard ran up to the fray, planted his front foot, and swung a giant club, delivering a lethal blow to the back of the creature's head.

Though Enoch had been repeatedly taught to expect exactly this type of initial diversion before a main attack, he momentarily forgot his duty. He stood marveling at his father, now delivering a last blow against the fallen creature. A guard grabbed Enoch's cloak and turned him toward the rear of the caravan, where the second part of the attack was underway.

A large rent now flapped through the canvas of the fourth wagon. The torn halves were flapping in the blustering wind and snow, exposing most of its contents. Enoch could see two protecs on a Cof that had apparently dove from the treetops through the roof of the wagon. Sabri had taken up her assigned position. Having climbed to the top of the third wagon, she was shouting the locations of the Cofs.

Sasha and her father ran back to the disabled wagon. Before they reached it, Sasha-protec leapt past them, lunging into the wagon to fight alongside his fellow protecs.

Amongst the chaos, Enoch saw the faintest hint of a Cof bounding from the tree line toward the road. It was kicking up snow and coming closer. He thrust a hand into the spike box, grabbed and twisted spikes into place. He threw as hard as he could as sounds of battle ceased around him. The Cof veered. The spike sailed past it, disappearing into a snowdrift at the side of the road with the strangest of sounds—metal into snow.

The animal turned and took flight over the treetops. Guards took up positions at the sides of each wagon, preparing for the next attack that never came.

People uttered sighs of relief after finding loved ones. An older guard, named Olaf, had been riding in the wagon pierced from the air attack. He had been struck in the head and knocked out, but was now able to sit up and ask, "Who hit me?" The problem was he would ask, hear the answer, and wait only a moment before asking the same question again…and again.

Berc came over to tell Enoch, "Glad we're not assigned to that wagon. Not only is it going to be a little breezy but imagine if he keeps asking that question for the next two days. I think I would volunteer to jump in front of the next Cof attack, just to put myself out of my misery."

As he and Enoch began to pick up fragments of the short battle, Sasha came from around the wagon with tears running from her eyes. Behind her, her father carried Sasha-protec.

Enoch's and Berc's jaws dropped open, but only for a moment as her father said, "Oh, don't worry about him. He has a little beak gouge in his leg. He was walking around fine, and would be still except for his owner here," tilting his head toward his daughter. "She believed he was mortally wounded and begged me to carry him back to what I'm sure will be a nice, padded spot in the wagon."

Berc chuckled at this and started to say something when Enoch slapped his hand over his brother's mouth.

"Let it go, brother. It was probably the first Cof her

protec has ever seen and, you must admit, he did charge headfirst right into the heart of the battle. So how about we give her a little while before you start in with all your jokes." Enoch paused another instant for Sasha and her father to walk to the other side of their wagon. He took his hand away slowly because Berc was still smirking.

They repaired the wagon. Guards put the horse from the lead team out of its misery. Enoch didn't ask, nor did he want to know how. They dragged the body to the side of the trail, along with the two dead Cofs, before restarting the wagons.

Enoch's mother hugged him—keeping her eyes trained ahead of her—as he slid back onto the front bench. She handed him the reins. They discussed all they had just witnessed, including his father earning another mark.

Sune quizzed him on several features of the attack. Enoch described the classic, initial attack by a single Cof, designed to draw attention and break the order of the caravan, as well as the second attack by multiple Cofs. He also described the placement of the horse carcass at the side of the road. The two Cof bodies were placed over the animal, in an act that always seemed a little revolting to Enoch, if not downright disrespectful to the horse. He knew however, this was done because the carcass of the horse would surely be consumed—probably just after the wagons were out of sight. This way, the wretched Cofs would have to at least see and acknowledge losses of their own to get to their meal. No one knew for sure if the Cofs had feelings such as these or were even smart enough to process this intended disrespect, but the practice continued, nonetheless.

Later, Enoch and Sune had traded positions with his father and the guard, when they heard a warning shouted from the lead wagon. A Cof bounded down the trail. It headed directly at the caravan before veering off to the side at the last moment. The drivers knew that this could be a preamble to the next attack. The strategy discussed after the first attack was then executed. The remaining three horses were urged into a gallop. The wagons behind also sped up as fast as possible with the idea being that they would react with exactly the opposite strategy undertaken with the first attack.

To the surprise of all, the Cof bounded by the wagons without even looking in their direction.

As the day turned into night the caravan stopped for the evening meal. This was the time when two out of every three caravanners were supposed to try and sleep while the others ate and kept watch.

Enoch tried to tell his parents he could take the first watch, but he was tired and drained. He sighed with relief when they told him he could rest between the supply boxes in the back of the wagon. He pondered the well-being of his family, Sasha, and her protec for only a moment before falling asleep.

Enoch dreamed he could latch onto the wings of pelicans or the fins of dolphins. All he had to do was hold on with all his might, just long enough to be carried up and over the mountains. He didn't care if it was the familiar eastern mountains just past the back edges of Verandale or the unexplored southern mountains beyond the long-abandoned landscape of Runal. He didn't even care if he had to travel alone to the dark and desolate areas northwest of Darnoc that had once spawned the striped animal and legend that was Olia-protec.

The others watched Enoch mumble in his sleep as he curled into a fetal position. He shivered and dreamt he was becoming colder as he ascended into heights never achieved in all the land. Boats sailed the Sea far below him. His left hand was holding on to the wing of a pelican, his right hand resting gently on the back of a talking dolphin. He thought this strange but relaxed as the dolphin told him they "were almost high enough."

He stopped focusing on his hands to look at the mountains. Climbing higher, Enoch realized he would soon see what no other human had ever seen—what lay beyond. They continued to rise, straight up into the sky. He asked the dolphin if they were going to fly closer to the top of the mountains so he could see even more.

"There will be no need, you can now look down at the top of the mountains and you will know what we know," the pelican answered.

Enoch saw they were higher than the tops of the mountains. Beyond the highest of the mountain ridges, he saw…nothing. No clouds, no trees growing on the other side of the mountains. In fact, there were no shapes or even colors. Enoch looked to the animals for an explanation.

"You will let go of us now," the pelican shouted over the wind. "You have been higher than any human and will now go deeper than any human."

Enoch felt the sudden rush of his insides leaping up into his chest as he plunged toward the waters of the Sea. He awoke startled and gasping, his arms flailing in front of him. He looked up, confused and embarrassed to see his parents looking down at him.

"Well son, that must have been some dream," his father said between bites of dried fish. "Did you save us from a whole flock of marauding Cofs?" Egard chuckled before rising to lift a side flap on the wagon cover and peer into the darkness.

"It was a strange dream. I was flying and thought I would be the first person to ever see the other side of the mountains, but then I saw there was nothing even there. Have you ever had those kinds of dreams?"

Sune nodded then announced they would soon resume their travels. Egard and Enoch took the next shift on the front bench.

Enoch kept a glove on the handbrake as the caravan rolled forward. He looked up at the night sky, now clearing and sending a few tardy snowflakes drifting to the ground. He contemplated how his father could still be awake, let alone driving the wagon. He looked up at the stars and wondered if there were other worlds, other mountains, and other Cofs.

Enoch stayed at the hand brake for longer than he thought possible—events of the day keeping him awake well into the night despite little sleep.

Sometime later, Egard hollered over the supplies for Sune to relieve him. Lack of sleep had finally rendered him a useless driver, and he would have to sleep from then until dawn…barring, of course any attacks.

With his father now cocooned amongst the supplies in the back, his mother surprised him by suggesting he travel back a couple of wagons and check on Sasha.

He approached the fourth wagon slowly, and with

exaggerated hand movements, so as not to be spiked. He saw two people on the driver's bench, Sasha's mother and father. They were happy to see him. They helped him up onto the wooden plank beside them while barely slowing the draft horses.

"Enoch, it is so good to see you," said her father.

"We thought you would be joining us long before now," Sasha's mother told him. "Sasha has been asleep, though pretty restless since her protec was hurt."

"Why don't you take the reins?" Sasha's father held out the three leather straps in front of Enoch.

He grabbed the reins and deftly drove the horses forward with occasional glances back at Sasha sleeping with one arm over her protec.

They continued like this until just before dawn, watching the night air crystallize before them. As the new day broke, Enoch was straining to see into the forest when he saw two Cofs a few trees in from the forest edge. One was curled around a tree and sleeping at the trunk. The other was pounding his horn directly into the mander tree, sending shards of bark flying in all directions. Oozing out from the bark and running down the trunk was a crawling river of amber-colored sap.

Enoch felt a shiver travel up his spine as they stared at the animal. Sasha's mother reached back to tug at her bedding and whisper to her to get up. She awoke, squinted her eyes at Enoch, then sat up and leaned her head out between her mother and Enoch. The upright Cof did not turn his head or in any way acknowledge the wagons. He continued striking the tree in a rhythmic beat: tap-tap, tap-tap-tap, tap-tap.

Everyone in the wagons, except for a few watchful

guards, watched in stunned silence as the wagons drove by. The Cof paused occasionally, long enough to turn its head and open its beak to drink sap.

Enoch stood to see up and over the wagon's cover and view the two Cofs for as long as possible. He turned back to the road as Sasha dressed in the back of the wagon. She then took her mother's place and talked to the others until the suns came up.

With everyone on edge, the day passed quickly. Enoch had run back and forth a couple of times between his family's and Sasha's wagons. The trail entered a long, gradual rightward climb. They could now see the northwest hills of Darnoc. Despite the increasing light of day, the air grew colder with their ascent.

The wagons began slowing, but not for an impending threat. This was for a scheduled stop that their father had discussed with them before the trip. Enoch had tried and failed to mentally prepare for this moment.

In the tall grass and drifting snow beside the road were the decaying wood and rusted metal frames of a caravan from some thirty-five years ago. The horses halted and began to nervously graze on vegetation in the road. Several guards took up standing positions around the wagons. Egard dismounted and grabbed a knapsack from underneath the bench. He broke the snow and walked to the gravesite of his parents, his uncle, and his two brothers, his only siblings.

Upon reaching the debris, he opened his pack and lifted out a rolled-up tlok-vine that had been painstakingly preserved while the flowers were in full bloom. He uncurled it, laying it out across the graves of his family. He weighed it down with an edge of a wheel on one end and a bundle of old cloths on the other. Enoch blinked away tears while seeing the stark contrast of the harsh winter landscape, the dilapidated remains of one of the worst attacks ever known, and the bright beauty of the flowers.

After a few moments alone, Egard looked back to Sune. She brought Enoch and Sabri forward with her and motioned to Berc to come from the lead wagon. They went to their father's side, seeing the remains of tears frozen below his eyes.

The winter caravan that carried Egard's family had been the first to leave Verandale and to never return. They had made it to Darnoc but were attacked soon after beginning their return journey. The only two survivors were two young girls who were able to escape and run the short distance back to Darnoc. They were never able to tell the family who took them in for the winter—or the investigating elders that arrived in the next year's caravan—any helpful details from the attack.

Before the caravan, young Egard had been left at the house of his grandfather Orgard. The hardships endured by a grandfather in charge of raising a small boy had caused all future caravans to be populated with whole families as much as possible, to try and prevent this type of orphaning. Despite the sorrow, Orgard had raised his grandson in a loving and dedicated home.

Egard hugged Sune and his children. They walked back toward the wagons and were relieved to stretch their legs, check the wheels, and talk in subdued tones with the other wagon teams. Egard brought the kids back over to have them stand upon the wagon's tongue behind the horses and look southward. Just over the thick forest, they could see the western cliffs, Egg Island, and the old docks used during the time of *The Chimera's* voyages.

They fed and rotated the horses. The caravan resumed its struggling climb for only a short while before approaching a summit. As each wagon cleared the peak, the occupants were able to see the wondrous red glow and the giant boulders forming the structure that crossed the valley of the Darnoc River. Ahead of them, all could now see the Darnocian Bridge.

OLIA
PROTE'S
LEGEND
ORIGIN
Lake of the Depths
DARNOC

Sounds of danger cower the young but awaken the brave.
—Posthumous

15

Enoch was unable to talk or even blink. To see the specter before him about which he had so oft read and upon which countless stories—probably most of them true—had been based, made him briefly forget about the surrounding danger. The valley forged by the Darnoc River was much wider and deeper than that of the Upper, Lower, or Salt Rivers of home.

Enoch could now see the misty, snow-covered outline of The Lake of the Depths and the myriad of winding switchback trails that connected it to the town. The town of Darnoc itself was much smaller than Enoch had always envisioned; one large, and seemingly translucent, structure in the middle surrounded by barely more than a dozen small hovels. Most of these plain brown homes looked as if they had been beaten down into the landscape by the wind and the drifting snow.

Enoch had expected the bridge itself to be somewhat unremarkable, given that it was built with roughly two-thirds of the stones initially intended. But the bridge's planners had an eye for detail that Enoch could never have imagined from the written accounts. The eastern end of the bridge began with stones that formed a buried porch of sorts. These appeared to erupt upward out of the dirt of the old road itself. The giant boulders then interconnected, locking with one another to continue arching up to span the gorge. A single massive stone pillar supported the structure at its midpoint and continued up and over the bridge to form a central bridge house.

The glowing red stones from Runal gave off more of an ochre hue here in the frigid north. They were interspersed with the stones extracted from the dull gray rock that was ubiquitous to the area between Verandale and Darnoc. Each of these gray stones was about twice the size of the Runal stones; each formed the base for a large opening in the side wall of the bridge. This gave the illusion—especially in the fading light of dusk—that the Runal stones making up the road of the bridge, cast a red light through the gray openings.

The drivers slowed their approach, knowing that the bridge itself would be one of the areas safest from attack. The danger, however, lay in the entering and exiting foyers. These provided a strategically impossible area to defend due to its steep slope, the Runal stones' ability to melt snow but form a sheet of ice on the coldest of nights, and the difficulty in backing up the wagons or releasing the horses if emergently needed.

Everyone was employed to scan the brush at the tree line, the treetops, and any large boulders nearby. When no one reported any sightings, they decided to proceed quickly—in order to outrun possible attack and complete the last part of the journey.

The wagon master in the lead gave a loud whistle

to start the wagons. Enoch braced himself and peered ahead. He soon found it ironic and sad that he was on the precipice of one of the most beautiful structures and one of the most long-awaited events in all his life and he was terrified.

The wagons swayed as wagon masters raised their reins and sent the horses lurching forward. Enoch hunkered down behind the front lip of the wagon, no longer caring about looking brave. He felt there was no way the wagon could travel across the bridge at this speed without flipping over into the chasm. The only question remaining in his mind was whether his death would come after the wagon flipped off the bridge to the right or after it careened out of control and plummeted to the left.

The speed of the horses and the descent of the hill now forced him harder against the front of the wagon as some of the crates pushed into him from behind. The horses snorted and whinnied as the tilt of the wagon suddenly shifted. The wooden wheels gave out a loud and horrible noise as they left the dirt road and rolled over the giant stones of the bridge.

Just barely over the noise, a voice yelled from the wagon ahead.

"Mommiiiiiiiiiiiiiiiie!" Berc screamed.

Enoch prayed he would live to remind his brother of this and tease him for many days. In fact, he wanted to live for any number of days, as long as he didn't wake up as a spirit, rising up—along with many other human, protec, and horse spirits—from the bottom of the Darnoc River Gorge.

Halfway across the bridge, the wagon passed through

the darkness of the central building and again sped downwards. Enoch held on tight. He knew he had to open his eyes now or lose any chance of seeing the bridge while crossing upon it. But they were travelling so fast, he had to stretch his forehead muscles just to open his eyelids against the rush of freezing wind.

Once opened, he saw his father wildly whipping reins. He was bouncing above the driver's bench and shouting commands to the horses—commands Enoch thought there was no way they could hear. As the bridge rushed by, Enoch noted how the red and gray stones, and the openings between, were now interrupted very briefly and intermittently by darker, human-sized shapes. Surely, there was no way anyone could be on the bridge during the crossing of twenty-three red-eyed horses pushed to their heart-pounding limits by maniacal wagon drivers and their terrified crews. There was much, Enoch figured, that was left out of the we-are-going-to-travel-to-Darnoc-in-a-caravan speech given by his parents.

The wagon was still tilted downward when the horrendous noise of wood versus stone suddenly ceased. Enoch's ears were ringing as he looked up to see that their wagon had left the bridge. But the speed of the wagons slowed only briefly on the upcoming hill. He also saw that there was no road, only a wide field of snow broken by occasional tufts of last year's crops.

A horn sounded from somewhere in the town.

What Enoch did not know was that the main driver of every wagon, though they had spent all their waking hours trying to keep their families and wagons safe, had also been preparing for this moment. The moment that would entitle the winner to bragging rights not only after reaching the relative safety of Darnoc, but also long after returning home and sitting outside Verandale's tavern—The Drunken Oswatt—the next growing season.

Egard stood up, pulled hard on the right reins, and quickly veered to the right of the lead wagon; but this path was blocked by its driver in an obvious pre-planned strategy. A third wagon lunged far to the left and took the lead. The race to the gates of Darnoc was on.

Enoch saw the guard, in a semi-standing position, trying to see through the spray of snow kicked up behind their wagon. The guard extended a hand to Enoch, helping him toward the back. Despite all the debris behind them, he could see one wagon that was gaining on the rest. It was driven by Sasha's father, barely recognizable due to his dirt-shielding headdress—probably, Enoch thought, kept in a secret bin or pocket all this time. He then saw Sasha cheering from behind her father, screaming for him to go faster. Next to her, jumping up and down, was Sabri. Sasha's eyes locked onto Enoch's for a moment. He mentally stumbled, but only for an instant, and then quickly ran forward to yell to his parents that this race must not, could not, be lost. They smiled—though glancing back not at all—and kept their eyes and hands focused on task.

The lead wagon was no match for the others. With only three horses, it was losing ground. As Berc's wagon was passed by their own, Enoch hurled himself back to the middle of their wagon and thrust his head through the flap.

He yelled as loud as he could. "Throw Berc out, he is dead weight!"

He laughed hard while stumbling his way back to the

front. Hanging on to the metal bow above him, he could hear the rumble of wheels from another wagon to their right. He recognized Sasha's wagon. It had pulled ever so slightly ahead of theirs. Standing tall, with their front paws on the back crates, were the fervently barking Sasha-protec and Dew.

Enoch leaned against the guard for support and peered between the shoulders of his parents. They were gaining again on the other wagons and racing to two giant, wooden gates now being opened by running and screaming Darnocians. More stood on top of the surrounding walls, waving bright red and orange cloths, shouting through the frozen air to cheer on the wagons.

With only a few wagon lengths to go, their wagon pulled ahead of Sasha's. Enoch yelled victoriously as they were the first—to speed with lunging horses and a shivering wagon—through the open gates of Darnoc.

His father leaned back, too exhausted to return the hugs from Sune. Enoch whooped and hollered, slapped the guard on the back, and jumped out the back of the wagon as the others slowed to a stop nearby. With the three horses of the last place wagon slowing to a stop, happy Darnocians pulled on robust leather ropes to winch the city gates closed behind them.

With a loud metallic clang and a vibration that spread through the ground, the gates were sealed shut, the howling winds now dampened by the barrier. Enoch sauntered over to the girls. The two of them stood with hands on their hips, their protecs standing between them licking their paws and cleaning their coats with long dark tongues.

"You guys are in awe of my superior wagon-driving abilities, aren't you?" Enoch boasted. "If the two of you show the proper respect, I will ask the award presenter if I can have a sister and a friend join me on the podium and stand behind me during my victory speech."

"Let me get this straight," Sabri mocked after sharing an eye-rolling moment with Sasha. "You are going to tell us that you had anything at all to do with driving the wagon other than screaming and trying not to wet your pants?"

This made Sasha crack up.

She stepped forward, whispering to Enoch, "You might want to pay attention to this, before you prepare your speech." She turned his shoulders around, so he was facing away from her. She rested an arm on Enoch's shoulder and pointed to the gathering throng of about two to three dozen people—all the inhabitants of Darnoc. "See that little guy in the middle?" Enoch looked and saw an older, portly man who was shorter than most of the adults surrounding him. "That is the Constable of Darnoc. See those people running up to him with papers in hand? They are bringing names of the people in each of the wagons. He'll take the names of the people, the number of the wagons and horses, and the starting positions we all held on the bridge. Then," Sasha paused for dramatic effect, "he will do the secret arithmetic that only he knows how to do."

This all just added confusion to Enoch's already confusing day. The crowd quieted as the Constable climbed onto several planks that had been assembled into a haphazard stage.

"Ladies, gentleman, and beasts of Verandale," his voice, though coming from such a tiny body, boomed across the valley, "the people of Darnoc give you a grand welcome!"

The crowd roared with applause.

"I am also most pleased to announce to my fellow townsfolk, that on this most magnificent but treacherous trail that connects our two lands, our brethren suffered no fatalities this year." More cheering.

"It is now my distinct pleasure to announce," he paused to bring a document up to just below his eyes, "that I have performed the arithmetic." Enoch joined in the clapping but wondered just how it was possible that he had performed anything in the short and confusing time it had taken to close the gates and quiet the crowd.

"The winners of this year's Race to Darnoc are…"

The crowd erupted into its loudest and wildest noise yet. Sasha and Sabri squealed and jumped up and down as their names—and the names of Sasha's parents and brothers—were announced to the crowd. The Constable asked them to come forward. As they ran away from Enoch, Sasha looked back. She smiled at him and shrugged her shoulders.

As Sasha's father was standing with his family and giving his victory speech, the Apprentice, who had been riding in Berc's wagon, came up to Enoch.

"So, I'm not so sure she is going to be impressed with just your mark and be your girlfriend for life. She is going to be trouble, that one."

Enoch could not agree more. He vaguely remembered Sasha telling him that the Apprentice had been on a previous caravan. Enoch decided he might be the one to help with the multiple explanations needed by a person on their first trip to Darnoc.

"Let me help you understand," the Apprentice said as if reading his mind. "What spot was your wagon in the caravan?"

"Second," Enoch answered.

"Right, and what spot was little miss yellow dress?"

"Fourth."

The Apprentice held up two fingers on one hand, four on the other. "Alright, so second and fourth," each hand now directly in front of Enoch, "and your wagon won by about this much." He moved his hands closer together. "So, there you go. A smaller brain would think that you won the race. A bigger brain knows that your wagon gave a good effort, but also came in third place."

Enoch looked down at the ground.

"The next thing you have to know is that you will be asked, upon leaving here in a few days, to never tell any of the children back home about the race that comes at the end of the trail." The Apprentice was obviously enjoying his rare time away from the shadow of the Healer. "Otherwise, they would know what was coming, and it wouldn't be exciting enough, see?" He said this while playfully punching Enoch in the arm.

"You have got to be kidding me. You mean to say that travelling non-stop for two days in the bitter cold, trying not to become dinner for a bunch of Cofs, then suddenly travelling twice as fast as you thought a wagon could go…"

Enoch's exasperation was interrupted by the closing comments of the Constable.

"Finally, my dear friends from Verandale, we welcome some of you back and some of you here for your very first time, but we welcome you all to the wonders of

Darnoc, the home of the manko!" This was followed by the loudest applause yet before the crowd began to disperse.

He quickly walked in the direction of his parents, deciding to avoid any more reveling from the girls for a while. They walked back to the wagon and started the tired horses. They traveled to the town's center as the suns dropped behind the tops of the mountains.

Your father knows most of what he speaks.
—Sune

16

They slept in the large building that had looked so strange to Enoch from outside Darnoc's walls. The nighttime torches had revealed little of the structure and the travelers were too exhausted to explore or even discuss much of their surroundings before collapsing onto their cots.

Upon awakening, Enoch felt like he was outside in the winter light of the suns, but he was still warm. The light was coming through the roof above him, and through the walls that surrounded the waking travelers. He rubbed sleep from his eyes and tried to focus.

He sat up and breathed in the aroma of hundreds of plants and crops that filled the building. Some were flowering, many still bore fruit in the middle of winter, and a few even stretched upward to brush against the high ceiling.

Enoch found his parents. They explained the building to him and Berc over a meal of fresh fruit and hot bread. The food was amazing, and he began to wonder about the wisdom behind sending people here for punishment.

The leaders of Darnoc, they told him, felt they needed a way to grow crops later in the year in the cold northern climate. They found that by grinding stones into sand and then mixing with water from The Lake of the Depths, they could heat the substance over a wind-stoked fire — into a thick, milky fluid. Upon cooling, it formed a hard, clear material that allowed light to pass, then trapped the heat inside. The building stayed warm and grew plants between growing seasons to feed the people much better than in previous winters. Egard explained this had been tried in Verandale but did not seem to work with water from any source other than The Lake of the Depths.

The boys wanted to explore the building further but were told they could not delay. It was time to hunt the manko.

The hunters were ushered between the cots which had been placed — more like jammed — into any piece of bare earth between the rows of crops and fruit trees of the indoor orchard. The Constable was waiting for them in a space between the sets of double doors that led to the outside.

He was dressed in a colored vest adorned with a bright red sash. He explained to the Darnocians and their guests that he would not be going with them today. He would be staying behind to attend to the affairs of the town.

"Besides," he said with a grin, "I am just the right size for a manko snack."

Some of the Darnocians thought this was quite hilarious. Enoch did not.

The Constable said he would be turning over the event to the man standing next to him. A man named Herol.

Herol was the unfortunate answer to the "guess who started the big fight at The Drunken Oswatt?" question. What actually started the melee is still debated, but witnesses did agree on one thing: Herol eventually brought forth a loaded spike and launched it in the tavern. Luckily, no one was hurt, but the spike tore through an enormous wooden cask and flooded the floor with some of the most aged and expensive tlok-vine tea in the land.

At trial, as one might imagine, The Legion did not look kindly upon his actions. They sentenced him to two years in Darnoc, time that would now be complete in just a few days. He would be travelling back home with the caravan.

"Talks down everybody, um, all the ones. I am the one called Herol." His red hair pointed out in front of him and bobbed up and down, like a rooster's comb, with every word. "I will be to in charge today."

"Great," Berc leaned close to Enoch's ear, "nothing could go wrong with this!"

"Today's hunt, we should will be staying on the tops of ice!" He found this statement amusing but was the only one who laughed.

Enoch found none of this reassuring. As Herol droned on, Enoch daydreamed about his future great moment in the suns after he passed his Ceremony. He would call a special meeting of the Legion. Appearing before them, he would announce with great fanfare that he had found a way to stop the population from declining, year after year.

It was simple, he would state to the hushed audience collected in the chamber. If the population were to increase, the people of Verandale and Darnoc would have to stop doing stupid stuff. The crowd amassed before him would scoot forward in their seats in wonder of Enoch's wisdom.

To be more specific, he would announce; no more wild wagon races over ancient bridges, no letting Kahdi out of his house, no running over girls with protecs, no visits to refuse buildings more than ten paces from the house in the middle of the night, no deciding buildings had to be made from rocks mined near Cof headquarters, and last, but not least, no going out on the ice with maniacs in charge.

As soon as they had traveled up the switchbacks, Enoch saw The Lake of the Depths and changed his mind.

They hiked past the final precipice to see a body of water frozen from end to end, but the top of the ice did not stop at the edges. Instead, it rose straight up to about the height of a grown man's thigh, giving the impression that the lake was a giant, crystal plateau. Unlike the small bodies of water back home and even the edges of the Sea in winter, the ice was absolutely clear. So clear in fact that Enoch could look through it and see fish—most, he had never seen before—as if they were swimming just under the surface. Enoch and Berc stood, stunned and still at the edge of the frozen body of water. Sasha and Sabri came up behind them. Enoch didn't have to turn around to know that his sister was also speechless.

Though there was snow drifting all around the lake, none of it stuck to the surface. Instead, it fell in blankets onto the ice, but quickly slid off, gaining speed with even the slightest gust of wind. The snow and sleet acted as if

He lay still for a moment, trying to make out the objects that arose from the middle of the lake.

Berc tugged at his arm to get his attention, and then whispered so that only Enoch could hear, "My nipples are numb."

Just when Enoch thought he was going to lie there forever, a horn sounded—like the one they had heard at the start of the wagon race. He felt a push, then began to slide on the ice and spin. As he did so, he found himself looking alternately at the structure ahead of him and the person who had pushed his knees. Glancing backwards, he was able to spy Sasha, jumping up and down, cheering him on.

The strange thing was, he continued to speed up while spinning toward the middle of the lake. In brief glimpses, he could see his sister, spinning to his left, and his brother to the right. The surface of the ice felt so smooth and fast, it felt more like falling than sliding. He continued to pick up speed until it no longer seemed possible to keep his eyes open or his orientation intact. Enoch could hear screaming but was no longer able to tell if it was coming from his mouth or from those around him.

Just as he started to worry about picking up speed all the way to the other side of the lake, his body hit a semi-solid structure with a loud thump. He came to a quick stop, breathing in a mouthful of dust. He listened to the sounds of other bodies hitting their targets. He opened his eyes to thousands of pieces of straw gently flitting back down, having been launched into the chill air upon impact of human and bale.

He leaned to his side in a careful attempt to right

himself. He again checked for any exposed skin. Finding none, he looked up to see that they were indeed now standing in the middle of the frozen lake. The next waves of people were sliding on the ice and headed swiftly in their direction. He crawled with Berc to an area where the ice was covered with tarps, so they would be shielded from the incoming sliders by the walls of hay bales.

Having made it to safety, he looked back to see Sasha, her family, and even his own parents, whizzing along the ice and screaming. Unlike Enoch and the other first-timers however, they were squealing shouts of joy, even as they occasionally collided with each other.

Their impacts into the barriers were even more impressive now that Enoch was able to stand back and take in the whole scene.

Sasha came over to stand next to him, still breathing hard while brushing herself off. Having looked herself over and disposed of all visible hay, she brushed some remnants off Enoch, pulling the last couple strands out from between his hood and hair.

"Pretty incredible, huh?" she asked him.

He just looked at her entranced, though he could see only her eyes.

"I'm not sure how many more of these surprises I can take," he admitted.

"Well, do you notice anything different about me?" she asked, holding out her mittened hands and twirling around in front of him.

Enoch had to admit, there was something out of the ordinary about her besides standing on a frozen lake that appeared to defy all laws of nature.

"Look over there silly," Sasha pointed back to the shore.

He looked over, along with Berc and a few others. They saw black shapes perched on a platform overlooking the edge of the lake. From this vantage point, six protecs—all the ones from both the caravan and Darnoc—would be able to oversee the manko hunt while keeping nervous eyes on their girls.

Enoch added this to the list of unbelievable sights he had witnessed in the last few days. He turned to Sabri. He didn't have to even open his mouth for her to answer his internal question.

"I know, little brother, I never thought I would see the day either, but Herol told us about it last night, and then he just led them all over to that raised-up thing and they all sat down. I heard a little bit of complaining from Dew as I was climbing up onto the ice, but it's just like they already knew there was no way they could touch the frozen waters of the lake and come with us."

Everybody contemplated this for a moment before Herol appeared in their midst. He was giving out instructions by using the wrong words—or by using the right words in the wrong order, Enoch couldn't tell which. Enoch knew there had to be somebody in Darnoc more qualified to lead the hunt.

Enoch took a moment to get his first full view of The Lake of the Depths. He walked over to the far edge of the tarp and looked down. The view was dizzying. He could see occasional air bubbles; otherwise, it was if he had no depth perception whatsoever. He looked through the ice and into the water below. He saw fish and other creatures swimming close to the surface, while at the same time seeing those that swam much farther down below.

He remembered a story told by an uncle or some other relative on his mother's side. Soon after the founding of Darnoc, people had put forth various theories and strategies to try and catch the giant manko. This effort had intensified after they netted a few smaller ones and people discovered the finest taste to ever reach their tongue.

It was many years before the idea of ice-fishing surfaced. Some even claimed that Darnoc was abandoned in the winters of long ago, though they couldn't explain how the townspeople made the trek back and forth from Verandale twice during the increased Cof activity of the warmer seasons.

Enoch looked down at a slow-moving fish, not much longer than his boot. It was black and covered with iridescent white spots. Whenever the fish turned or rolled, the spots turned dark as the body turned white. Enoch had never seen anything like this before.

"Baby manko," said a voice from behind him.

Enoch half-turned to see one of the native Darnocians, but quickly looked back at the fish. It intermittently stretched its mouth open to a width that surpassed that of the rest of its body.

"See, they don't really chase anything, and they don't even scavenge anything. They just open their mouth and filter all the tiny creatures in the water. That is why," the man stopped to gesture at the fishing apparatuses all around them, "you can't just put some food on a hook and hope to catch one. That is why we serenade the oldest of them to strike, just after they have spawned and just before they die."

Enoch barely noted the increased activity behind him as he kept his eye on the baby manko.

"Don't worry son, everybody gets the stares the first time they come here. It was many years ago—the first time I stepped out onto this ice—but I can still remember when my parents gave up on me being useful. They let me just stare through the ice all day, until they carted me off when it was time to go back into town. Nobody's really going to bother you much unless one of them is hooked. It is then that we will need your strength."

Enoch looked around to see two other fishing set-ups nearby. Each had a central area cut out of the tarp. This surrounded a large hole cut into the ice, and towering directly over this, a pyramid of logs, buttressed up to support a sturdy rope extending straight down into the water. Each area was populated by small groups of people, most of whom were carrying and assembling ropes and lumber.

Egard called the family over to one of the holes that did not yet have a rope in the water. One of the locals brought out a giant hook from a "fermenting barrel." The barrel contained a black oily substance that looked to be a mixture of rotting entrails and mold. Even through his face cloths, Enoch could not imagine a more putrid smell.

The man explained that the hook—which appeared to be almost as thick and heavy as the anchor of *The Indomitable*, had been sharpened to such a fine point that "you could bleed just by looking at it." He smiled the smile that gave away the special sense of humor that apparently was essential for surviving a Darnocian winter.

He tied the rope through the eyelet of the large hook. Enoch noted that the point of the hook did indeed appear sharper than the points of any knife, scythe, or spike he had ever seen. The hook was then fed up and around a pulley suspended from the logs above the hole.

The man raised a hand and signaled a group stationed near a giant wooden spool. The spool was at least thirty paces away, was taller than the people who surrounded it, and contained what appeared to be enough rope to stretch all the way back to town.

Several of the townsfolk grabbed the large metal prongs that extended from the edges of the spool. They pushed the prongs while digging their spikes into the clear ice beneath them. As the spool turned, it released more rope and the empty hook descended into the water.

Enoch snarled a confused look onto his face. His father turned to him.

"I know what you are thinking son, but you must remember what you have been told." He continued, "The mighty manko are the biggest animals known to exist. Yet they exist by eating creatures smaller than our eyes can see. So, we cannot fish for them using bait, nor can we catch them in a net that would be strong enough to hold them. You see the manko must be attracted to the hook not because it is disguised by food. Instead, the hook smells like death's portal to this tired old animal that has completed its last spawn and is searching for the path to the great beyond. We must accept that we play a part in the life of the manko that is more complex than any normal relationship between predator and prey. In fact, in the minds of the secretive manko...we may be their creators.

As his father spoke, Enoch concentrated on the rope. It descended faster and faster, splashing into the freezing water at the middle of the hole in the ice, and sending the tiniest of waves to lap at the hole's edge.

Enoch stared at the rope and wondered how long its descent would continue. He looked back to the spinning spool. The handlers surrounding the spool stood back as it spun faster, less than half of its girth now remaining.

Enoch paused to take it all in. He stared at his boots. They touched the ice but appeared to float over the transparency of The Lake of the Depths. Enoch looked up to avoid the dizziness associated with this view. The rope's descent came to an abrupt halt and a new flurry of activity began around him.

A guard grabbed the rope and began to pry a knife between the strands. Others came forward to hold the strands apart as one of the Darnocians produced a long, cylindrical, shrouded object. As he approached, he removed the shroud, revealing a hewn metal rod that was polished to an extent which Enoch had never seen. It caught and amplified the light of the winter suns.

The men began to position and twist the rod between the fibers of the rope. Though the object was mesmerizing, Enoch occasionally had to look away as it caught and reflected a blinding amount of light.

Both ends of the rod were buried in the rope and secured with extra ties while the middle remained exposed. Herol appeared out of the surrounding crowd and walked forward with a small wand. Egard whispered to his children that these wands were melted and cooled repeatedly from a precise mixture of mander sap, ground stone and various local plants. It produced a wand that appeared solid but gave way to pressure, bending in a slight almost semi-liquid way with the right amount of applied force.

"Listen very closely my children," Egard said as he put his arms behind them. "At first you will hear the music only with your ears, but if you let the music move inside your head, you will understand The Serenade of the Manko."

Herol stepped forward, mumbling as he held up the wand. The guard adjusted the pulley and the rope ever so slightly to raise the hook from the depths below just enough to again be suspended in the waters. Enoch doubted that Herol could produce any meaningful musical sound.

With a glance to the wand holders at the two surrounding holes, Herol positioned his feet on either side of the gap in the ice. He grasped a supporting timber with his right hand. With his left, he positioned the wand against the rod and rope. He cocked his head slightly and began to play.

At first, Enoch heard a straining type of squeal, but a melody soon emerged. It joined the slightly deeper sounds coming from the surrounding holes and Enoch, Berc, and Sabri stopped their whispering to listen to the music. Enoch was speechless. He closed his eyes and let the sound overwhelm him.

He opened one eye hesitantly, fearing that Berc might notice and tease him, but even Berc's eyes were closed. Enoch thought that this sound was the most beautiful he had ever heard; then he noticed Herol. He was holding on to the rope with his right hand and causing a sort of voluntary convulsion with his left hand as the embedded rod gyrated against the bending wand. Herol was in a trance. Enoch could not believe this action produced such a sweet sound.

Sune and Egard motioned for their children to follow them across the ice and away from the holes. On the way, Sune explained how hard it was for Herol and the others to create this sound. She retold stories she had learned the night before from some of the Darnocians.

Herol had been assigned to learn this task after his arrival two years ago. Despite his odd persona and persistent misuse of words, he had quickly taken to his assignment—learning the mastery of the wand. He had not only learned the skill of making music, but also the physical stamina required in what could often turn into an all-day task.

His reward for completing his two-year sentence was to be named the leader of the hunt and granted permission to travel back to his home. For all his faults, Herol had dedicated himself to the task and excelled in his training.

"So, you are saying that he is not actually dumb?" Berc asked, cracking up his siblings.

"No, Berc," his mother grabbed him by the shoulders and turned him to look directly at her. "He is not dumb. He had some problems and worked hard to resolve them. Do not be so quick to judge."

"Alright," Egard sighed. "We need to talk about our assignments. Otherwise, our bodies and brains are going to get much colder, standing out here and listening to the wisdom of Berc.

"Our task, if and when, a manko is hooked, will be to control the rope. If we get the signal, our job will be to pounce upon the rope between the spool and the hole.

We will need to dig in with our spikes to stop the rope and to keep ourselves from being thrust into the hole and to a certain death."

"But we are not small enough to fit through the hole," countered Sabri.

"You have been told, and no doubt you have read, about the size of the manko. The hole in the ice will need to be extended significantly before the manko is to be brought forth from its world into our own. The way this is done will be a pleasure to your eyes and other senses, and I shall not ruin it for you."

"Great, another surprise," Berc said to Enoch, who tried to ignore him and pretend that he was not listening to anybody but his father.

Egard was not fooled. "Since the two of you are so interested in the details of the hunt, I feel that you should get a more intimate feel for the proceedings." Their father started to look in the direction of the other holes, obviously searching for someone.

Enoch held his mitten palms up and shot an annoyed look at his brother. "Thanks a lot, who knows what you've gotten us into now."

"Nonsense, boys," Egard said as he found what he was looking for. He herded both his sons forward with a hand at their upper backs. "The two of you will now be master strainers."

They approached a pair of glum looking boys, seemingly in a hurry and running between two of the holes. Egard had a short conversation with them, whereupon they visibly rejoiced, thanked Egard profusely, then handed over two large ladles and scampered away.

Egard led his two boys to the closest hole and explained that their job was to position themselves beneath the wand-wielder, the rope, and the wooden apparatus in order to break any ice forming on the water at the top of the hole. They were to first use the blunt end of the ladle—taking care not to come in contact with any of the water or ice—and then strain the ice out with the other end. They were to accomplish this forthwith and then run to the other holes before the ice there became too thick and their slowness impeded the whole hunt. In these colder temperatures, they would need to perform each ice removal as quickly as possible to avoid jeers, or worse, from the "real hunters."

They were completing their second round at each of the three active holes and were already winded when Sasha and Sabri caught them.

"Alright, let's hear it for the strainers!" Sabri shouted as they knelt at the hole in the ice.

A derisive cheer went up from the crowd. Enoch restated how Berc should not open his mouth ever again.

The boys soon lost count of how many times they had de-iced the three holes. Though the running kept them warmer in the howling wind, Enoch was glad to see his father finally approaching them to relieve them of their duty.

Enoch and Berc leaned over with their hands on their knees, catching their breath for a moment. They held up their ice-breaking ladles to hand over to their father. Except he didn't take the ladles. Instead, he placed his hands on his hips and slowly shook his head from side to side.

"Boys, to look at you, one would think that you

had never done a day's work in your life. I think if we actually are able to carry you back to Verandale and lay you safely into your cradles, I will ask the Legion for special permission to hire two full-time babysitters to spoon feed you goat's milk and swaddle you in warm blankets…because you are obviously unfit to wear the title of a one who has passed his Ceremony or one who bears the mark of a Cof kill!"

Enoch realized that their job as "master strainers" was far from over.

"…so, I will consider summing up the courage to allow our wagons to return to Verandale, not just with the ever hoped-for manko meat but also the worthless weight of Berc and Enoch as I somehow convince the elders that you really are worthy…"

Enoch tried to keep listening but also concentrated on not looking at Berc, afraid of the giggling that could ensue and the extra punishment that it could bring. As the parental lecture droned on, one thing was apparent; they were definitely not done with their assigned job.

In fact, Enoch pictured himself succumbing to exhaustion, freezing, and eventually becoming a part of the inhumanly cold ice of The Lake of the Depths. He would then become a mere side-story to future legends of the hunt for the manko. Something along the lines of "now let me tell you children, the tale of the one boy from Verandale who was lucky enough to receive a mark for a confirmed Cof kill but was too dumb to actually help the magnificent people of Darnoc in their annual Serenade of the Manko. May you learn from his story and never repeat his dumbness."

After Egard finished his lecture, he told them that

he would be travelling back to Darnoc, along with Sune, Sabri, and Sasha, to gather the mid-day meal for those that remained upon the ice. He also reminded the boys that the ice forming over the holes—and around the ropes connecting them to the realm of the manko—would take extra expedient attention now that they "had wasted time standing around." Enoch swore he saw the earliest hint of a smile as his father turned away from them and summoned the girls.

He quickly conferred with Berc, and they decided to split up and attend to the two closest holes before meeting at the third. He ran, high-stepping with his spikes so that they came down straight onto the ice surface to try and prevent a slip and fall which could possibly propel a person, Enoch thought, all the way off the lake's edge. He felt he was even becoming good at the business of getting around on the ice between the tarps. He did an exaggerated high step, catching himself showing off a little as he approached the crowd and the music emanating from one of the two "non-Herol" holes.

"Hey, look everybody," Enoch recognized the gravelly, shouting voice of one of the oldest Darnocian men, "the ice-strainer is here. See I told you he gives an oswatt's behind about the success of the hunt. Look at the concern on the lad's face as he arrives late to his hole, wondering if his lateness will ruin the entire hunt for all of us. I say make way, let him through as easily as possible so he doesn't *strain* himself!"

Everyone laughed but Enoch. He did his best to ignore them and dropped to his knees. He threw himself, and the stout end of his ladle, directly at the ice around the singing rope. He dodged the legs of the wand-wielder, gyrating above him. He felt a twinge of relief as his first thrust formed a crack that split the ice between the rope and the edge of the hole. His second thrust missed, and the metal painfully rebounded off the hardened ice surrounding the hole, shooting shards of pain up into his shoulders. He focused his third attempt, and the metal broke through, releasing a slow current of water to bubble up through the crack.

Trying to stay focused, he hacked repeatedly to break the ice into small floating floes. He turned the strainer around and used it to lift the fragments and pile them next to the hole and in front of the many pairs of unhelpful boots facing him.

With the rope now freed again, he righted himself and dodged between the onlookers. He ran and saw Berc do the same. Enoch naturally began to pick up his speed but then thought better of it, believing that he didn't need to take a chance of slipping and also being thankful just to have his brother's help with the ice below Herol's feet.

As he was racing across the ice, he saw the mass of people surrounding Herol move as one. Enoch picked up his pace. The crowd formed an enlarging circle, as the people ran off of the tarps. As they did this, Enoch saw Herol. Having thrown the wand aside, Herol hacked at the ties to release the timbers. The rope was singing as it sped past him and into the hole.

A manko had been hooked!

Enoch dropped his strainer and ran toward the rope. The timbers crashed to the side as the remaining crowd quickly assembled on either side of the rope. Enoch couldn't believe that they were going to throw themselves upon something that was moving this fast.

But as the signal was shouted from the man closest to the spool, they did exactly that.

Enoch hit the rope and felt it lurch beneath him. He saw people around him turn their bodies so that they were facing the hole. They dug in their heels, attempting to slow the rope. Some were successful, but some, like the man immediately behind him, lost their balance and tumbled forward when the pull became too great and their heels became a fulcrum rather than a brake, causing their bodies to flip head over heels. Enoch felt a mass strike his back and was able to turn his head just enough to recognize Olaf, who offered a slurred apology as he jumped back on the rope.

The rope slowed. Enoch felt a burning in the backs of his arms and wondered how much longer he could hold on. His father had arrived, having been partway across the ice and carrying two large satchels of food when the manko was hooked. He had dropped the food and come running, eventually jumping into the small space just ahead of Enoch on the rope line.

"Alright son, this is where we find out what we are made of." He paused to take a few panting breaths between words. "All of us are holding onto this rope against a much larger and much stronger beast. It is now time for each of us to decide if we have the will to maintain the fight for as long as possible. That is, will we hold on until we are too tired or until we have won?"

Enoch pondered this for a moment. He felt he could hold on for now, but he also wondered about the fate of the rope and those around him if most or all the people were to loosen their grip at the same time. He looked at the people in front of and behind him on the rope—counting thirty-six in all.

"Has a manko ever been stronger than all the people trying to land it, and it pulled them into the hole?"

"Maybe," his father answered him. "There is a tale, many years back, about the fish that pulled the rope free of all the handlers. They jumped off the rope to avoid being dragged into the hole. Legend has it the rope screamed across the ice until there was only the last little bit of rope tied around the center of the spool. The fish then dragged the spool until it went crashing down through the hole, sending splinters of wood and ice flying in all directions. The astonished hunters were able to run along the ice and follow the progress of the damaged spool as it was dragged under water. The hooked fish, the rope, and the spool were finally recovered several days later when the manko expired and they chopped a new hole into the ice for retrieval."

Egard paused to readjust his tight grip on the rope. Enoch had many questions in his head and was about to ask another when his father motioned him to be still and watch Herol. The two other ice holes were abandoned as soon as the giant fish had been hooked. Everyone had come running to their positions at the rope, except for the original two wand-wielders. They now worked with Herol to clear the timbers and throw back the surrounding tarps.

With the tarps removed, the ice underneath was exposed, and Enoch saw that, without the trampling effect of dozens of spiked shoes, it was the clearest ice of all. It was scarred only by a deep circle drawn several paces outside of the ice hole. Other dark lines extended from the circle back toward the hole itself, giving the rough appearance of a wagon wheel etched into the ice.

Egard explained that there was no way to fit a manko through the original hole and there was no way to use the cutting axes to cut a larger hole in a timely manner. Generations ago, the Darnocians had come up with a solution. They would attempt to secure the rope and tire out the manko. When it was clear that the manko was near the hole, one of the wand wielders would ignite a mixture of wood shavings, sap, and tar that had been poured into the carefully dug perimeter that was previously covered by the tarps. If this task was done properly, the explosion would produce several pie-shaped ice fragments that would be loosely floating by the time the fish was hauled to the surface.

Herol gave the order for the tenders of the rope to begin pulling. This initially caused the manko to make another run and the rope sped toward the hole. But they were able to gradually control the rope with their synchronized heaves.

Enoch asked his father what they would need to do once a live manko was pulled out through the ice.

An unfamiliar voice, from a man behind Enoch, answered him instead, "Young man, there has never been a live giant manko pulled up through the ice. They have spent many years in the deepest depths by the time they are approaching the end of their lives. Some people believe it gives up at some point after it has been hooked. I think it is more accurate to say that it simply succumbs to the lesser pressures near the top of the waters. This causes its outer skin to undergo a strange transformation where it instantly hardens—some would say freezes or crystallizes. Nobody can explain exactly how or why this happens, but we do know it forms a hardened shell that is not seen on the younger manko. The good news for us is this causes a type of barrier and seals in the best tasting meat our world has ever known.

As he listened to the man and they all strained to haul the fish closer to the surface, Herol raised a torch above his head. A small cheer went up from the exhausted crowd holding the rope.

Herol brought the torch slowly down to waist level. The two other wand-wielders jumped outside of the outlined circle and the brave souls at the front of the rope shielded their eyes.

"For the ices to be with the waters and by way of ours fire," He shouted to the throng, who interpreted this as a toast of sorts and tried unsuccessfully to shout the scrambled words back to him.

Enoch saw Berc, three people ahead of him on the rope, fall over laughing before Egard yelled at him to right himself.

Herol stood poised for another instant to be dramatic. He then touched the flame to the black substance. A blinding flash of light and smoke erupted, followed by a deep cracking sound. One of the large pieces of ice within the circle tipped sideways and splashed back down before two men, armed with a lasso-like apparatus, hauled it out. The hole was now as wide across as three people laid end-to-end. If the manko could be brought up to the surface, the hunt would be successful.

The work of all the people increased to a feverish pitch as they pulled the rope upward. Only Herol remained at the spot where the rope and water met, looking down into the enlarged hole.

Just as suddenly as the frenzy had begun, the rope suddenly stopped twitching and pulling. Enoch stopped and stared, as did several other first-timers. He realized that the pull of the fish did not change because it was off the hook; it changed because the manko no longer moved. They now retrieved the rope in a much more orderly fashion. Enoch discovered a second wind and felt like his strength was actually contributing to the task.

As he continued to pull, he saw the outline of the giant beast appear beneath him. It had an underlying dark green color with darker brown reflective spots. The lifeless shape moved solemnly beneath them until it reached the opening.

Herol and several others held the rope out in front of them to allow the head of the beast—bigger than several humans—to be eased upward and into the center of the hole. Herol gave the signal for the people to stop pulling the rope. Enoch gasped when he saw the fish break the water's surface.

The mouth was placid and expressionless, showing no teeth but appearing fearsome, nonetheless. All members of the hunting party came forward to haul it out of the water. It was easier to get the massive weight onto the ice than Enoch would have imagined. Once the head was out and the hook grasped, the rest of the body slid out on a thin layer of water between it and the transparent ice surface.

Enoch stepped back to gaze at the animal that was bigger than his house. He sat quietly for a moment, thinking of all the stories he had ever heard about the manko. He took off his glove to touch the hardened exterior until he remembered the dangers of human skin touching the waters of The Lake of the Depths.

Enoch contemplated the strength and force that could be generated by an animal that only ate creatures smaller than bugs. Enoch made a mental note to ask Ibrakrim about the life and the death of the manko upon completing his hoped-for return to Verandale.

Berc came up behind him. "Did you ever think you would see anything like this, little brother?"

"Uh, well I'm still not sure I know what I saw."

They both stared ahead at the fish as Herol emerged from the crowd. He stepped forward and pushed one of the fish's eyelids closed with a gloved hand. He said a few words that seemed to be honoring the creature before giving way to workers who had converted the tarps into a sort of sled.

As the fish was positioned for quartering and transport, the order was given to bring up the ropes of the other two holes. There would be no other fish caught this day. Enoch overheard one of the older ladies explaining to the Apprentice that she and some of the others would be staying back at the hot house—Enoch supposed this was the large, transparent building where they had slept the night before—during tomorrow's hunt, to prepare the fish. Most of the meat would be packed into crates for the trip back to Verandale, but some would be cooked fresh for the next evening's send-off feast.

Enoch walked off the ice exhausted but recovered as Sasha came next to him.

"I have to tell you, as amazing as this day was, I miss my protec," she confided. "I don't even want to come out here tomorrow. I wouldn't complain if we could just go home now."

"Well, you know what they say, the trip home is always more dangerous…though I don't know why. But if you think about it, we didn't even get attacked on the second day of the trip." Enoch stopped, distracted by the sight of the restless protecs, as they gingerly approached the edge of the ice along with the rest of the townspeople. "Do you think Cofs actually know what we are doing or which direction we are going?"

"Maybe they like manko meat, too."

When Sasha's father helped her off the edge of the ice, Sasha-protec was instantly at her side. With her protec now back at her hip, she made her way down along the switchbacks, next to Enoch.

They arrived back at town to find the townspeople excited at the news of the manko, but also solemn with the news of a Cof attack. One of the older residents of Darnoc, a farmer named Athos who tended livestock and had a home just beyond the western walls, had not arrived, during the hunt for his planned assignment. A party was sent to his farm and found signs of a struggle. Shredded blood-stained clothes and remains of several cattle were strewn under a covering of light snow, as was a loaded spike. The official funeral would be after the departure of the caravan in two days, but Enoch knew all Verandalians would find a way to show their respect before they left.

The nighttime meal was modest, but the warmth of the building was extra comfortable after the long day upon the ice. Enoch said goodnight to Sasha and found sleep just moments after finding his bed roll and looking at the stars through the clear ceiling. He was too tired to even dream.

The second morning of the hunt brought slicing cold and heavier snow. The weather, combined with dampened excitement compared to the previous day, caused Enoch to start shivering shortly after his first step onto the ice.

Enoch was thankful that he and Berc were not reassigned to the job of strainers, but the day dragged, nonetheless. Berc claimed to be delirious from the cold and volunteered to "go update the others back at the hot house." Having failed at this, he joined Enoch in jumping up and down at the edges of one of the tarps, trying to use the crowd as a wind break.

They also grumbled about Sabri and Sasha being assigned to the food preparation work detail back in town.

"I bet they are close enough to the ovens that they have had to shed layers of clothes," Enoch said.

"Yeah, probably sneaking a few bites of manko while filling the pots, too," Berc added.

It was well after the midday meal. The brothers' moods were becoming foul as Herol took time away from the wand to run around shouting orders at people, then becoming angered if they did not comprehend his special Heroldian language.

With the suns sliding lower in the sky, and the winds blowing chilled knives through their clothes, the hunters were finally rewarded with another manko catch. Enoch and Berc dove immediately on the rope. This time, there was no pausing. They realized the sooner they got the fish out of the water, the sooner they would be back in the glow of the hot house for the farewell meal.

They pulled as hard as they could until the fish, even larger than the one the day before, was on the ice. The boys were leaning over with their hands on their knees when another manko was hooked. They overcame their exhaustion long enough to haul the third and last fish of the trip out of the water.

They were assigned to be part of the quartering team and put in charge of pulling one sled back down the switchbacks but didn't complain since they were headed back into town.

Upon arriving at the hot house, they were allowed to pull their heavily laden sled into the back-kitchen entrance and give it over to the warmer workers. They took off their outer layers of clothes. Enoch walked over to the ovens, trying to figure out which was better, the heat or the smell of fresh manko wafting out of them.

Just as he was beginning to get feeling back in his hands and feet, Sasha made her way over and grabbed his arm, leading him out to the main room.

"You have to see this," she said.

They turned the corner and Enoch saw an amazing site. All the cots and bed rolls had been pushed aside and large tables with ornate tablecloths were lined end to end across the room. In the middle of the hot house, a large post supported a roaring flame that extended halfway to the ceiling. Enoch hadn't noticed this the last two nights, but a long thin cord dangled from the ceiling and allowed the central panes of the ceiling to be opened. Smoky trails wafted upward before sneaking out into the chill of the night.

"Whoa," whispered Enoch.

"I wish I could tell you how good the feast is going to be. The people of Darnoc spend a lot of time skimping and conserving food throughout the year, but they go all out on this one night."

"So, you spent all day preparing the food and never snuck one piece?" Enoch asked in an accusatory tone.

"A good cook never shares her secrets." Sasha batted her eyelids and looked away, hiding a smile while managing to put a neatly wrapped morsel into Enoch's pocket.

Before Enoch could thank her, the rest of the people filed in and the Constable made his way to the head of the table, gently striking a glass.

He gave a pretty standard Constable-like speech. It was also plenty long, Enoch thought as his belly growled.

When the speech was over, and the feast began, Enoch understood why so many hoped to make the annual trip to Darnoc. The first course was a small cup of manko soup, served with an identical cup that contained water from a spring that fed the far side of The Lake of the Depths. Sasha helped explain to him that the cups of water were set outside just before the dinner to have the finest sheen of ice across the top. The tradition was to take one's spoon, dip it into the iced spring water briefly, and then drop it into the steaming soup. The soup was then sipped from the spoon. This was meant to duplicate the process that the live manko had endured at the moment of death when heat escaped from its body and the frozen shell was formed.

"Are you sure this makes any difference?" Enoch asked.

"Just try it," Sasha pushed his hand toward the cup, "you won't be sorry."

Enoch's spoon broke the ice, and he quickly transferred it to the steaming soup. The interaction of water and soup, cold and hot, caused sizzling and bubbling. Though he briefly fumbled the spoon, he spilled only a few drops before tasting the liquid. He then realized it really was possible to taste soup better than the soup at the end-of-the-school-year banquet.

He started to tell Sasha, but she just cut him off with an, "I know, but this is not even the best part."

They finished every drop before the cups were cleared. The cooks brought forth pieces of seared manko meat. Each was impaled through its length by a thick stalk of winter wheat. Each end was tied by a stringy dark green leaf that smelled like mint. Though the appearance was strange, the taste proved to be as fantastic as the soup.

Fresh greens, grown in the hot house and cut earlier in the day, were served on the side. Near the end of the meal, carved stone mugs filled with tlok-vine tea were placed in front of the adults, while smaller mugs of "twice-cooked tea," containing much less of the distilled intoxicant, were given to the young. The great dining hall was filled with warmth, the clanking of mugs, and friendships new and old.

The feast and merriment continued to increase until the Constable rose upon a dais near the main doors. No spoons rang against mugs. No one had to tell anyone to quiet or put down their utensils. The Constable was wearing the black robe of a departure ceremony.

He paused before the crowd, and then started with a solemn voice.

"The news undoubtedly has reached and touched everyone in this hall. I knew Athos as a quiet and solitary man. He didn't talk much, but he had a way of caring for anything that ran on four legs. As you know he spent a fair amount of time alone and within sight of the forest. We all spent a good amount of time worrying about him and trying to persuade him to stay closer to the gates, or at least enlist a guard for his protection while in the fields. Having said that, I never saw him in the fields with anyone but the animals, unless it was one of us pestering him to come back to town.

"I would like to share with you, two of his favorite responses that he spat at me or anyone who tried to impose their idea of safe farming onto his own. One early morning, I saw him far out in a pasture. He had just finished coaxing a calf out of some bramble. He was walking, in no hurry, back toward the herd with one hand on the calf's back. His back was turned to the edge of the forest, but he wasn't looking back; just chewing on a piece of grass and occasionally saying short words of encouragement to the animal. I ran up to him—while keeping my own nervous eyes on the tree line—to see if he was hurt or perhaps dazed. He was neither. In fact, he wasn't concerned at all. I said, 'Athos, you have got to be more careful, man, do you want to get eaten?' He stopped and looked at me for a moment and said, 'Those Cofs won't ever wanna eat me…the meat is too tough.'

"Another time, we were out in a blinding storm, trying to steer some sheep out of a normally dry depression that had filled up after several days of rain. We were both well past muddy and miserable when I told him that I was counting on the suns for a much better day tomorrow. He looked up and simply said, 'Sunshine always follows rain.' He paused just long enough to know that he had me, and then added, 'unless you drown in a puddle.'"

The Constable paused for laughter and nods from the Darnocians who knew Athos. He grabbed his mug and held it up to the crowd.

"To Athos: may your life on the other side be filled with more sunslight than you ever imagined. May the Cofs be only as big as your hand, and…maybe even tasty when boiled with a ripe head of cabbage." The Constable tried to gather himself before continuing, "May every animal you have ever cared for and all of us whom you have ever made smile, stop by for a visit…though we promise to keep it short."

He thrust his mug above his head and out toward the crowd. "To Athos," he said through tears.

"To Athos," the crowd yelled back. They raised their glasses to the ceiling and to the darkened sky above.

Enoch and Sasha stayed at the table for a while longer. They listened to fantastic tales that pre-dated the era of the written word and had probably been embellished by several generations of people and several thousand mugs of tea.

They left their seats and walked along the table in search of the others. Enoch glanced in front of him and could not believe what he saw; someone had dropped a thumb-sized piece of manko meat onto the floor. He moved a chair quickly aside, but Sasha-protec lunged in front of him and gulped down the meat.

Sasha stood in front of him with one hand on her hip, trying not to smile. "Don't worry. He knows that you were picking it up to give to him anyway, right?" Sasha-protec licked a tusk with a giant slurp and looked at Enoch.

"Absolutely," Enoch replied, grabbing her hand and walking toward a darkened corner of the hall. There, they found Berc, Sabri, the Apprentice, and a smattering of younger children telling ghost stories and trying to scare one another.

Enoch heard fables presented as true and true stories enhanced to a point where they sounded like fables. Enoch thought about retelling the story of Ibrakrim's first mark, but he was too tired to do proper justice to the tale.

Children were allowed to spread their bed rolls out together as the adults carried on. Berc told the most fearsome tales but also insisted his sleeping spot be safely in the middle of all the others. They were all soon asleep. The adults snuffed the candles shortly thereafter, none wishing to be short on sleep or long on drink prior to the morning, and the return trip to Verandale.

Boys are tasked with reason but strained with boyhood.
—Overheard from conversation between
Sabri, Sasha, and Falo

17

The town gates closed behind them as the caravan approached the Darnocian Bridge. Sabri used an increasingly agitated tone to ask Herol to please be quiet. Her mother just smiled and settled into a nook between two crates that gave her a view out the front, between the occupants of the driver's bench: Enoch, Sasha, and her protec.

Sitting in the back between crates packed with manko meat, Sabri already regretted volunteering for this wagon. She felt like she was doing the right thing at the time. When the wagon assignments came out, Berc was to be in this wagon. She thought the combination of Berc and Herol would be painful enough, but to have Berc there pestering Enoch and Sasha when they had been promised a chance to ride in the same wagon...that would be too much.

"Why name not to like you, and not to protec?" He asked her while pointing at Dew.

Sabri started to offer up another explanation but decided instead to remind Herol that he had the first shift to watch the rear of the wagon. Up front, Enoch gripped the reins tighter as they approached the Darnoc Bridge.

Before they left the warmth of the hot house for the last time this morning, he learned there would be no races and no surprises on the return trip. Instead, there was one simple plan: get all the wagons, all the people, and this year's supply of manko meat safely back to Verandale.

Enoch tried to scan the trail, the wagon ahead of them, and the decreasing width of the open fields between them and the forest, but it was hard to pull his eyes away from the bridge. The wagons were travelling much slower than their first trip over the bridge. Up close, Enoch could see the imperfections in the quarried rock and could see what little remained of the light given off by the Runal rocks during the long winter's night. As the lead wagon passed through the building covering the center of the bridge, an order came for the caravan to stop.

Enoch and Sasha dismounted while Sasha-protec jumped down between them. Enoch felt the heat of the stones all around them. Sasha grabbed his hand, and they walked between the wagons ahead of them. After just a few paces, Enoch saw an intricate life-sized statue, made of regular stone but standing in a crevice that had been carved into the high Runal-stone walls of the bridge.

"You have to see this," Sasha said.

She pointed to the name "Olia" carved into the base of the first statue. Next to a young Olia was her protec complete with stripe, a fierce snarl, and a Cof horn in his mouth. They walked down the row, and saw statue after statue, all labeled with legendary names. Many were from long ago, such as Acetr. But they also came across Ibrakrim in his long librarian robe and a few statues bearing names neither of them recognized.

The caravan leaders made sure the stop was short, but also allowed time for a few of the travelers to leave plants or other mementos upon the statues of long-lost relatives.

Enoch helped Sasha and then climbed back up onto the driver's bench. His father stopped on the path back to the rear wagon to make sure his son was still comfortable in his role as driver. As he answered his father, Enoch felt the fear that—unbeknownst to him—was shared by all the members of the caravan.

Sasha talked to her protec, nudging and coercing him until he finally settled on the far right of the bench allowing Enoch and Sasha to sit next to each other. Enoch held the reins, waiting patiently for the wagons in front of them to start moving.

"I don't know about you, but I would be totally happy to be back in our classroom, learning about crops or something," Sasha said.

"I am with you. I don't think I will complain about being bored, ever again."

"And not to be a part of what the Cofs have on their plates," came a voice from the back of the wagon.

Enoch and Sasha smiled at each other as the wagons began to move forward. Enoch wondered what their life would be like the next time they saw Darnoc.

The first day of the return trip was nearing an end. The larger of the suns was touching the rim of the western mountains and illuminating the path and the forest ahead of them. Though no part of the day had been warm, it had at least been free of snow and free of the kind of cold that made skin numb, and bones hurt.

A rare sight had both mesmerized and terrorized the wagons late in the morning when the driver of the lead wagon saw a large Cof sailing above the trees to their north. Every possible person was placed on lookout, whether it was from driver's bench, beneath the canopies, or from the sideboard near the hand brake. No attack occurred however until after dark.

The wagons had stopped in a large clearing in order to rest and feed the animals. One of the watchmen sounded an alarm after hearing a disturbance in the nearby darkness. The horses were quickly started as people ran back to their positions. A Cof bounded out from the direction of the original noise.

Another dove from the treetops on the other side of the trail.

It may have started its descent from even higher than the treetops, for it crashed with a heavy thud, sending snow and rocks spraying in all directions but missing the wagons. Fortunately, many of the well-trained guards and others knew to look in both directions during a Cof assault. A guard riding in front was the first to let a spike fly and they heard another thud, followed only by silence.

All were on edge as darkness ringed their wagons. The drivers and their relief teams were able to keep moving for most all the night. Enoch, Sasha, and her protec were eventually convinced to give up their positions on the bench to those in the back. To Enoch's relief, he found that Herol was either too tired or too preoccupied to keep talking after taking the reins. After a brief repositioning when he found his nose too close to the hind quarters of Sasha-protec, Enoch nestled among bed rolls lodged between crates and slept longer than he would have guessed possible.

He was startled to find the darkness of the night already fading when he next opened his eyes. But he knew the dawn of the last day usually brought smiles and vastly increased happiness to all the members of the caravan.

However, he found the whole team in an even more somber mood than the night before. For a moment, he frantically imagined he may have slumbered through an attack. He stuck his head out of the front of the wagon long enough to make sure the wagon count was steady, and to receive confirmation from his mother that he had not missed anything of significance.

"Why all the long faces then?" he asked his mom, trying to hold back a smile as he realized he would see his home and sleep in his bed at the conclusion of the day. Without interrupting her constant scrutiny of the tree lines on either side, she directed him to look out the back and past the other wagons for the answer.

Enoch moved carefully, trying not to step on the sleeping forms of Sasha or her protec. When he reached the back, he understood the cause for the caravan's concern.

As the suns broke over the eastern horizon, they

shone upon one of the most feared sights for any wagon team. The clouds approaching from the west were towering, dark, and stretched ominously from northern to southern horizons. Winds violently beat at the cloth of their wagons and foretold of an oncoming storm that would catch them long before they reached Verandale.

Enoch sat down, embarrassed at yet another thing that he did not figure out on his own. He stretched to get some blood moving in his limbs before offering to relieve his mother and sister and take the next forward watch while Herol drove.

He heard Sasha stirring behind him but responded to her "good morning" without looking back, determined to keep his focus unbroken, looking for any dangers lurking in the storm. He talked to Herol, anything to make him less nervous.

One of the topics they discussed was Kahdi. Enoch thought it interesting and a little perplexing that the merits and downfalls of Kahdi were a fairly regular topic around the mugs in the Darnoc hot house. According to Herol, the Kahdi updates were an important part of the information provided by those in the annual caravan. Herol also explained, Enoch thought, that Kahdi might someday have his own statue on the bridge.

"Wait, wait. You're trying to tell me that the same Kahdi that sinks boats and bites people will one day be immortalized forever along with all those other statues we saw?"

"You do not know with the statues, that you know with the person," Herol said in his still booming voice, unchanged from his time in command of the manko hunt.

"I'm not sure what that means Herol, but I do know that

everybody who has a statue there has done something really amazing. Kahdi is not even stable enough to join the caravan to Darnoc, let alone…" Enoch paused as the first snowflakes blew sideways from behind their wagon. "…Let alone be immortalized as a statue."

"We cannot be to future knows, what Kahdi knows."

Sabri poked her head up between them, placed one hand on Herol's shoulder, but looked at Enoch.

"You just keep watching the tree line little brother. I'm going to try and mentally process that one," she nodded her head toward Herol, "for a little while." She retreated back behind them while Enoch also tried to decipher this latest Herolism.

Enoch stopped talking as the snow turned into a blizzard and made it nearly impossible to see the wagon ruts in the road. The lead wagon team announced there would be no further stops; they would continue through until they reached the western edge of Verandale, still about half a day away. By doing this, they hoped to outrun the worst of the storm and avoid any chance of being snowed in on the trail.

Enoch felt as if he was getting a second wind when Herol handed him the reins and stepped back over the bench to trade places with Sasha. She and Sabri had already been at work making an overlook for their protecs. It enabled them to sit right behind the driver's bench, maintain a view of everything in front of the wagon, and still be within short reach of their charges.

After positioning her protec and Dew side-by-side, Sabri braced her hands on Enoch's shoulder and lowered herself next to him on the driver's bench.

As Enoch took his eyes off the road to smile at her,

two dark shapes materialized out of the blanket of snow above their heads.

The first Cof hit the sideboards of the wagon with enough force to tip it for a moment onto its two left wheels. The second animal was diving directly at Sasha, but the tipping of the wagon threw her over the front and between two of the horses.

Enoch couldn't tell if she was hurt. He desperately pulled the horses to a stop. He grabbed his weapons bag as shouts and screams erupted all around.

He jumped down to the space between the horses, landing on top of Sasha as her protec dove against her attacker.

He thought she might be unconscious.

"Stay down," he screamed at her, hoping she could still hear him.

The Cof landed and struck its horn against the frantically tangled horse—the only object between it and Sasha. Enoch grabbed a scythe and lunged over the horse, aiming at the tough hide covering the Cof's chest. The animal did not seem to even notice. Only the frantic bucking of the horse prevented it from impaling Enoch.

Enoch was grasping for another weapon when Herol, having jumped out the back of the wagon, threw a spike directly into the Cof's neck. It dropped to the ground motionless as Sasha protec thrust its tusks into the animal's side.

Enoch was grabbing at Sasha, trying to get her upright as he called for his mother and sister. He heard his father's voice shouting orders above the many panicked voices behind them. He saw only a blur of activity between the snowflakes and grey of the blizzard.

As Herol ran along the right side of the wagon, a thunderous force slammed him against the wagon then into the ground. Spikes were let loose against the beast but missed high as the throwers tried to avoid hitting Herol. Enoch jumped up to the bench with a mander club in hand. He was about to use the bench as a platform to launch himself up and over the side when the next volley of spikes came whistling out of the snow from the rear wagons. He had to duck as one ripped into the canopy of the wagon itself. He also heard one strike a Cof. He watched as the beast fell between the wheels of the wagon. It was bleeding but not dead.

It tried to right itself but was now below the wagon. As Enoch tried to see if Sasha was hurt, the Cof lunged forward, striking the bottom of the driver's bench with its head, sending boards and splinters flying upward.

Enoch froze as the path to get Sasha back into the safety of the wagon was blocked. They pulled each other upright as a horse crashed into the side of his knee. He winced in pain as Sabri appeared, yelling for them to run to the wagon in front of them.

Enoch and Sasha tried to run into the blinding snow and away from the Cof. But the panicked horses had run forward, pulling the wagon with them. Enoch knew that they would be trampled or worse if they didn't get out of the midst of the horses.

"Hold on!" Sasha grabbed at him as he tried to run on a bad leg.

As they both dove under the back canopy of the wagon, Enoch cried out in pain as he felt his injured knee strike a crate. He winced and tried to right himself as soon as possible in order to face the open space behind him. Sasha was screaming as loud as she could for her protec until she heard a bark and he came sprinting at full speed, out of the snow. Convinced they were safe, and the wagons were again under way, Enoch turned to a voice behind him.

"Who is there?"

It was Olaf. His voice was ragged, and his breathing came in gasps, but he looked to be uninjured.

"It's me Enoch, and my girlfriend, Sasha." That sounded wrong right away, even in the midst of chaos.

"I can tell you one thing, sonny. I am getting way too old for this dung heap of an idea they call a caravan. This time next year, I'm going to be sitting home next to a fire surrounded by people who are paid to cut up my dinner!"

Sasha scooted over next to Enoch and asked if he was alright. He told her about his knee. She said she had been clobbered in the head. Enoch confirmed she had a bruise but no blood.

Sasha's father appeared running through the snow from the wagon before them. He hugged his daughter and told them that her mother and brothers were safe, and he was doing a head count.

There were all kinds of people in the wrong wagons. Some of them were injured and the count was far from complete. He promised to return or send someone back up to their wagon as soon as he knew about Enoch's family.

Enoch stretched to look behind them, carefully measuring the distance he would have to run to make it back to their original wagon. He finally jumped out into the snow. Enoch could make out the front two horses but strained his eyes—unable to see if her father made it.

Enoch and Sasha checked in with the two drivers of the wagon to see if they needed any help. They were relieved when they were asked only to keep watch out the back and tend to Olaf.

They braced against each other as much from the fear of news from the rest of the caravan as from the cold of the blizzard. It seemed to Enoch waiting had never felt this long.

Both of their hearts jumped when a figure ran toward them. It was Enoch's father, and they both shrieked with relief. But his face was dour as he pulled himself up and hugged them both tightly.

Sune, Berc, Sabri, and Dew were all safe and had no major injuries. But the attack had been ferocious, and the snow had proved to be perfect cover for an ambush by multiple Cofs. All grew quiet as Egard hung his head and announced that both Herol and the Apprentice had lost their lives to the evil brought forth by the creatures of the forest.

18

A mixture of dead leaves, pine needles, and blood-soaked frost were caked in the hair of the lifeless head. An ever-decreasing rivulet of bright red blood oozed from a gaping chest wound. The head and neck bounced up and down as the body was dragged up the side of the mountain and left a red stain across the rocks and snow. The upper appendage under the Cof's wing gripped tightly around the ankle at the other end of the prey.

Ricit steadied his lower body, leaned into the upslope of the mountain, and dragged the human forward. He conveyed it with a lumbering heave to the waiting grip of his hunting partner. With the ankle firmly transferred to Tucir, Ricit bounded twice up the mountain and reached back to receive the body, repeating the process by heaving it forward.

They repeated this process countless times. Several paces behind, two other hunters quietly mimicked Ricit and Tucir's actions with a kill of their own. As the four approached the camp, they were helped by the other hunters of the group who had already flown back after the successful ambush.

They arranged the bodies next to each other, arms laid neatly at the sides. They draped two tlok vines from neck to thigh on each side of each corpse. The grunts and whistles used by the Cofs for communication ceased as the group grew silent—in the frigid growing darkness that surrounded their meal—and awaited the Commander.

Hearing the wind separated above him, Ricit looked up quickly to see the Commander swoop down from the snow-covered trees near the mountain's rim. As the oldest Cof, the Commander had long ago lost his ability to camouflage. He appeared amongst the silent Cofs in his original bluish-green hue. He bounded to the small space between the bodies, and then looked at each of his subjects, counting to himself as he rotated in the middle of the circle.

"I count eleven members of the original expedition."

"Yes Commander," Ricit nervously volunteered, "one of the members of the ambush was hit with a cutting rock. He was not wounded badly at first, but then stumbled in front of one of the charging animals that pull the carts. Another died instantly, Commander, and has gone to meet the being who gave him life. There were other injuries but no other loss of life."

The Commander looked over the carcasses and spoke from within the circle of his followers.

"Comrades, we have lost two of our own on this blessed day. They have given up the vessels of their souls so that our extended family can continue to nourish itself. It is only through the goodness of the Maker that we are given the gift of another meal and the right to another breath. Please honor her memory and pray the prayer of honor for our prey. As with their cousins, the deer and oswatts, they do not know the power of the Maker. They do not know how greatly they have honored the Maker as they have once again given the gift of nourishment to us and our offspring."

The tunic was ripped and removed, first from Herol's body and then from the Apprentice. As the hunting party anxiously peered upward at their leader from bowed heads, he gave the signal with a raised wing and backed away. Other Cofs joined the gathering from outlying regions, beneath the darkening canopy of the forest. They kept a respectful distance until the hunting party had supped first on the flesh of their honored victims.

The Cofs removed the last remnants of flesh after first feeding the soft entrails to the young. At the end of the meal, long bones were broken with a reverberating snap. The richness and the warmth of the marrow was released and presented to the Commander as he came forward from the darkness to sup and signify the end of a successful hunt. In this way, the final honor was paid to the meal supplied by the Maker from the other side of the mountain.

The sated northern colony scattered the last remnants of the Apprentice and Herol. Several leagues away, the blizzard began to clear. A wounded and lessened winter caravan crossed the Upper River Bridge and entered the western edge of Verandale, illuminated by the last vestige of the late day suns.

Living amongst the Cofs is beautiful,
for those who remain amongst the living.
— Professor Andrew

19

noch felt the tingling progress to deadness in his left arm as he tried not to move and awaken Sasha. Her head lay atop his shoulder and her shoulder pressed against the midpoint of his arm. The two rode on the back of the wagon, beneath heavy blankets. The view behind them was difficult in the fading snow and twilight, but Enoch frequently caught the somber glances of the rest of his family and others in the wagons behind them. He wouldn't learn until much later the details and horrors they had witnessed during Herol's last fight.

Though he treasured the moment they would reenter the familiarity and the relative safety of Verandale, Enoch could not imagine the pain he would see as friends and family members were told of the loss of two more of their own.

He did not want to grow up and face the responsibilities of adulthood. At the same time, he resolved to find a way out of this land and out of the danger that was ever present while living amongst the Cofs.

Everyone in the caravan shared his sorrow and the

dread that were necessarily mixed with the relief of arriving back home. They would soon all discover that theirs was not the only population that had changed. The population of Verandale had also changed in their absence, but a member had been added rather than subtracted.

As the caravan entered the town, the welcoming crowd surrounded the wagons. At the back, an animal was standing next to the largest of all the people. The animal looked cautious but strong. The human looked bewildered, but also resigned to the constant companionship of the animal and the extra attention it had brought from all the mystified inhabitants of Verandale over the last two days.

The man reached down and scratched at the space behind the animal's ears and near the beginning of the large stripe that ran along its back. It paused its panting to look back up at him.

Kahdi-protec had arrived.

Part III

~

What Kahdi Knows

We cannot be to future knows, what Kahdi knows.

—Herol

20

Enoch kept his chest pressed against the short grass of the new growing season. He was between Berc and Sabri. They had been lying here for so long the condensation had not only soaked through the front of their clothes but now covered their backs also. The three siblings tried to stay as quiet and hunched down as possible. Sabri kept an arm over Dew, who reluctantly kept his head down but pointed his ears in alarm at each and every sound.

The foursome had been in this position ever since arriving at first light to spy on Kahdi leaving his house. The day began with a lot of giggling as the three of them "camouflaged" Dew by sticking grass and twigs into his thick fur until he looked like a gigantic porcupine. But the humor had dissipated as they grew wet and cold. Boredom set in as the morning progressed with no sign of Kahdi.

"If we are here much longer," Berc complained, "the grass is going to start growing *over* us."

"Stop whining," his sister scolded him. "For all we

know, maybe he only goes into the forest on days when he sleeps in."

"You know, this being our third day of sitting up here," Enoch paused to stifle a yawn, "we may just have to admit we're never going to predict any of his actions. Kahdi will just go into the forest whenever he wants to. In the meantime, we will sit around and wonder why he is the only man to ever get a protec, not to mention a striped protec, and why the laws of the forest seem to apply to everyone but him."

While they sat pondering this, the front door of Kahdi's house opened. Kahdi-protec ran out, rolled on the dusty path, and then stood to shake his bi-colored fur all over. He turned back to the house, but first raised his nose to the air and turned his head ever so slightly toward the distant kids. He sniffed Dew a silent hello, and Dew lifted his own nose in a form of protec answer.

Kahdi-protec turned back, obviously awaiting his charge, but instead faced only the darkness of an open door.

"I bet he has decided this is the craziest protec job ever," Berc smirked. "He is saying goodbye to Kahdi, before travelling back across the mountains and demanding to be reassigned."

"Shush, will you? His protec has already sensed us. Do you want Kahdi to see us and leave us forever without our answer?" Sabri pleaded.

Berc reluctantly took her advice, as did Enoch. They continued to be as still as possible until they saw a shadow move within the house.

Kahdi slung his head lower in order to avoid hitting

the door's top frame. He stepped outside and squinted his eyes against the harshness of the mid-morning suns.

Enoch stared at the mountainous figure. He looked... well, he just looked dumb, Enoch decided. There was no way around it. He looked dumb and like there was no way he could hold the secret to entering the forest, let alone any other secret that could affect the future of Verandale.

Kahdi shook his head back and forth, mimicking the action his protec had just completed. Enoch noted his hair was still long on one side of his head, short on the other—the victim of giving himself a half-haircut several days earlier. This, along with an unfortunate small fire he had started when assigned to wash dishes at the palace, convinced the residents of Verandale that Kahdi may be safer from the Cofs now that he had a protec, but Verandale was not any safer from him.

He lumbered down the path, just behind his protec. They walked a short distance until they came to a small stick that lay across the path. Kahdi stared at the object until the animal picked it up and carefully held it between his powerful jaws.

"Surely," Sabri paused, unsure of what she was seeing, "the once mighty race of protecs has not degraded itself to fetching a stick for that towering body of ever-confused flesh?"

Enoch and Berc held their breath. Kahdi stopped to look at the offering held in front of him. He bent down with an outstretched arm reaching for the stick. But before he could reach it, the protec hurled his head forcefully to the side and let the stick fly. It landed in some short green foliage, several paces off the path. Kahdi looked at it and then back at the animal. They both froze for just a moment.

Then Kahdi ran to the stick.

He picked it up and brought it back, placing it gently on the ground at the feet of his protec.

Kahdi-protec bent down and turned his head sideways, maneuvering his jaws and tusks to pick up the stick. Once completed, he repeated the process and landed the stick even farther off the path, where Kahdi gladly ran after it once again.

"I have no words," Sabri winced, shaking her head.

Dew rose up and looked at the display, his head cocked ever so slightly to one side.

Berc and Enoch could take it no longer. They tried to stand, no longer caring about blowing their cover, but made it only partway before rolling over each other, laughing and holding their sides.

"I have never…," Berc squealed while pounding the ground with an open palm.

"I know," Enoch tried to finish his brother's thought. "What's next, the protec fills a bowl with water and Kahdi drinks from it?"

Sabri thought about trying to get them to be still, but one look at the scene to her left—two merry bodies rolling, slobbering, and slapping each other—convinced her that any attempted intervention would be futile. She resigned herself to holding onto Dew and directed her attention back to the distant scene playing out in front of her.

Kahdi fetched the stick a third time. But this time, the protec and his charge stood, just facing each other, and panting, neither appearing sure of what they would do next until Kahdi's mother came out the front door.

She swung two wooden pails, one from each hand. She walked up to her son as if the scene in front of her was completely normal.

Keeping her eyes fixed on Kahdi's mother, Sabri frantically slapped at her wrestling brothers. She was finally able to get their attention as Kahdi took the pails and headed away from the house.

Kahdi-protec brushed against the right leg of his charge as they climbed up the mountain and beneath the boughs of the first trees at the edge of the endless forest. All three kids and Dew watched the pair disappear into the dark green shadows.

"I'm not sure I can make sense out of anything that my eyes just saw. We might as well just go have breakfast on Egg Island."

"I know what you mean, little brother. I just wonder where they are going to come out of the forest," Berc said.

"What I would like to know," Sabri interrupted, "is if they are going to come out of the forest. I mean, how do you just walk into the area that we all fear and expect to come out whole, or even come out at all?"

"Maybe the fear is only there if the knowing is there." Enoch paused as his siblings turned to him. "I mean, what if you can only fear what your head recognizes as scary? And if your head is not good at recognizing scary, your body may be able to walk into things without your brain telling it not to."

The three sat and contemplated all they had just seen. No one was ready to take the first step. It was not until Dew arose—complete with all his extra ornamentation— and started forward, that they knew exactly what they had to do. They needed to go to Kahdi's house and talk to his mother. They would try to talk to her and understand the mysteries that were wrapped up in the man child, her son.

Sabri tried to keep her eyes on the forest but was distracted by her brothers. Berc removed a twig from Dew's coat and bounced it off the top of Enoch's head. Enoch bent over quickly to grab the biggest stick he could see. He whipped it sideways, hard enough to make a *thwack* against his brother's thigh. Berc tried to act like it didn't hurt but gave in to an urge to rub the area with his hand.

"Oh, everybody stop, we've got a serious injury here!" Enoch shouted happily. "Dew, lick Berc's wound. Sabri, bring him some flowers."

Berc grabbed Enoch's hair and yanked downwards.

"Come on you guys, cut it out!" Sabri yelled at them. "One of these days, I'm going to get eaten by a diving Cof because I'm yelling at you two and not paying attention."

The four of them resumed walking in relative silence, Sabri and Dew now having positioned themselves between the boys. They approached the house, finding the front door still ajar. Sabri peered inside and yelled a friendly hello.

Kahdi's mother appeared, wiping her hands on an apron, and looking as if nothing remarkable had happened.

"Oh, just look at you fine young people, all growing up and getting bigger!"

She reached forward and grabbed Berc by the cheek before noting a scrape and fresh blood on his arm, incurred from the just completed battle.

"Oh, my dear, you're bleeding! Don't tell me that Dew is going around biting everybody again?"

Sabri frowned. She started to defend her protec and make sure everyone understood Dew would never do that unless really, really provoked. She let it drop as Enoch began questioning.

"Can you tell us, um, Kahdi's mother…I'm sorry, mam, I don't know your real name."

"That's alright dear. You can certainly call me 'Kahdi's mother.' After all no one is going to confuse themselves with me since there is only one Kahdi."

"That's for sure," Berc mumbled behind his brother, before Sabri thrust an elbow at him and silenced him with a glare.

"Well see, we were wondering," Enoch continued. "You know how he just ran into the forest just now?"

"Oh, sure, some days he just leaves with a couple of buckets and comes back later that day or that evening with them full of fruit or filled with sap."

Berc was petting Dew but stopped to look up incredulously. "So, he is in the forest in the evenings also?"

"Oh yes, in fact just a few days ago, he was supposed to go spend a day with that nice old man in the library, Ibrakrim."

Now Berc had to turn and face the other direction and even Sabri had to bite her lip to keep from laughing as she continued.

"The problem was that we were on our way down the road and a wagon was coming toward us. So, we stepped out of the way to let it pass but my little Kahdi, do you know what he did?" she asked, as she bent closer to them, and her eyes became wider.

No one was able to answer her.

Berc's mouth was about to explode.

"Well, I'll tell you. He stepped off the road and then he just kept on stepping right up into the trees and took his little animal with him. I certainly didn't know what to do. You know I called him a couple of times, but he didn't answer. He is not a big talker. So, I kept on going up to the palace and met with Mister Ibrakrim myself and told him the whole story. And do you know what he told me?"

There was still no way that anyone was going to be able to answer her while maintaining a straight face. Enoch was at least able to shake his head no in response.

"Well, at first he just gets a funny look on his face like I'm talking in words he can't understand, but then he tells me that we could save everybody a lot of trouble if we just sent Kahdi to Darnoc every winter and told him to bring the manko back himself."

Enoch looked at her, waiting for the rest of the story, but realized it was never going to come. "So, I guess what we need to ask you is; how do you know when your son is going to go into the forest?"

"Oh, Enoch, I don't think we ever know until he gets there."

At this point, Sabri and Berc were ready to give up on any more questions, but Enoch had one more.

"Do you know how many days ago your son went into the forest?"

"Hmm, well no young man," she stopped to look up at the sky. "There was today of course. Before that, I know it was more than a couple of days or so, and I know it was the day that I ran into your mother down at the mollusk fields. She is such a nice lady, your mother. Why I remember her when she was just knee-high to an oswatt. She was the cutest little loaf of happiness…"

Enoch tried to be polite while they were backing away. But he knew they were unlikely to get any more information out of Kahdi's mother. He tried to combine waving with "goodbyes" and any other words that would get the three of them down the road so they could develop a plan.

They had already started to discuss the possibility they had learned absolutely nothing from all their days of silently watching Kahdi's house and their just completed conversation with their mother, when they heard her voice once more.

"Goodbye you youngins," she hollered as the kids once more rolled their eyes upwards, "and congratulations Enoch…" This stopped the kids in their tracks. They turned back toward the boisterous lady still standing and yelling from her doorway. "…on being named the new Apprentice."

She walked back into her house and quietly closed the door. All three siblings and a protec stood speechless in the middle of the road.

Healing is paramount when health falls or trauma rises.
— The Healer

21

Enoch and his father walked through the old gate. Its creaking hinges still held but had long ago bled a rusty orange coating down the post and into the dirt below. The wood itself was so splintered it looked dangerous to touch.

The gate and fence surrounded a darkened house that occupied the most northerly spot in all Verandale. It appeared much older than any other and resembled other houses in name only. It was built upon fertile ground next to the Upper River and was less than a stone's throw from the forest.

At the back of the house a large water wheel groaned rhythmically while splashing worn and moss-covered paddles into the river below.

Enoch turned his head, trying to decide if it was the house or the land upon which it stood that was not quite straight. They came upon the front door. His father knocked loudly to overcome the roar of the water and the turning of the wheel.

"Maybe he's not home," Enoch said quietly, but hoped loudly.

His hope grew as moments passed and he heard no footsteps. He started to ask his father how he was ever going to learn anything from a man who spoke so little. He was interrupted as the door opened and small puffs of dust danced in circles on the entryway floor.

The Healer stood before them. Enoch thought he appeared much smaller—or maybe just more hunched over—than the last time he had seen him, the day he had received his mark. But his robe and vibrant colors of his hair looked as if they had changed not at all. With a gesture of the Healer's upturned hand and a tiny grunt of sound from between his lips, he ushered them inside.

The door closed behind them, deafening the sounds of the river and the water wheel. Enoch saw the walls to his left were covered with shelves containing all sorts of liquids in all sorts of containers, and many dried plants— some recognizable and some not—hanging from long strings suspended from the ceiling.

On his right, a large black pot hung over the flame in a stone fireplace. Herky fish were drying on the hearth. The Healer pulled out a chair for Enoch to sit before a table that supported a single bowl. He did this as his father bade him goodbye, bowed slightly to his non-speaking host, and was gone out the front door.

Enoch looked at the soup, briefly hoping it was manko, but it had more of a green color and a texture he had not seen before. The Healer pulled out his own small stool. He sat across the table and stared at Enoch.

Enoch thought this could turn out to be the longest day of his life. He tried to think back to the position of the suns as they walked the long path from their house to the Healer's. He wondered if it was possible to be dismissed from his new apprenticeship and wished that he had somehow thought to ask the last Apprentice more about his job before his untimely demise.

He picked up the spoon to lift the first of the liquid. The Healer sat across the table, continuing to say nothing.

The liquid gave off an aroma that Enoch could not identify. Looking across at his host, he received no further guidance. As the warm soup hit his tongue, he detected a faint vegetable odor first, but then was assaulted by a deep pungency as he attempted to swallow.

He leaned forward as his insides retched and he struggled to keep the liquid down. His eyes clouded, his vision blurred, and his palm involuntarily struck the table as he tried to focus.

"I would say that it is not good, what about you?" Came the steady voice from across the table.

"So…you talk?" Enoch looked up with watering eyes.

"Of course, I talk." The Healer sounded almost amused.

Enoch stared at him with his own mouth open.

"In your new job, there will be many things to realize. The first is that my job, that you now share, is to heal people. Some of these people can be helped by roots and other concoctions such as the slightly repulsive one which you just sampled."

He pulled himself up from his stool and walked over to Enoch. "But the art of healing, Enoch, is really much more about making the patient believe in you. Come with me and we will go see our first patient. You must remember that they are usually either sick or injured. At this moment in their lives, their natural instinct is not to believe. But, for reasons hard to discern, it is easier for people to believe a mysterious man who wears a shiny white robe, has hair of many colors, and never speaks. It took me quite a while to appreciate this, but once I transformed from regular Verandalian to strange, silent, man, I found that people more readily accepted their treatments."

They walked over to two untethered horses feeding on grass near the front gate. Enoch had not remembered seeing them when he had arrived earlier. They secured the packs, hoisted themselves upon the horses, and started off at a quick trot through the roads of Verandale.

As they crossed the Salt River Bridge, the suns were high overhead and beginning a final burn through the scant remaining clouds. An increasing number of people coming to and from the palace stopped in their tracks to watch the Healer and his newly appointed Apprentice. Some congratulated Enoch while others shouted greetings at the Healer, who said nothing. Enoch felt the first twinge of pride in his new job and sat a little higher in his saddle.

"I suppose the reason why we are taking horses instead of a wagon like everybody else is to look…mysterious?"

The Healer checked behind and in front of them, to ensure that they were now out of earshot of all onlookers.

"Exactly, Apprentice." He said this quietly under his breath and stared straight ahead with a satisfied look across his ruddy face. "I do believe that you will be a capable student. When I see my old friend, Ibrakrim, I might need to tell him that he was right, and I was wrong."

Enoch smiled briefly, but then contemplated whether this was a compliment from his new boss. He stared ahead and guided his mare along the ruts of the winding roads.

His pack was beginning to weigh heavily upon his shoulders by the time they could see Olaf's house down by the Sea.

"Do you know why Olaf was struck upon his head by the diving Cof?"

Enoch contemplated for a moment. He had not thought much about this particular part of the winter caravan, as it paled in comparison to the many other triumphs and tragedies.

"I thought he was just unlucky," Enoch offered.

"This, like so many other happenings is just like the skin of an apple. You see the outside of the apple and—if you had never thought to peel or slice into one—you would think it is red all the way through. But it is not."

The Healer paused in his teaching to look upon the forest. They were passing a section of the forest that contained many trees supporting Tlok vines—now at the peak of their multi-colored blooms. The aroma mixed with the salty wetness of the Sea and filled the air.

"Here is what you may not know about Olaf. He is a fine man who loves his family, works hard on his farm, and is the owner of a few Cof kills. Many years ago, however, he decided the intoxicating liquid of the tlok-vines was not just good, it was essential. You see, by the time the caravan was attacked, he was without the daily amount of tea his body needed.

"As a result, his heart beat faster and he became irritable. By the time his wagon was attacked, he had been pacing small laps around the inside of the wagon, working himself and the other poor people in the wagon into a frenzy. It's possible the Cof heard him in the blizzard and dove in his direction simply because he was making the most noise."

Enoch tried to take in all this information and combine it with his memories of the caravan.

"I am unable to explain why Olaf survived the attack. I can tell you, however, that no one in this land is going to do well if they are often intoxicated, or in any other way impaired." The Healer continued, "There is another problem one's body must deal with when only tlok vine tea is poured into it. See, it is not only the tea itself that will kill you; it is the lack of nutrients from fruits and vegetables that his body is doing without. We are taking our concentrated 'soup' to Olaf so that he will drink it and repair his body for at least a little while longer."

As they approached the cluster of houses by the Sea's edge, the Healer explained the symptoms they were likely to see once they saw Olaf.

"We will likely come upon a man who is sitting or lying down. His sense of balance will be eroded so he will avoid walking unless absolutely necessary. He will have trouble focusing his eyes and might be confused. Whether his confusion is from having a few drinks already in this young day or a longer-lasting and more difficult confusion brought on by a lack of proper food..." the Healer paused to look behind them as they turned their horses to face away from the forest and started down the lane between the houses, "...will be hard to know."

They slowed the horses as they came across the small hut. Unlike the neighboring homes, it was surrounded only by tall, dry shards of grass and a spot where an old chair had been placed, and the earth worn down in front of it.

Olaf slumped in the chair. His head tilted back, and his mouth was open, facing upward to the sky. The Healer motioned for Enoch to dismount, and they approached. Enoch was relieved to see Olaf's chest rise and fall, in contrast to the rest of his body which appeared lifeless.

The Healer asked Enoch if he remembered everything they had discussed during their trip. Enoch swallowed hard but nodded his head. The Healer found another chair and quietly put it in front of Olaf's. He sat back and stared at the patient and the new Apprentice.

"Olaf, uhm, Olaf sir." Enoch grabbed his shoulder and shook it gently a couple of times and then much harder until his whole body shook. Olaf's head bobbed forward until his chin hit his chest. Enoch grimaced. He looked to the Healer for guidance, but just then Olaf awoke enough to open his eyes—struggling to shield them from the brightness of the day.

"What the," a coughing fit interrupted his attempt at a question. "What are you doing, I'm sleeping in my own house." He looked around at the building behind him. "…or in front of my own house. Why did you have to…?" He focused on Enoch, scrunched up his face a little more, and then focused on the colors of the Healer, directly in front of him.

"Oh, no. Oh, no, no, no! You didn't bring me that stuff again, did you? That wretched stuff smells like an oswatt's butt!"

The Healer smiled at Enoch, then pointed at Olaf.

Enoch pulled the flask from his pack and watched Olaf's eyes flit back and forth, from the Healer to himself.

"Hey, you're Enoch. What are you doing here?"

"Actually, sir, I am the new Apprentice."

"Well, kick me over and call me Cof bait. I'm going to need to shake the hand of the man…" He lurched forward, attempting to stand but only managed to knock his walking staff over before slumping back into the chair.

Enoch undid the cap from the medicine flask and held it in front of Olaf.

"Bah, get that away from me, I'm not drinking it." He swiped a hand at it and missed.

"Healer says you have to drink this."

Olaf put a finger and thumb on his top and bottom lips and squeezed them closed. Enoch looked at the Healer who continued to silently watch.

Enoch contemplated wrestling Olaf to the ground and forcing him to drink, but then had a better idea.

"Healer says, if you do not drink this whole flask in front of us, right now, he will summon palace guards to come and take all the tea out of your house. And even the fermenting vats out back!"

Enoch again held the flask before Olaf.

"You couldn't woulda do that?" Olaf mumbled in a nervous, childlike tone.

"Healer says we certainly would."

Olaf looked to the Healer then took the flask from Enoch. He drained the flask as a grimace spread across his face. Out of the corner of his eye, Enoch could see the Healer nod and smile, ever so slightly.

Olaf's loud swallowing stopped. He dropped the

empty flask into the dirt at his feet. Enoch picked it up and looked back to the Healer. Receiving no guidance, Enoch turned to Olaf who had green remnants around his mouth and nose, some still running down his chin.

"Healer says we will be back in two days to check on you. In the meantime, try to cut down on the tlok-vine tea a little bit. Healer says if you sit around intoxicated all the time, one day a Cof will come and you won't even wake up until after you are eaten."

Olaf mumbled a response and forced himself to pick up his staff and stand to extend a tremulous hand to his caregivers. Enoch told him he was welcome and then followed the Healer to the horses. They rode a short distance until they were out of the range of Olaf's hearing.

"So, I did well, right?"

There was a pause, just long enough for Enoch to worry about the Healer's answer.

"Yes Enoch, for your first day on the job, you did well. Nice improvising on the palace guard threat also."

"Thank you," Enoch said proudly.

They rode for a while longer, as Enoch thought through all the things he had seen and heard. He realized he was now going to be in the service of a man who could answer many of the questions so plentiful in Verandale.

"You know how you were saying…" Enoch felt briefly over-brazen but was too interested to back out of his question. He cleared his throat before going on, "You were saying that some people are too intoxicated or impaired to survive in our land. Yet, Kahdi has to be the most impaired person in the whole population, and he not only survives, he even goes into the forest and survives."

"That is not actually a question Enoch, but I will answer the question that I believe you intended. You see, everybody looks at Kahdi—and the destruction and mayhem he brings to all his surroundings—and says, 'I can't believe all the things he doesn't know.' Put more simply, they believe Kahdi is stupid. I think, by making this over-simplified assumption, they are missing many possibilities. I personally believe Kahdi has a hard, if not impossible time communicating with people. This probably means he can't form the words he needs, but it does not necessarily mean that words and thoughts are not neatly organized inside his own mind."

He pulled on his horse's reins and Enoch did the same. They stopped, each in the middle of their respective wagon rut. They overlooked much of Verandale as the Healer continued.

"I think we should be asking ourselves; what does Kahdi know? Then work on ways to find out. I broke my public silence last winter. I went to the Legion and suggested a simple plan—that they assign an observer to him full time. As evidence for my case, I simply pointed out what they and everybody else already knew—that he can go into the forest after fruit, after rocks, or maybe even to climb a mountain and see what is on the other side. The fact is, by definition, Kahdi knows *more* than we know. And we don't even know where to start with him being the first man to ever have a Protec. Therefore, we should spend our time and resources not on 'what poor soul has to babysit Kahdi today,' but instead, 'who will be smart enough and brave enough to finally learn Kahdi's secrets?' With Ibrakrim as the lone exception, they unanimously voted against my proposal, and I was told to kindly stick to the art of healing."

Enoch tried to picture the Legion, including his great grandfather listening to somebody as smart as the Healer and turning down his ideas. He made a mental note to ask Orgard the next time he saw him.

"You must understand, I do not think they are being malicious—at least not on purpose. But I do think they are failing to look beyond Kahdi's outwardly imposing exterior. Why, the same people that think Kahdi is worthless, and should be shipped off to Darnoc and forgotten, will see a raven cawing from the treetops, and be convinced that they have somehow been singled out by a pure evil from the nether world that will haunt them for the next year...if they even live that long. You know what I think? I think the ravens are looking for food—just like all the other animals, no more and no less. The point is they might have it all backwards. I think Kahdi has something to teach us, and the ravens...well, they are just birds."

The Healer let himself down from the saddle to adjust his horse's bit before continuing.

"Just this morning, before you and your father arrived at my house, a group of men were assembled at the edge of the forest. I went over to see if there was some kind of disturbance and they told me that Kahdi was going into the forest and hauling out the deadfall for them. There was a tremendous noise and sure enough, Kahdi and his protec came trudging out from the trees. He had a strap wound around a log that was bigger than any two normal men could drag and an axe hanging from a rope at his waist. He deposited his tree between a couple of men and waited just long enough for them to slap him on the back and watch him disappear once more beneath the canopy. There they all stood, completely happy to not put themselves through the normally dangerous day with half of them clearing logs and the other half nervously standing guard. No one thought to inquire how Kahdi accomplished this feat over and over, emerging unscathed each time."

They mounted their horses and made their way slowly back up the road in silence. When they neared Enoch's house, the Healer told Enoch that he was done for the day and that he would be happy to take his horse the rest of the way back to the stables.

Enoch dismounted and bade the Healer goodbye. As he walked toward the front door of the house, his mind raced. He felt even more perplexed than before he had heard the Healer's first words.

Little did he know that by the next morning, he would know what Kahdi knew.

Mirk!
—Kahdi

22

Enoch awoke with a start.

Drenched in sweat, he threw off his bedding. It was the darkest and middle-est part of the night. He jumped out of bed, causing a sudden movement from outside his window. He whispered to the guard to warn him that he would be opening his shutters. The guard shot Enoch an annoyed sideways glance but asked him if he needed any help. Enoch told him he was alright; he just needed "to sit up and think."

"Great," gruffed the guard, "maybe I will be lucky enough to keep you alive for another year, and I can be promoted up to guarding the potatoes!"

Enoch left the window and sat down on the edge of his bed.

He pictured all the times he had seen Kahdi go into the forest. He relived the first time at the spike-throwing fields, as well as the day with Berc and Sabri at the school. He went over the details the Healer had told him, and all the episodes he had heard about, but not actually witnessed. He also replayed the incident with the farmer's pig and Kahdi's reluctance to enter the forest at that spot...or was it that day?

Enoch leaned over the edge of the bed and put his hands on either side of his head. He grimaced and tried to think. He thought about asking the guard, but decided he was already too annoyed.

He wished Berc, Sabri, or even Sasha were awake for him to talk to. He tried to remember each of the conversations they had had over the last year. He moved slowly from the bed, feeling in front of him until his hands found a piece of parchment and a writing stick. He bumped against a chair and froze. The guard muttered something mean as he pushed Enoch's shutters closed once again.

Enoch gave his eyes a moment to adjust, then stepped out of his room and into the hallway. He was just passing Berc's and Sabri's rooms when he spied the remaining light from the dining pit. The last slow embers from the evening fire were still burning.

Enoch quietly stoked the coals before taking a seat on warm stones of the floor.

He began to write down everything he knew about Kahdi and the forest. He wrote at the top: "1. Kahdi wants new rocks at the spike fields—runs into forest at start of growing season." He placed a number 2 on the line below it, trying to think back to which incident would have been the second time. He then remembered that there was actually a time before the spike fields—Sasha had told him about Kahdi making a forest trip the very next day after the banquet. Enoch looked at the words. He crossed them out and started over.

1. Sasha's friend sees Kahdi go into forest…day after end-of-school banquet.
2. Kahdi runs into forest to get rocks…last day of me doing Berc's chores.
3.

Enoch stopped writing—tapping on the paper and wondering how he was ever going to remember back to all the Kahdi forest excursions he had heard of over the last two years. He read the words again. He read them one more time and his heart began to race.

He stood up, but his eyes had adjusted to the firepit, and he could see nothing. He nearly tripped trying to get a candle, then dropped it before finally lighting it against the small flames of the fire.

With the candle held softly out before him, he shuffled to his brother's room. He pulled back the covers from the head of the bed to reveal Berc's feet. Undaunted, he pulled the other end of the covers and held the light of the candle near the closed eyes of his brother.

"Berc, wake up." Enoch stood in silence for a moment before shaking his brother's shoulders. Berc emitted only a slight groan and tried to roll away from him. Enoch placed a fingertip onto one of his brother's eyelids. He lifted it up and moved the candle a little closer, watching Berc's pupil constrict from large to small.

"What the…what are you…?" Berc pushed the flame away and tried unsuccessfully to sit up. "Why are you burning my eyeball with a candle in the morning?"

"Because it is not morning, it is nighttime, and you have to listen to me."

Berc groaned and fell back against the bed, pulling the covers back over his face.

Enoch gave him just a moment before continuing, "I know how Kahdi goes into the forest!"

Berc stayed motionless, but Enoch stared for only the briefest of moments before Berc sat straight up. The covers stayed on his head until he was able to reach up and pull them down.

"What did you say?" Berc now appeared to be fully awake.

"I know how Kahdi goes into the forest."

Enoch excitedly ran to the largest candle in the middle of the room and held his flame against it. Once it was lit, he handed his own candle to his brother. Berc closed the door to his room while Enoch ran over to the wall. He pointed at Kahdi's kitten picture and pulled out the nail that was holding it in place.

"See, this drawing tells us everything. We have been thinking all along that Kahdi just runs into the forest at random, or he just knows the safe spots to go into the forest. It is actually neither one. Remember how he ran into the forest when I was training him at the spike fields? That was the last of the ten days that I did your chores for you. Sasha told me about his trip into the forest the day after the banquet, which was the *first* day I did chores for you." He dropped the picture into Berc's lap and pointed at the kittens. Enoch tried to catch his breath before speaking the words that felt like the most important ones to ever come out of his mouth.

"Kahdi goes into the forest every ninth day, because it is safe every ninth day. That is why he drew this picture. Eight kittens sitting outside the trees, representing the eight days when it is unsafe to go in and the ninth kitten just all kinds of happy because he is in the forest on the 'safe day.'"

"Whoa," Berc muttered as he stood up to face his brother. "So Kahdi knows there are days when the Cofs aren't going to bother him, or they're busy taking baths or who knows what. But then when the hog is running loose, and we all get the brilliant idea to get Kahdi into the forest to rescue him…"

"Exactly!" Enoch shouted, interrupting him. "Kahdi knows it is not a safe day and refuses to go after the hog, leading to wrestling, protec bites and general mayhem."

The boys sat silent for a while. The only sounds were the flickering of the candle flames inside, and the wind merging with distant Cofian sounds outside.

They eventually sat down to complete the list Enoch had started. They worked on it through the rest of the night, ending with Kahdi's trip into the forest they had witnessed while spying on him from the hillside, and the logging episode the Healer had described to Enoch.

They decided they were going to need good Kahdi surveillance over the next few days, and continuous surveillance eight days from now. If the "theory of the nine kittens" proved to be true, they could carry out a plan on the ninth day that could save the people of Verandale. They quickly promised each other that no one else would be told until they had absolute proof.

Just when it felt as if they could finally fall back asleep, they heard their father's footsteps coming down the hall.

"Time to get up boys, lots of work to do today." Egard stood, one hand on the door latch, looking at them for a moment, his mind comparing the bedraggled spectacle before him with what he normally saw from his boys first thing in the morning. He closed the door and walked down the hall towards Sabri's room.

The brothers looked at each other and sighed. It was going to be a long day.

Enoch and Berc made it through the rest of the day, barely awake enough to stand, let alone work, but they made it—both asking to grab just a handful of dinner on the way to bed.

The next day, Berc learned from Falo that she had been with Kahdi all day as they had both been assigned to a crew working on repairs at the Salt River Bridge. Kahdi had mostly behaved himself except for one episode in the late morning when he ate three workers' lunches. Per her report, he definitely had not gone into the forest that day.

The day after was a training-pit day for Enoch. Berc was to tutor him for his upcoming Ceremony. They went by Kahdi's house and asked if they could take Kahdi with them. His mother gave them a confused look but took it as a sign that Kahdi was making new friends. The boys had taken special care to pack Kahdi a large lunch and he behaved quite well for most of the day.

At one point, Berc laid out nine rocks for Kahdi, who launched the first eight as expertly and viciously as always—seven of them hitting their target. Berc held the ninth in his hand and asked Kahdi if he could throw it himself. Kahdi stared at him, not answering of course.

Berc turned his back from Kahdi and launched the rock into the shadows at the end of the forest. Kahdi stared at him some more. Enoch fought the urge to see the scene behind him.

"You're on your own big brother," Enoch yelled. "I have to make sure we didn't wake anybody out of the trees."

Berc looked at Kahdi and Kahdi looked at Berc.

"Mirk!" Kahdi struck one open palm against each of Berc's shoulders and sent him flying downwards into the dirt. Berc quickly righted himself and strained to clear the dust cloud from around him in case of another attack; but Kahdi was already running out of the field, back toward his house.

Berc cupped a hand on either side of his mouth after he was able to stand, "We know about the nine chickens."

Enoch arrived next to him and slapped him on the back. "That's kitten's you dolt."

Berc squinted for a second, before cupping hands again and yelling even louder, "I mean kittens!"

But Kahdi was now just a distant speck on the road back into town.

"That went well," Enoch said as he helped brush dirt and plant fragments off his brother's back.

"I can tell you one thing," Berc responded while rubbing his shoulder, "I can't survive day after day of mirkings."

The boys discussed days one and two of their new surveillance and began to formulate a plan for day nine that would leave no doubt in anyone's mind about the Kahdi theory of safety in the forest.

After they made it home for the evening, Enoch

quizzed his father about the schedule for the upcoming days. He tried to act nonchalant but knew he would be unlikely to hide his level of increased curiosity and sense of urgency from him—especially after their staying up all night episode. But his father did not press him further and Enoch was able to find out that he had at least four—maybe five days straight—of training and studying scheduled at the library, and Berc was to be his chaperone.

He was mentally preparing his back-up plan until he found out that Sabri would be fishing out on the boat with their parents for each of those days. Enoch knew he and Berc were going to have to divulge their secret in order to conduct the proper Kahdi watch over the next few days.

Being already worried that his father, Sabri, or Falo would know something was going on, Enoch was hesitant to tell anyone at all of his and Berc's plans. He knew that if he had to tell someone, he could trust Sasha.

He knew her family was supposed to be at the village square the next day. He ran down early in the morning before he was due to leave for his training session. He had to wait for only a short time. He passed the time sitting on a wall and watching the peddlers trade and haggle with their neighbors—the mothers and fathers of Verandale.

He spied Sasha walking into the square. She was being pinched and generally harassed by her little twin brothers, until she was able to grab one of them with an arm wrapped around his head and squished against her side. She was exerting some impressive strength—completely incapacitating him and his flailing arms while laughing and fending off the wild strikes of his twin—while her protec barked and gently nipped at her attackers.

Enoch snuck up behind and grabbed the second brother, mimicking Sasha by also placing his head in a human vise. Sasha was shocked to see him at first but then giggled as they both tried to outdo each other in twin-squishing.

It wasn't long before Sasha's parents caught up to them and firmly told them to let the boys go. One of them was able to land a medium sized kick against Sasha's shin as he was getting away.

She was laughing as she hopped on one leg. She leaned against Enoch for support as she bent over to rub her future bruise.

"You know when they get a little bigger and figure out how to attack their prey on opposite sides…"

"I know, I know, Enoch. I can still handle them for now, though. Plus, you know they're plenty scared of you." She looked up at him. "I'll have to forget to tell them you are not as mean as you look. What are you doing here anyway? I thought you had training today."

Enoch waited for her parents to travel farther down the road and out of earshot before whispering his plan to Sasha. She produced the response he had expected, backing away from him with a gasp.

"That is the worst and most dangerous…and worst plan I have ever heard!" she yelled.

She took another step back and then ran down the road to her parents. He worried that she had just decided he was crazy and was never coming back. But she had simply asked for permission to talk to Enoch for a while before joining her family back at the square.

They sat on a couple of boulders at the side of the road while Enoch laid out the details of the nine kittens, the forest excursions, and what he felt to be the thought process of Kahdi…and his protec. It took much explaining and a little bit of pleading, but he was eventually able to convince Sasha that he and Berc had thought out—even written down—all the known trips into the forest, the possible implications for the land, and their plans to prove the theory six days hence.

It was Sasha's turn to surprise Enoch as she not only agreed to spy on Kahdi and record his actions for the next several days but agreed on one condition; that she travel with them to prove their quest on the ninth day.

Enoch tried to protest but she would have nothing of it. She would be travelling with them, or she would not agree to be Kahdi's keeper for the next few days. He eventually gave in before seeing her off to the square.

He walked away scared of what lay ahead and scared to have involved others in his quest. He would attempt to prove a theory that had never been considered by the greatest of Verandale's leaders and scholars.

As he turned and walked back along the road, a big part of him hoped that Sasha would see Kahdi go into the forest in the next few days. She would share this with Enoch and Berc and they could forget about their plan once and for all—assigning no further credence to Kahdi's nonsensical drawings and leaving the big decisions to the Legion and others; those old enough and wise enough to dismiss these kinds of wild ideas.

But Kahdi didn't go into the forest. Sasha spent two of the days directly by his side and he didn't do anything the slightest bit interesting. In fact, he did what he was told all day long by his various supervisors, stopping only at the end of the day to walk home, his striped protec by his side.

On the ninth day, Enoch and Berc traveled to Kahdi's house at dawn with the intention of taking Kahdi out in the morning. Their plan was to witness him going into the forest, at which point their journey would commence. When they knocked on the door however, his mother answered and told them Kahdi had been up early, had taken two pails from the front doorstep, muttered a word that even she couldn't decipher, and walked beneath the boughs of the trees that marked the point where Verandale stopped, and the forested mountain began.

Their theory confirmed, the boys ran home to gather their supplies and carry out their plan.

The dumbest person on the safest road, is still in danger.
—Professor Andrew

23

Enoch stood next to Berc at the stern of *The Indomitable*, trying not to shiver. He proceeded with his charade—carefully folding and stacking the fishing nets with meticulously falsified attention, though they would never be touched once they left the dock. In fact, Enoch wondered if they would ever be used again.

Few people were out during this time of day, normally set aside for the morning meal, but every person who did pass along the dock seemed to stare at the brothers with suspicious eyes. Enoch simply looked down to hide his guilt. Berc tried to compensate in a different way—gleefully greeting each party that passed within earshot, with a "hi, how are you on this fine sunny day?" or a "have a great day on the Sea?"...whether they appeared to be heading to their boats or not.

Enoch elbowed his brother.

"Berc, cut that out. We're already gonna be in enough trouble without you drawing the attention of all of Verandale!"

"Relax little brother. We have as our trusty and

unchallengeable resource, none other than the superior intellect and the always trusty decision-making of the amazing Kahdi. Oh, and of course, the number nine symbolized in a drawing of kittens. On the bright side, if we are wrong then we will soon be dead. If we are right, just think how impressed the girls are going to be."

As if on cue, two girls and two protecs began their descent from land to dock. Enoch looked up the hill at Sasha. She already had the tan of the growing season. Her dress was just a shade darker than her skin. She looked amazing, but also appeared at least as scared as Enoch.

Falo walked next to her. She also appeared tan and fit but was acting like only Falo could—a little spacey, a little oblivious, and Enoch could not tell if she was scared or not.

Falo-protec, having been on Falo's family boat many times before, ran a little ahead of his owner and jumped up and over the side of the boat.

Sasha-protec was much more cautious. He walked slowly along the dock then sniffed the side of the vessel before finally loading in. He didn't even growl or react when Sasha hugged Enoch hello.

"You sure he's going to be okay?" Enoch asked, pointing in the animal's direction.

"Well, he has been on a boat a couple of times before, but we were just goofing around down here. We never even took the boat out onto the water."

"I think he will do great, but what about you?"

"I'm scared Enoch," her eyes had just begun to well with water.

"I'm scared too. But you have to promise not to tell anyone about my scaredness, alright?"

"I'll make you a deal," Sasha whispered, with her chin just over his shoulder, "you make it so we actually have a chance to talk to somebody ever again. In return, I'll make sure that when we do actually talk to them, they will know you have never been scared a day in your whole life." Sasha looked at him with as close to a smile as she could muster under the circumstances. "That is of course, assuming that they didn't see you receive your mark."

Enoch just looked at her, amazed that she could crack a joke on what could be the last day of their lives.

"So, when are we going to go to this town or whatever?" Falo was somehow able to say this while chewing on her fingernails and looking bored.

Berc rolled his eyes just a little but continued preparing the boat with the strange indifference that had always helped him put up with Falo being Falo.

With an unspoken signal between the brothers, they raised the anchor and untied the moorings. Falo placed her right foot on the dock's pylon and gave the final push to launch the boat.

Enoch and Sasha raised sails as Berc tended to the rudder. He guided the ship to the south and to the west. The four traveled through barely rippled waters and had to work vigorously to catch wind in the sails. They passed one other small vessel whose nets were in the water. Berc greeted them across the bow, but they otherwise traveled in silence while contemplating the weight of their unassigned burden.

They thought about the secrecy of their quest and the fate of future breaches should their theory prove correct. Should their theory be incorrect, of course, their fate would be swift and final.

This day would prove or disprove the theory of the ninth day of Cof rest, once and for all. To demonstrate the safe refuge of the ninth day, the four travelers set out for the one place from which their safe exit could not be misconstrued. *The Indomitable* and its crew of four humans and two protecs were headed to the ruins of Runal, where the ill-fated Chimera had been the last boat to dock some eighty years before.

The boat continued to break the waves before it, the sails pushed by invisible wisps of wind. Verandale had fallen out of sight. The kids sat on either side of the sails. Sasha leaned into Enoch, and he placed his arm around her.

"I wrote a note and placed it under my sleeping pad," Sasha said quietly.

"What?" Berc asked, raising his eyes up from the planks on the other side of the boat.

"I said I left a letter explaining what we set out to do today."

"Why would you do that? You could have put our whole trip in danger." Berc looked at her mystified.

"Oh, come on genius. No one is going to look underneath my bedclothes today. It is there so if we don't return, then my parents will one day find the note and know that we were trying to save the land, and not just sneaking off on a boat with dumb boys!"

Smirking, Falo took her finger out of her mouth long

enough to poke it at Berc, leaving a wet spot on his sleeve. "Did you hear that, you big bunch of muscles? That's the first time that someone has ever called you a genius."

Berc decided to ignore both of them and just stick to sailing the boat.

"I have to tell you guys about this old speech I copied down when we were doing our research at the library. It is titled 'A Warrior's Oath.'" Enoch pulled a piece of parchment from his tunic, cleared his throat, and read aloud.

Tomorrow may find my bloodied ribs
scattered far from each other across the mountainside

Tomorrow may find oswatts
nesting within my broken skull

But today is the day
the Cofs will feel the heat of my breath

Today is the day
they will know the vengeance of my soul

Berc looked at the girls. They looked back at him knowing he would have something to say. He stood up and slapped his brother on the back.

"Well, thanks a lot for that bit of happiness, because we weren't scared enough on our own. How about next time you read us something that cheerful, you read it right before you go off on a solo adventure?"

Enoch refolded the page and put it back into his

pocket. "I just thought it was kind of inspiring to see this really old writing and know that one day someone might write something great about us, that's all."

No one answered him.

Enoch stayed quiet and looked out at the dolphins playing in their wake.

The high mountains of the south were now clearly visible and Berc brought out the map they had drafted from their research. It had taken several days to trace. The boys had been assigned to the library as part of Enoch's ceremony preparation. They had occupied the darkest corner of the library and kept the old wood of one of the tables covered with enough scrolls to keep their project hidden from the watchful eyes of Ibrakrim and his assistants.

Legend claimed the voyage to Runal was easiest at night. Many sailors of old had timed their voyages to end in the late evening to use the red glow of the quarry as the final landmark on their journey—though of course they never docked until the dawn of the next day.

The kids strained their eyes as the once distant shoreline came into view. They knew their chances of finding any of the ancient wooden dock structure intact was unlikely this many years later. All sets of nervous eyes scanned the trees and the steep shore for any sign of quarry or sand dune—and especially, for any signs of life.

Their attention was so diverted by the mountainside— the mander trees and tlok vines were fully leaved, the evergreens were at their deepest green—and so frayed by the importance of their quest, that they were almost on top of the docks before they saw them.

The boys' research had led them to the wrong conclusion. They believed the old wooden docks, unused and even unseen now for several generations, would be in total disrepair, if not completely fallen into the Sea.

What they found instead was red docks made of chiseled Runal rocks. They were the same giant size as those quarried for the palace. They rose out of the water and extended back to meet the shore. Though the first stone dock towered above the kids and *The Indomitable*, they rowed past it until they saw smaller rocks with iron docking rings. As the boat came closer, Enoch could see the slight staining and a perceptible disintegration where the rocks had stood against the Sea for many years. Gentle waves played against the rocks at the water line, oblivious to the humans that would be the first to dock there in this lifetime.

They stopped rowing and grew quiet as the boat drifted toward shore. They strained their eyes for hints of movement in the thick vegetation that covered the mountainside behind the docks.

"I can't believe we are going up there," Berc whispered beneath his breath.

No one spoke another word. The only sound came from the waves—like liquid hands pushing their boat closer toward the shore. The kids soon realized they would not have to row any more. In fact, it seemed as if they wouldn't even have to steer *The Indomitable* for it to cozy itself into the rocky berth.

Enoch leaned over the edge of the boat, feeling sick to his stomach but also trying to look past the surface of the water for a hint of any structures hidden below. He told himself he was going to have to summon up all his courage now, or plan on it hiding forever. He followed the direction of the waves, past the dock and to the shoreline.

There he saw stone steps intricately carved into the mountainside. Though the old maps showed a rather barren area between the Sea and Runal, the lower steps rose straight out of the water, covered by moss and algae. The steps rose steeply from the water, merged with the landing on the dock, and continued upward. Enoch counted thirty-six steps before they were overgrown with plants and disappeared behind the foliage.

Beyond this, shadows took over and thousands of tall trees blanketed the high mountains and hid the ghost town of Runal.

"Well, we can't turn back now," Enoch said as he grabbed his backpack. "We would still get banished for travelling to Runal, but without actually figuring out anything that we could tell the Legion in our defense."

"I'm not even worried about the Legion because either the Cofs or my parents are going to kill me first," Sasha answered.

Berc lassoed the first iron ring and secured their vessel, noting that the dock came up to the exact height of the side of their boat.

"If you were a hungry Cof, which of us would you eat first?" Berc asked.

Enoch leaned his palms against the warm stones of the dock and looked up the mountain.

Sasha-protec leapt out of the boat but stayed in a crouch facing the trees—whether from Sea legs or fear of what lay ahead, Enoch couldn't tell.

The rest of the crew stepped from the boat and opened their weapons bags. The bags were much heavier than usual, having been "double packed" by Berc and Enoch. They each loaded a spike and handed a scythe to each of the girls.

They went over the details discussed the day before and added a plan for jumping into the boat if they were fleeing from pursuit. The boys would use axes—one was left near each rope that secured *The Indomitable* to the docking rings—to free the boat as quickly as possible. Falo would raise the sails and Sasha would be the first to get an oar into the water. No one mentioned what everybody was thinking; *what if there were less than four humans and two protecs jumping into the boat?*

Berc took an extra big breath and let it out before walking up the dock and stepping up the first stairs. The girls and their protecs fell in behind him. Enoch took up his assigned position guarding the group's rear. His heart was pounding in his ears. He started up the steps, telling himself to maintain alternating views to the sides and behind and resist the temptation to look ahead, past his brother and the girls.

He took one last glance at the other dock that still towered above them after they had ascended several steps. He tried to imagine *The Chimera*, picturing a boat that would be large enough to fit into the giant berth. He tried unsuccessfully to prevent the shiver that arose in his lower back and traveled to his neck and shoulders.

Berc stopped as they came to the spot where the bushes covered the higher steps. He was the first to see that there were no more steps. There was only the nearly imperceptible remnant of a stone path; encroached on all sides by plants and bushes, even a few blackish flowers splattered with spots of bright red and poised to catch the light of the midday suns.

The kids looked at the path and realized they would have to travel single file as they entered the forest. To make matters worse, the undergrowth was thick enough and tall enough to obscure their vision, and the branches were sure to scratch and tug at their clothes, making a quiet approach impossible.

Seeing no alternate routes, they decided to aim for a spot in the shadowy distance that appeared to be a false peak and looked to be a bit more than a hundred paces ahead of them. Enoch took the lead.

After one particularly sharp turn on the ancient path, they heard breaking branches to their right. The first three readied their weapons, straining to see the source of the sound. Berc fought the nearly irresistible urge to look in the same direction; remembering his duty as "tailer" and alternating his watch to cover the left flank and the rear.

They were able to relax only slightly as they heard the still unseen creature less and less and could safely assume it had scampered away. Enoch looked over each of the others and the protecs before plunging again between the branches. The tops of the shrubs now met the lowest hanging branches of the evergreens to create a botanical tunnel above them.

Enoch continued pushing up the mountain, holding his left forearm before his face, trying to keep the branches from scratching at his eyes. He kept the spike in his right palm, though he thought it likely futile to attempt any kind of a throw in this confined and ever-darkening space.

He again checked on those behind him, then proceeded up the hill. He hunched over and identified the tracks of ani deer. He realized this was likely a game trail now. Enoch heard a sound come down through the tunnel of trees. He held up a stop signal to the others. He looked up to see traces of daylight from up ahead and…heard a voice.

"Hellllp…Help!"

The kids hit the ground. Sasha threw an arm heavily over her protec as he emitted a low growl.

"What the…there is no possible way," Berc whispered.

"How can there possibly be people here? Every last one of them went on *The Chimera* for her last voyage," Enoch added. "To take the shipment to Darnoc and then they were all supposed to go back home to Verandale for the last time."

"It has to be a trick." Everyone looked at Sasha. "I mean there is no way there are people still here. Could the Cofs be doing this?"

"Hellllp!"

All of them looked at Falo, mostly because she was the only one who had yet to offer a theory. "Don't ask me, I'm thinking it has to be a ghost or something. I would have to say a girl ghost by the sounds of it, though." Enoch noted she had lost whatever it was that she was normally chewing on. She crouched behind her protec and looked scared—the first time he had ever seen fear on her face.

"I think I should go up there first," Sasha whispered. "It is only a few more steps and my protec will be able to sniff out a Cof long before any of the rest of us."

Silence followed as no one disagreed with her. She started slowly up the trail, trembling toward the brighter daylight ahead.

After only a few steps, Sasha put up a hand behind her, motioning for the others to come beside her. Enoch could see that her head was now at a height where she would just be able to see into the brighter area ahead. He fought the urge to hurry past the others and crouch at her side. He watched her protec paw at the dirt and stare ahead, his attention locked in the same direction as Sasha's.

Sasha hunched down and motioned for each of the others to do the same.

Enoch took one last cautionary view behind him before he put his head between Berc's and Falo's and squinted into the brightness ahead. No book or tale about Runal could have possibly prepared him for what he saw.

Fate comes knocking when your door is not paying attention.
—Berc

24

A cavernous lake stretched out before them. It was red and shimmering from shore to shore.

All their lives they had seen Runal rocks only as one size and shape. They were chiseled squares—whether they lined the walls of the palace, the Darnoc Bridge, or were placed into the roads and paths leading to either of those structures.

What they now saw was a giant expanse of stone that dwarfed any of the structures ever cut from it. Scattered about were hundreds of house-sized red boulders that had never been scarred by metal. The mountain that formed the back of the quarry was also pure red. The part of Runal that most caught their eyes was also the part that none could have predicted. Filling in the deepest parts of the quarry, and extending into many crevices and valleys, was the clearest water that they had ever seen, clearer even than the ice at The Lake of the Depths.

Perched on many of the uncarved boulders—and some of the stones that had been carved but never removed—were dozens of large birds covered in iridescent blue and green feathers.

"Peacocks" muttered Enoch under his breath. His brother shot him a confused look. Both took a moment to again scan their entire perimeter before Enoch clarified further.

"Remember that day in the empty school? We read about the green birds of Runal that used to warn the miners of any approaching danger.

"Hellllp" one of the birds yelled as if responding directly to Enoch's words.

The kids sank down into the dirt and froze, before realizing the sound came from one of the peacocks. They let out nervous sighs.

"I can't believe we are actually standing at the edge of Runal," Sasha whispered.

Poking their heads a little farther out, they saw the whole quarry, the rolling dunes of red sand, and the decaying ruins of what was once the town of Runal.

The girls stepped forward, edging toward the water. The boys followed them while eyeing the trees surrounding the ancient quarry. Falo-protec dropped his head, looked at his own reflection briefly, and then stuck a tentative tongue out to lap up some of the warm water. Falo edged a little closer, undoing the leather straps around her ankles, and sticking a bare foot into the water.

"Oh!" She pulled her foot back quickly. She shifted her weight to dunk the toes of her other foot into the water. A smooth ripple spread silently away from her, disappearing only after it reached the middle of the lake.

She grabbed Berc by the arm and pulled him

downwards. "You are not going to believe this." She dunked his hand into the water. Sasha and Enoch quickly followed. The water was warmer than any they had ever felt before, except water coming from a pot off a stove.

"You realize this could be the greatest swimming hole ever? And look," Enoch swept a hand in front of them and motioned to all of Runal, "there is not a Cof in sight. You guys realize this means Kahdi is probably right, and every ninth day we can go anywhere in the forest or even up a mountain."

No one answered.

"Well, come on, what do you think the deeper meaning of all of this is?" Enoch pleaded.

"I think," yelled Berc, "that this means we can go swimming and not be eaten!" He took off his shirt and threw it at Enoch's face.

Enoch caught it and tried to throw it back at his brother all in one fluid motion. In doing so, it sailed past the others and into the water. Berc paused just long enough for Enoch to lunge past him. He picked up the dripping garment and whipped it toward the others, hitting Falo directly across her midriff with a loud "whack" and covering everyone with a warm spray of water.

In no time, shoes and clothes were flying, protecs were barking and everyone splashed down into the lake.

"Can you believe how great this feels?" Sasha screamed, while Enoch took one last glance at the trees and swam as fast as he could to the middle of the lake. He reveled briefly at being first. He then took a deep breath and dove under the surface.

His whole life he had been accustomed to the biting cold felt with immersion into any body of water. It took a moment for Enoch to absorb the feel of the hot water and realize that this was different than any water he'd been in before.

He dove down deep enough so that he was totally submerged before he allowed himself to open his eyes. When he did, his senses were pounded from all sides with a surreal underwater view that was somehow even sharper and clearer than when he was on the land. He saw schools of fish darting between endless columns of green plants waving up from the depths below and catching the rays of the suns. When he looked more to the exact middle of the lake, he saw depths that were too deep for even these massive plants to take root, but he could still see all the way to the bottom and the carved-rock rectangles made by men long before the quarry had filled with water.

Enoch surfaced long enough to take a deep breath and then re-submerge himself. He turned to face Berc and the girls. He saw three lithe bodies still a fair distance away but splashing and swimming in his direction. He stopped blowing air out long enough to realize that he could hear their conversation—more like their taunting—just as if his head was above the water.

"Berc, if you try to dunk either one of us one more time, we will tell both protecs to consider you their dinner," Sasha warned him but sounded far from stern.

Falo added, "Yeah," before playfully slapping him.

"You know, from my vantage point, swimming does not seem to be a protec strong point." He exclaimed this just before getting a face full of water splashed from Sasha.

Enoch figured there was no way the others would yet

know about the ability to hear underwater. He decided to come up for a couple more breaths of air in order to try and stay underwater even longer and continue eavesdropping. He swam straight downwards until he felt the increased pressure against his ears. He then took off in the direction of the others and listened.

"Hey, look at the ring of water where Enoch used to be," his brother said.

Silence for a moment, and then "I see him, he's going to come up right under us."

"If he tries to scare me, I will wait 'til he comes up for air then pour water down his throat," he heard Falo's voice.

Berc laughed at her and more rounds of splashing and wrestling ensued.

Enoch stopped short of the others and came up for air.

He looked back to the shoreline. The protecs had tired of their less efficient form of swimming and returned to shore. They stood watch on the tree line after shaking their fur free of most of the warm water.

The kids stopped and looked at their surroundings. Everyone gently treaded water while marveling at its warmth. Comparisons were made to a giant bowl of soup.

"The problem with that image is it would make us giant floating bits of meat," Berc chided.

"No one is ever going to believe this day," Sasha said, swimming over to position herself next to Enoch. He decided that this moment and this day were the most amazing of his whole life.

"Hellllp!"

Everybody looked to one of the birds sunning itself on the mountain side of the lake.

"You know," Enoch told Sasha, "they seem to do their yell, not as warning or for any great reason but just because the suns are shining, or the winds are blowing, or who knows what."

They both studied the trees behind the bird, just in case.

"Do you find it strange that nobody ever thought to bring a couple of peacocks back to Verandale?"

"That is strange, especially if they are such great watch birds," Enoch mused. "Maybe it is not possible to port a peacock."

They both laughed as Sasha treaded water behind Enoch and then jumped up on his back. His head went under briefly but then he was able to get his head—and surprisingly, most of his shoulders—above the water. She whispered for him to head in the direction of Berc and Falo, who were treading quietly, facing away from them, and pointing at the remnants of the town that still stood at the western edge of the water.

Enoch told her to hold her breath then took both of them underwater, so she could experience his discovery.

"…saw something move in that second building."

"Berc, if you are trying to scare me, you are doing a good job of it. You know my protec would have a fit, trying to move around between all those buildings, or half buildings, whatever you call a bunch of falling down places like that. Besides, I don't even want to go over there."

Enoch and Sasha came up gasping for air.

"Okay, that is one of the most amazing things I have ever heard, and this water is…I don't even know how to describe it," Sasha paused, at a loss for words. "Couldn't you just stay out here all day?"

Enoch looked at her. "You know, since our plan is working, I guess we could stay here all day. But of course, we could stay here for none of tomorrow."

They swam over to Berc and Falo. Just before arriving, Sasha climbed up on Enoch's shoulders. Falo shrieked when she turned and saw what they were up to. She quickly clamored up on Berc's shoulders and the challenge was on.

Enoch kicked his legs, trying to hold Sasha higher while moving toward the imposing tower of Berc and Falo. He approached his brother carefully, but once he was in close proximity, Berc turned and saw them. He charged and rammed the top of his head into Enoch's chest. Enoch splashed backwards. He closed his eyes, sure that he and Sasha were going to topple over. But his fall was stopped, and the imminent submersion never happened.

He heard a shriek in front of him and opened his eyes. Sasha had reached for anything she could to keep them from going over. She had grabbed a handful of Falo's hair, who was now screaming about unfair tactics.

Enoch reached up with a hand to tap Sasha's side and try to tell her to let go so he could try and maneuver them behind the other two, but when she let go Falo was able to grab her arm and fling them under the water.

All came up gasping for air. Enoch was prepared for a good fight. He lunged one hand toward Berc and one toward Falo, but then became silent as his eye caught the sight behind them.

Some of the peacocks that had cautiously moved away from them when they had first emerged from the foliage of the lower mountain, now startled, yelled, and took to a lumbering flight.

They both heard and felt a disturbance from the trees at the steeper southern border of the lake. Enoch saw the head horn first, followed by the beak, the head plumage, and the body of a larger than normal Cof. The creature thrust his leg forward causing his body to rise slightly in the air behind it and the tail to drag forward—almost as an afterthought—until the entire body came to rest with a thump, and the leg again thrust forward, repeating the process.

All fell silent, unsure if they had been spotted. All fell silent that is except for the protecs, who began splitting the silence with their barks and growls from the other side of the water. The Cof slowly lifted his head and turned it to the side, one eye focusing on the mortal enemy of his race, not seen in Runal for generations. Falo-protec stepped to the side and began to run around the water's edge. Sasha-protec followed, and the kids began to swim to that side of the lake, yelling for them to stop.

Enoch swam for several strokes then glanced back at the Cof. Enoch stopped as the creature looked from the running protecs, to the swimming kids, and back to the protecs. Its wings had been slightly opened in the way that they sometimes were when the animal was preparing to strike, but each wing relaxed as the creature looked down at Enoch one last time, turned, and bounded back into the forest.

"Hey guys!" Enoch yelled to the others now well in front of him. He had to yell one more time before getting their attention. They turned to him. He simply pointed behind him and up the now silent mountain. No one could see any sign of the creature that had just terrified them. The protecs fell silent.

They swam back to shore and Enoch laid flat on his back, between the others. They divided a loaf of bread into six equal parts and devoured it. As the suns beat down upon them, Enoch decided that the trees, the water, or Runal itself made it the best tasting bread ever.

"You know, I would say that this just about proves the theory, don't you think?" Sasha said to the others, lying all around her.

Everyone contemplated this in silence for a moment until Enoch sat straight upright.

"What is wrong little brother, you don't agree?"

"Actually, I do agree" Enoch paused to swallow his latest bite of bread, "In fact, I just thought of something that proves our theory even more."

"So, you are going to tell us something that means more than…" Falo waved a hand around her head, "…everything we have seen all around us here today?"

"Sabri told me about this time that she had seen Kahdi run for the trees. Right before he went in, he said, 'Co frist.' I didn't really know what it meant at the time. Maybe it is the warm water, or the ruins we are about to see, but it just now hit me. Kahdi not only knows about the ninth day, but he also knows about the ninth day of 'Cof rest.'"

"Whoa!" Berc said while keeping his eyes closed and laying back against the warm rocks. "To think, all this time everybody thought that Cofs caused havoc basically every day but we have actually had all these days off and only Kahdi knew about it."

"Remember that second day of the winter caravan," Sasha added. "No one attacked us, and when we actually saw some Cofs; they were just working some sap out of that tree and barely even paid any attention to us."

"Exactly!" screamed Enoch. That was probably one of the Cof rest days. There are going to be some big, huge changes back in Verandale once we get back and tell them."

"What if we make it out of here but Berc sinks the boat on the way back?"

Berc stared at Falo before poking a finger into her side. A brief tussle ensued but soon all the kids were again quiet. They watched the ripples on the water and listened to the wind dancing through the forest.

Enoch propped himself up on one elbow and looked to the east. "You know we are going to have to go over there."

The other three looked to the dunes and the buildings, some of which had already collapsed into the sand.

"Oh yeah. That looks *real* safe!" mocked Falo.

"Yeah, but just think, it can't be much scarier than what we have already been through today." Berc added, "Basically, we took my parents' boat without asking, stole away to a place that is totally forbidden, and we still have to go back and explain ourselves to parents and maybe even the Legion."

"Maybe we should just save everybody the trouble and sail straight to the old port by the Darnoc Cliffs," Sasha said with only a hint of a smile at the corner of her lips. "They are just going to send us there anyway."

The others smiled nervously at this while they gathered up clothes, weapons bags, and protecs.

Enoch took one last look behind them and then at the ruins scattered along the rolling dunes at the eastern end of the quarry lake. Sasha came up next to him while wringing the last of the water from her hair.

"Well, I think the right thing to do at this point would be to let the Apprentice lead us into the ghost town."

"Very funny," Enoch said, leading them toward the ruins.

Enoch's feet left the hard rock and sunk into the blowing sand at the edge of the former town of Runal. A wind swirled around the kids as they stepped closer to the first of the abandoned buildings.

The wooden door of the small building had fallen from its stone frame and split, partially sinking into the sand. Small, struggling tufts of grass had taken advantage of the decaying wood and sprouted in the midst of the otherwise inhospitable dunes. Much of the roof had fallen in behind the doorway.

Falo stepped past the others to peer inside the window, but found the collapsed ceiling obscured any further view of the inside.

Moving to the next building, they found the words "Guard shack" engraved into a stone set near the entrance. The structure looked as if it may have supported a balcony at one time—possibly fashioned after the towers that held the guards and tocsins back in Verandale. Unlike the first building, there was no remnant of a door, and the kids could peek inside at the remains of a dining area, table, and chairs.

One of the protecs began a drawn-out growl as the girls stepped into the doorway.

Berc held an authoritative arm out in front of the girls. "Wait just a...," he started but stopped abruptly and let out a shriek as a family of oswatts darted out the door, around and through his legs.

Enoch and the girls looked at him. Smiles started to turn up at the edges of their lips.

"That's the sound that scares them away…The oswatts, I mean," Berc protested.

Now everyone was laughing at him, and he couldn't even pretend that he hadn't been frightened.

"Hey big guy, if the next thing that pops out of there is a Cof, how about you make a bigger scream so you can also scare them away," Falo chided as she elbowed ahead of him and walked through the doorway.

The ceiling of this building remained intact and, despite a covering of fine red dust and the absence of shutters on the windows, Enoch could imagine the historic comings and goings of the men once charged with protecting the quarry and the town.

Inside the doorway, a scythe leaned against the wall. Enoch looked at the rusted metal of the blade. He touched the wooden grip and the wood disintegrated, creating a shower of wood dust, and causing the metal blade to clang to the floor. Echoes pounded against the inside of the stone walls, and everyone froze.

"Sorry," Enoch whispered as he tiptoed to the stacked slabs of Runal rock that served as the central table in the room. He blew dust off a square of smaller stone that sat on the middle of the table. This revealed two handprints drawn on the top of the object.

"Hey guys, look at this."

The others came over to his side. He placed one hand over each of the prints.

"What do you suppose that is supposed to do?" asked Sasha.

"I don't know," Enoch said as he bent down for a closer look at the front and sides, "but look how the handprints cover most of the top and then the fourth and fifth fingers curl around the side."

The girls and Berc crowded around him to look at the sides and the back of the stone. Enoch placed his hands onto the handprints and leaned back. All of the kids and both protecs stood silent within the abandoned building and looked at Enoch. He continued to focus on the object in the center of the table.

Finally, Berc could stand it no longer. "You think you are just going to put your hands against the tablet and a magic path will open up to take us through the mountains?"

"No, but you have to admit, if there ever was a day where that seemed possible…today would be that day," Enoch said and the girls nodded in agreement.

But nothing happened until Enoch leaned forward and grasped the stone tighter, curling his fingers around the edges. He strengthened his grip on the rock, concentrating on the fingers curled at the sides. As he did this, he felt the cover shift beneath his fingers.

Enoch moved the cover to the side to reveal a hollowed-out container of stone. Sasha reached beneath his hands to an aged piece of parchment. It contained few recognizable words, only multiple symbols without further explanation. Sasha carefully held it up for the others to see.

"Can't say I've ever seen anything like that before," she said.

"Wow," Falo added, "what do you suppose the chances are it is important, like a recipe or something?"

Berc looked at her. "Yeah, a recipe written in code and left behind in Runal. Does the fact that it is one of the very few things still intact, and the fact that it was carefully left in an object that looks like a tiny stone coffin, suggest anything to you?"

"All right, all of a sudden it feels darker in here and I'm getting that feeling that runs up my spine again." Sasha turned to the rest, "Can we get out of here?"

Enoch was looking around the remains of the room. "I have to agree. I don't know what is creepier; somebody from *The Chimera* leaving a note, or somebody leaving a bunch of symbols that might be a note. Who did they think would ever be back here in this room to read it?"

"I say we grab the note and the coffin-thingy and get out of here," Falo said in a serious voice. "I don't know what the fastest way to the ship is, but I say we just head in the direction of the water. The day is only getting later."

Berc ignored her and stood at the back of the room. He stared up at some deteriorating hand holds that looked to have once led up to the rooftop. Enoch turned the contents of the box over and over in his hand.

"I think I can climb up there," Berc declared.

"Of course, you do," Enoch faced him with an incredulous look on his face, "because it is not dangerous enough being in a falling down building in the middle of Runal where we are not supposed to go in the forest, and where we are not supposed to ever be there anyway."

Enoch tried to stay serious through his stammering, but the girls were between smiling and laughing. Berc had already hoisted himself up the first couple of rickety handholds and disappeared above them.

Enoch resigned himself to stand guard at the doorway. He allowed himself a brief moment where he fingered a spike and imagined it was the middle of the night—he was the last guard remaining on the outskirts of a dying town. Women and children huddled behind him along with the last of the pigs and chickens. Enoch loaded a second spike for his left hand and held a scabbard in his teeth. Mixed within the whimpers behind him, he heard a mother tell her small children, "Master Guard Enoch is as strong as four loyal protecs, maybe five on a good day."

"Enoch!" Sasha's voice was raised as she shook his shoulder from behind. "You're not having one of those daydreams where you are the last guard alive again are you?"

He turned to see her standing with her hands on her hips.

"Well, no... I mean yes." Enoch gave up pretending just as Berc came down from the rooftop.

"None of you are ever going to believe what I found to take back to Verandale." Berc said as he held out his hand and revealed several charred stones.

Falo allowed herself a quick glance away from her lookout. She leaned a hand against Berc's shoulder and looked into his hand.

"Great, because there are no rocks back in Verandale, maybe we could scoop up some sand to take back, too!"

Berc shrugged and emptied them carefully into a pocket as the others prepared to leave.

The girls directed their protecs through the former door of the building. Enoch grabbed the parchment and secured it between his tunic and chest. Berc followed the others after he grabbed the interlocking stones and carefully forced them back together—not knowing the object would never make it back to *The Indomitable*.

The eight feet of the kids and the eight feet of the protecs sank with each step as they tried to run in the fine red sands. They slowed for an instant until Enoch found a shorter, albeit steeper, course down to the Sea.

The others followed his gaze down the mountain to their right, but all eyes jerked upwards in unison as large shadows soared across the sands and overtook them from behind.

"Holy…!" They gasped and hit the ground as shadows flew directly over them. Enoch slowly turned his head to the sky. A Cof was gliding over the town but remained high in the shifting colors of the late-day sky. Well behind it was a larger Cof. It stood out much more to the observers on land as its body lacked the camouflage of every other live Cof they had ever seen.

Enoch grabbed a spike from his weapons bag.

The first Cof passed over the western edge of Runal and arched its body to perform a slow banking turn to the left. The strangely colored one did a more labored and less exacting turn to the right. They came together and again flew over the trespassers.

The kids scrambled back until they were again in the deepest sands of the dunes. Each took up a position, so they backed to the others. Enoch had the eastern view. His eyes scanned the buildings of the deserted town they had just left.

Time stretched unmercifully. He tried to keep watch for a ground attack while the soaring Cofs looked down at the top of his head.

"Will someone please tell me what they are doing so I don't have to turn around and look for myself," he pleaded.

"Amazing," came Sasha's voice from behind him. "They are just soaring and looking down at us, like they are the most peaceful beings in the land."

"Wait, are you kidding me?" Berc interrupted. "This is the ninth day—they are not allowed to attack."

"That will sound great when you are quoted at our death rites service…not that our bodies would ever be found. Just keep an eye on your assigned direction; in case we counted our days wrong, or Cof days end sooner than people days, or who knows." Enoch struggled to keep his eyes scanning the broken and empty buildings until the Cofs again flew into view.

"They really are majestic," Sasha whispered behind him as he felt her protec nudge his leg. "I mean when they are that far away."

"You know all this time…" Enoch stopped his words as the Cofs started to descend.

"Let's get out of heeeeere!" Berc shouted, the protecs barked, and everyone started running down the hill. Berc dropped the stone tablets that had endlessly protected the parchment in the abandoned building. They shattered into the dust as the kids and protecs fled.

Enoch darted downward between the trees. He was able to see *The Indomitable*—its bow and stern teetering against the solid backdrop of the dock—after only a few steps but had to concentrate on his feet to jump from rock to rock without falling.

All six made it to the dock and jumped on board. Nervous shouts filled the air as they untied the docking ropes and raised the sails to put distance between *The Indomitable* and the shore.

No one on board could say a word as they tried to slow their hearts and lungs and think about what they had just accomplished.

Enoch finally broke the silence, "I want to tell everyone what I started to tell Sasha before our race back to the boat. We thought we knew a lot. Even the things we didn't know, we thought we at least knew the smartest people in the land—the people who knew the most that there was to know." He paused, trying to find a way to express his surging thoughts.

"Turns out that all the people and the beings who knew the least…they may have actually known the most. Look at all the brightest minds in our land: there is Ibrakrim, the Healer, Professor Andrew, even our great grandfather. None can tell us how to leave this land or even how to get the number of births to exceed the number of deaths from one year to the next. But then look at what today proved. We proved that Kahdi—the dumbest guy we know—taught us what years of history and years of history's scholars were unable to teach us. From him we learned that the Cofs either can't or won't attack us on every ninth day. In fact, today has proven that Kahdi knows more than the scholars. Tomorrow may reveal that the dolphins know more than Kahdi, and the trees know more than the dolphins."

The others said nothing. The ship sailed on in silence

as Enoch's words floated out over the waves and the sea spray leapt over the edges and onto the deck.

Enoch waited for some kind of confirmation of his thoughts. Berc finally looked straight into his brother's eyes.

"Hey, do we have any food stored away on this thing? Because the suns are just about over the mountains, I'm starving, and you know once we get back people are going to be asking all kinds of questions and all the wisest fathers will be asking me to marry their daughters. It's going to be a lot of work without much time to eat."

"You wish," Falo mocked as she grabbed a slab of jerky and slapped it into his midsection.

Berc chewed while Enoch adjusted the sails one last time. Satisfied that the ship was oriented toward Verandale, they sat quietly huddled against each other as the fading light of the suns reflected off the Sea. They braced for the human storm that would envelop them once they told their story and forever changed the lives of all who lived in the land.

Ezrini Emnchimera

25

The Commander felt each muscle contract as he forced his wings down into the wind beneath him. He tried with every breath to inhale more air into his lungs, hoping to relieve some of his exhaustion and hide it from all of those who served under him. He knew his ability to fly would soon be lost—just as his ability to camouflage was lost a few seasons ago.

He reluctantly marked the days. Though he had not discussed giving up his command with any of those around him, all knew that the day would soon come. As he struggled to stay high above Runal, he knew any flight could be his last.

He had not believed Ricit at first, when he had been awakened from his high-suns slumber curled around the tallest tree—the one they called the Mother Tree and the one from which he ruled. Ricit had leaned forward and tapped his horn three times lightly against the bark just above the Commander's head, trying to stay respectful and silent despite the urgency of his message.

"Commander, it is true. They have sailed their ship to the red lands. They have trespassed upon them—

the first to do so since the time of our forebearers. I am afraid, Commander…I am afraid they have knowledge of the Sabbath Day. They know because they were told by The One Who Sees into Our Lands. If you please, I will take you over the red lands now so that you may view this yourself."

Now, from his high vantage point, the Commander could indeed make out the heat prints of nine animals within the former human town. Three were smaller and still scurrying away from the others—likely rodents. But the rest appeared to be four humans and two of their protector animals, exactly as he had been told.

The Commander banked to his left and Ricit also turned in flight.

As they passed the team of humans one more time, they dove to get a closer view. Ricit recognized at least one of them as a member of the wagon team that they had hunted on the Darnoc trail. He asked the Commander if he wanted to survey the scene and the trespassers one more time.

"There will be no need, Ricit. Their knowledge has reached a level never before known by our prey. We all know who gave them this knowledge. We also know what must now be done."

Ricit nodded in agreement, and they turned to fly for home.

Just as the red sun follows the yellow sun, danger follows joy.
— Athos

26

Though they had little daylight left with which to navigate, the kids extinguished all the torches on their ship and even hid all their brightly colored clothing and objects. They did this to maximize their chances of sneaking the boat back into its berth at the fishing village and making it home to tell each set of parents before the story began to spread.

Just as they sailed close enough to make out the shoreline, however, a light appeared on Berc's tunic. They immediately turned their heads to the shoreline to see the source of the light but saw none. The light came from Berc's pocket. He jabbed his hand downward between the layers of fabric and pulled out the blackened rocks he had found in the ruins. From the side of one of them, the blackened charcoal had been rubbed off. He placed a finger into the path of the light and began to dance up and down in pain. He flung the rock overboard and dropped the rest of the rocks. They fell from his hands and clattered onto the wooden deck. The light coming out of the sinking rock continued to shine even as Falo,

Sasha, and Enoch stood openmouthed and watched it fall into the depths below.

"What in the world was that?" Enoch shouted to his brother who was holding his burned finger into the cold waves at the opposite side of the boat.

"I have no idea, but it hurts as bad as a Kahdi bite!"

When the light finally faded down into the darkness of the waters, the protecs began to bark. Two boats approached with full sails. They heard angry parental shouts from both the boats and the shoreline. Enoch knew the plan to sneak back into Verandale had now failed.

The docks of the fishing village were full of all sorts of Verandalians and their torches. Many more lined the roads leading from the docks. Some were even sitting in their boats—either in the berths or anchored in the waters beyond—Enoch couldn't yet tell. What he could tell was that every last soul in Verandale seemed to be waiting for them.

As they came closer, he began to recognize people in the crowd. First was Sasha's family; there was not a bit of happiness on her parents' faces. Her brothers' faces, on the other hand, were alive with giddiness and anticipation.

He looked away. He tried to get Sasha to do the same, but it was too late.

"I don't think we should go back home after all," Enoch whispered.

"It would be safer if we sailed to Egg Island and nestled between hatchlings," his brother answered.

Falo peered from behind Berc's shoulder. "Do you think it is too late for the three of you to hide me in the live well of this thing and tell everyone I died?"

Enoch took a sail down as they came between two of the ships that had sailed out to confront them.

"I've seen a lot of things in my day," said the crackling voice of the blacksmith, "but never seen anyone with this much gumption who lived to tell about it."

They took down the final sails and took up their oars. As they came to within a few paces of a family—all staring at them from their own ship's rails—one of the wide-eyed kids could stand the silence no longer.

"My mother says you guys are in more trouble than you could ever imagine." The young mouth was quickly covered with a parental hand.

All four were too scared to speak. Even the protecs kept their heads down as the boat was gently directed into the dock. Berc reached for the ropes, but several people were already on hand to secure the boat for them.

Enoch looked up into the eyes of Sasha's parents. The letter, found beneath her pillow, was in her mother's hand.

Standing with them were Orgard, the Healer, and several other Legion members fronting most of the population. They unloaded from the boat. No one spoke until the crowd parted and Ibrakrim stepped forward. The only sound behind him was from the distant rush of the Salt River.

He looked at the four of them as they stood on the worn wood of the dock.

"I do not need to tell you of the seriousness of your actions today. I will ask the Apprentice to step forward and explain the reasoning behind travelling to a forbidden land and endangering the lives of yourselves and all those around you."

Enoch was caught off guard as he had always pictured Berc explaining their actions. He felt hundreds of eyes upon him as he stepped forward and cleared his throat.

"Mister Ibrakrim, sir, we have indeed just returned from Runal."

Gasps were heard all around from those nearby on the dock, as well as those up the hill. Enoch figured there was no way he could possibly get them all in any more trouble now.

"We take full responsibility for our actions today. We did this to prove the theory originally demonstrated to us by Kahdi."

This was too much for many of the bystanders who let out nervous laughs, then repeated Enoch's words for those who were too far away to hear. All edged closer as Enoch continued.

"It might not seem possible, but Kahdi goes into the forest every ninth day because that is a day when the Cofs will not attack us. In fact, we believe they will not even attack the deer, the oswatts, or any of our farm animals because it is their day of rest. We studied and recorded Kahdi's actions before travelling to Runal to prove our theory."

Enoch continued until well after dark. Chairs were produced for some of the older Legion members as the three other kids also explained their roles in the mission. The entire crowd was stunned even more when Enoch produced the coded message, and Berc brought forth one of the charred rocks to present to the Legion.

After only a short while, Ibrakrim announced they would hold an emergency meeting the next morning. This would include the Runal transgressors and their families. He did not need to tell the wide-eyed observers they would soon witness the biggest proceedings to take place in Verandale during their lifetime.

The exhausted brothers grabbed their supplies and began their trek home. Their parents were no longer glaring, but remained silent, nonetheless. Sabri came up between the two brothers and mouthed the words, "Way to go." It wasn't until they were back at home that Egard finally told them he was both angry and proud. Enoch gave in to sleep knowing that no dream could come close to the real events of the day.

If you don't catch a falling leaf in autumn,
you will not survive the winter.
—Debunked schoolyard legend

27

The morning meal began quietly—almost as if everyone was afraid to acknowledge the events of the day before, or the importance of the upcoming meeting.

When their mother finally spoke, Berc dropped his spoon.

"You boys need to know that whatever happens today, we are completely behind you," she said while pouring milk from an urn.

Silence returned.

Enoch tried to eat but was just going through the motions. Out of the corner of his eye, he could see Berc, also just pushing food around on his plate. When their father pushed his own plate away and stood to leave for the palace, they did the same.

While walking along the road just past the school, they came upon several people surrounding a person lying on the ground. He was large enough that his identity was certain even at a distance. Upon closer inspection, they found Kahdi—protec at his side—holding both hands over his forehead, apparently dazed. An older woman explained that he had been chasing a butterfly and had somehow smashed his head against a log.

"Great, this is certainly going to help our case," Berc mumbled.

Dew looked over and gave a perfunctory growl as they kept walking.

Climbing the southern steps to the palace, Sabri took advantage of the water's deafening sound to needle her brothers. "You know, looking on the bright side, the Legion will either exile you to Darnoc or they are going to assemble statues of you on the bridge to Darnoc. Either way, you will be famous."

The boys smiled at her but remained unable to respond.

They entered the doors at the back of the palace foyer; they noticed many familiar faces in a crowd of people lining the hallway. They represented the multitudes that had arrived too late to gain a seat in the Legion's main hall. As Enoch followed his family and pushed through the crowd, he heard varying words—some encouraging and some not—from people that Enoch knew would have never given him even a second glance before yesterday.

A giant archway framed the entrance to the meeting hall. The crowd became even tighter. Enoch placed a hand on the back of Berc's shoulder so he could move forward without stumbling, but still look up at the dais from which the Legion ruled.

Upon reaching the front of the hall, Egard gently pushed his boys forward. The last of the onlookers parted so Enoch could see Falo and Sasha already standing at the front of the throng.

"Well, we can't be as nervous as we were at this time yesterday, right?" Enoch asked.

"We just have to tell our story," Sasha paused, "and hopefully that will be enough."

Enoch felt a renewed sense of confidence that was shattered immediately with the head Legion member's first words. His aged head had no visible trace of hair. Though he was in no way obese, the skin on his face hung in layers from his dark eye sockets, down past his jaws where it merged into his neck.

He was the ranking member of the Legion; he was looking directly at Enoch as he spoke, and Enoch had completely forgotten his name. "I would like to ask the Apprentice if he has the desire to one day be a perpetual resident in the land of Darnoc, or if he wishes for his body to be buried before it has even stopped growing?"

The hall was instantly silent, except for the sounds of Enoch's heart pounding through his ears.

"Um, well actually…Sir," Sasha's head turned. Enoch could feel her looking at the side of his head and figured she already knew he had forgotten the leader's name.

Small beads of sweat started above each of Enoch's eyebrows as the gaze of Hanging Face failed to waver from his own.

"What we did, we did to help all the people of this land. We have spent many days with Kahdi, and we have seen him go into the forest many times. When we started to, um…talk to others and map out these days." Enoch gulped even though his throat was dry. "That was when we discovered the ninth day of Cof rest. In fact, Kahdi has tried to tell us this, but when you only speak one or two words every day, it is kind of hard to speak these important things."

"You are referencing the same large fellow whom we saw outside the palace this morning? The boy felled by a log while chasing an insect?" Hanging Face asked amid scattered snickers from the crowd.

"Yes, Sir." Enoch paused to retell the story of the nine/eighteen kittens for what felt like the one-hundredth time, then had to catch his breath. "It didn't make any sense to me either, but we all know there must be something special about Kahdi. Either that or he just happened to be the first boy to ever get a protec—the first striped protec that anyone now alive has ever been alive to see one."

Falo recognized the start of Enoch-rambling and nudged Berc.

Berc stepped forward next to his brother. "I know there are some who have questioned our journey to Runal. Some are skeptical of our reasons, and some are even questioning the fact that we made it there and back. I would like to offer this piece of scorched Runal rock as evidence of our quest."

Berc handed the rock forward and it was passed along to the hands of each of the seven Legion members.

"Berc," his great-grandfather echoed from his seat to the right of Hanging Face, "I would like to ask you about this parchment that you also presented upon returning to Verandale last evening. Do any of you have a theory to explain the strange symbols written here?" He asked while holding it up in front of the crowd.

"We do not."

Ibrakrim held out his hand to Orgard, and the

document was transferred to him as he spoke. "I have seen this only briefly. I do not yet know what these symbols represent. I did go back to the ancient scrolls last night and was able to confirm that Ezrin was indeed the first mate on the final ill-fated voyage of *The Chimera*. I plan to lock myself away amongst the ancient book stacks tonight until I can decipher this document."

"I must interject some wisdom at this point," Hanging Face interrupted him in a desultory tone. "We could make monumental decisions in this hall on this very day that could affect the rest of our lives. I will not ask the Legion to make decisions based on a piece of paper that any of us could have drawn and a burned rock that could have been chipped from the back of this very building. As I look upon the four young people standing before us, I see great potential. But I also see fervent young minds with equal parts imagination and careless ambition. These same minds believe the way for us to finally leave this land is to entrust our efforts to Kahdi, the sinker of boats. We were all on hand last night to hear the wonderful—almost magical—tales of *The Indomitable*'s journey to Runal. I would like to believe these tales, but I will need further proof."

Enoch had no argument to disprove his skepticism. As he looked at the others, he knew they were equally dumbfounded. That is, he knew until Sasha looked up at him and smiled. She stepped forward into the silence.

"If I may address the Legion," her voice came out slightly squeaky at first until she cleared her throat. "I would like to present proof of our trip to Runal. I will show the Legion and all the people in this hall an object that has never before been seen in Verandale."

Sasha now had every set of eyes upon her as she raised her left arm up above her head. Enoch had not noticed that she was wearing a long-sleeved dress on a warm day. A small white object protruded just under her wrist. It was about the size and shape of a writing stick, but it also appeared to be almost translucent. She reached into the sleeve with the fingers of her right hand—as if she had spent much of last night practicing for this very moment—and the white turned into the brilliant, shimmering green peacock feather as long as her arm. Oohs and aahs arose from the crowd, then all quieted as she held in her hands proof of their visit to the Runal quarry.

Hanging Face requested that the feather be passed up to him and Sasha lifted it up. The eye at the top of the feather appeared to gaze at him as if offering the proof he had requested.

Sasha stepped back to stand next to the others. Enoch beamed at her and wondered how she had managed to keep the feather secret during their frantic retreat from the quarry and the ghost town.

The feather was passed to all seven Legion members upon the dais. The crowd again grew quiet as the Legion members announced they would recess to the back chamber and return shortly with a decision on the fate of the kids—and likely the future of all Verandale.

With the retreat of the last robed figure, chaos erupted in the great hall and the crowd surged forward to surround the four.

"Sasha, that was amazing," Falo said while hugging her. "The only decision they could come back with now would be for you to replace one of those old men as one of the seven members of the Legion!"

Enoch and the others bobbed with the force of congratulatory pats upon their backs and tussles of their hair. Even the Healer came forward to tell Enoch—whispering so that only the Apprentice could hear, of course—that he could take as many days off as he needed in order to "get the old badgers to come to their senses."

Some of those in attendance had retreated outside, knowing that this would likely be a long break. Even the kids themselves had begun to make their way to the back and toward the dimmer torches of the hallway, when they snapped their heads back to the sound of rustling from the front of the room.

They saw the members of the Legion already filing back to their seats as murmurs spread through the great hall. They had barely made it back to their place at the front of the crowd when Professor Andrew—now seated in the center of the seven—began to speak.

"I believe we should recognize that these four young people have brought us information today that was hard fought, well thought-out, and achieved with great bravery in the face of immeasurable danger. Their actions, and the information and evidence they have presented, have demonstrated a level of maturity and intelligence that far exceeds their infantile antics I witnessed, on a daily basis, within the confines of the school walls."

The professor looked up only briefly from his paper to acknowledge the scattered snickers from the nervous throng.

"With this information in hand, we believe several actions should be commenced in the coming days. First, we will monitor closely the actions of Kahdi and attempt—may the stars and suns help us—to interview him in order to further glean some of his…knowledge. Next, we will organize an attempted breach of the forest, the twelfth to ever be undertaken. This will start on the next day of Cof rest and will be composed of ten volunteers. Our only stipulation will be that it contains at least one member of the four adventurers standing now before us, one protec, and one member of the Legion of Elders.

"Finally, on the matter of punishment for those standing before us," the Professor continued. "Sasha, Berc, and Falo will receive no punishment for violating one of the oldest and most important laws of Verandale. We believe the consequences of their actions outweigh their ignorance of the rule of law. The Apprentice, on the other hand, I will ask to approach the Legion."

Enoch had no idea how many steps he could take but felt even one was an accomplishment given how fast his heart was racing and how weak the muscles in his legs now felt. He suddenly felt as scared in the middle of the great hall as he had when docking at Runal the day before.

"For you, we believe that special care was necessary in determining the appropriate response to your actions," the professor continued while his gaze stared straight through to the back of Enoch's eyes. "Your physical skills previously demonstrated during the Cof attack on your boat, and the mental skills demonstrated by your deciphering the safe days of the forest are, we believe, not only commendable but require quick and extraordinary action from this Legion. As I speak, we have asked the craftsmen to travel to your home."

A stunned hush rippled through the crowd behind him.

Enoch's knees buckled.

"Enoch, we will now ask all of those in this hall, as well as all the others outside, to consider your Ceremony completed. You will return to your home to find that a door is being crafted from the window into your room. We will, of course, ask you to respond from now on to each and every danger that threatens this land. Accolades and gratitude should be extended from all your neighbors for what you have brought to our future. Notices will be posted here at the palace and at multiple locations throughout Verandale to coordinate what we can only hope is the first successful breach of the great forest. This meeting is adjourned."

Enoch sat down in the middle of the floor. The great hall—and the entire palace, for that matter—began to spin and his hands and face went numb. He closed his eyes and was surprised that he could still hear pieces of frantic conversation around him.

"What a little teacher's pet you have turned out to be." Enoch picked out the voice of his brother. "To think that I spent all that time training you just so you could be the first boy to ever skip his testing for the Ceremony."

Enoch felt a tugging at his ear, interrupted by another hand that fought to protect him. He knew the tugging was from Berc, he hoped the other was from Sasha. One thing was clear; there was now chaos all around him.

After much effort, Enoch was helped up by Sasha and Falo. There were congratulatory slaps on his back as well as grasps at his hands. He looked through the melee and was able to see his father, clearing a partial path for Enoch to leave the great hall.

"Son, the only way you could create a greater

disturbance is if you had brought a pet Cof into the hall with you. Come, let us swim our way out of here."

After waiting an uncomfortable amount of time for the crowd to clear out before them, Enoch and Sasha walked the corridor back to the palace's entrance. They stood together in the brackish mist billowing through the foyer. Though he felt spent, Enoch's senses were carried away—as they always were—the moment he came near to the birthplace of the Salt River.

Enoch took Sasha's hand and they gazed at the crowd scattering before them. In the middle of what looked like every single inhabitant of Verandale, they saw Berc and Falo. Berc was looking directly into Falo's eyes, and his usual smirk was gone. He was holding both her hands, and she was holding his. Enoch and Sasha would later confirm what they had already guessed— Berc had asked Falo to be his wife, and she had said yes.

In the next couple of days, they also learned Berc and Falo had volunteered for assignment in the scheduled breach of the forest. This was not the first time they had discussed becoming husband and wife, but it was the first time they had ever considered being a part of an attempted breach—a fate that had resulted in death for every single person who had ever decided the same.

Enoch walked out of the palace, no longer trying to hide the fact that he and Sasha were holding hands. They both knew any chiding they might receive would pale in comparison to the events of the last few days.

"Well, there is no denying it now," Sasha broke the silence.

"What, that we are holding hands?"

"No, Enoch," she sighed. "You can no longer deny that you are going to be a very big thing around these parts. Why, I'll bet they are going to be measuring you tomorrow."

She paused, and Enoch looked at her before taking the bait. "Measuring me? What in the name of the other side of the mountain are you talking about?"

"For your statue on the Darnoc Bridge, they are going to want to get all the features right: your big muscles, your mark, the big brains you have that figured out the code of Kahdi…you know, everything."

Sasha swung her hands, looking straight ahead and smiling with the knowledge that she had rendered him speechless.

After descending the palace steps, they rejoined his parents. The looks on their faces, and Sabri's, changed when they saw Enoch and Sasha approaching.

They were promptly mobbed with more hugs and kisses.

"Well, just look at you son," his mother gushed while planting a kiss on the side of his head. "It seems like it was only yesterday that you were crawling around and babbling. Why for the longest time, you couldn't even tell your food from a pile of…"

"Mother!" Enoch interrupted while Sasha and Sabri giggled.

Berc and Falo joined them as they left the grounds of the palace. They wanted to know what had caused the snickering from the girls. To Enoch's dismay, his mother repeated what she had said before and added a few more specifics.

The seven of them walked into a cheering crowd.

Many were genuinely interested in congratulating him, but also trying to stall so that he would not arrive back at the house before his door was completed.

Eventually, he even gave in to one or two invitations to enter a house for tea. As they came closer to their own home, they were passed on the road by a palace guard who was running from building to building—even tree to tree—handing out and posting papers that described the breach attempt that would commence in eight days—the next day of Cof rest.

They eventually came upon the mass of people that surrounded their house. Enoch looked at the new door that rendered the rest of his room unrecognizable. The craftsmen had already blended into the crowd, but Enoch recognized one familiar face standing directly at the side of his window-turned-door. The palace guard took a step in Enoch's direction. He was the same one that Enoch had startled—the night he jumped out of bed as knowledge of the kittens hatched within his mind. In the guard's gloved left hand, he held a freshly forged spike. He offered it to Enoch. He placed his right hand upon Enoch's shoulder and whispered so that only Enoch could hear.

"This is my best and newest spike. Though it flies the straightest and the longest, my wish is that it will sit in your weapons bag and grow rust for nigh these next many years."

Enoch took the weapon and turned to face the crowd. He tried to speak but could not.

He opened his new door and illuminated parts of his room that had never before felt the direct light of the two suns.

The boisterous crowd finally dispersed only after Enoch had fallen into his bed.

He slept clear through the mid-day meal, oblivious to the scores of townsfolk that now found an excuse to walk by his door—whether it was on their normal route or not. He awoke as the shadows were growing long. His family had protected him from congratulations in the form of food, gifts, and even one newborn lamb.

The only person they eventually allowed in was a young messenger from the library, sent with specific instructions to deliver a parcel only to Enoch. He brought two parchments from Ibrakrim who had been locked within the stacks of books, refusing to acknowledge anything but the coded message found in Runal and occasional sips of water.

Enoch accepted the parchments and sat down to read them while his family looked over his shoulders.

One was the same notice that had been posted all around Verandale. It described the upcoming breach attempt in detail—including the plan to enter the eastern forest on the next day of Cof rest. The long-standing estimate was that the mountains were high enough to require two days of travel. The first day, the ten volunteers would leave at dawn, followed by a night in which the party would travel with the protection of several larger than normal lit torches, and then a last—hopefully shorter—day that would take them to their first ever view of the other side of the mountains.

The second was a copy of the coded message, along with a message scrawled in Ibrakrim's hand. It described various theories the librarian was working on, along with a note requesting Enoch's presence the next day, when Kahdi was to be brought to the palace for formal questioning by the Legion.

Sometimes, it is better to just not go and get Kahdi.
—Kahdi's mother

28

Except, Kahdi decided he wasn't going to the palace. His parents had attempted to awaken him at first light as instructed by the Legion. Kahdi had responded with a typical confused look at first but would not get out of bed even after his eyes and his furrowed forehead had adjusted to the morning light. When his parents increased their efforts, by tugging and pulling, Kahdi's response was to stop breathing.

They had seen this before, starting with episodes as a toddler that had garnered him a diagnosis of a "not at all normal child" from the Healer. But this time Kahdi kept his mouth closed and one fist pushed against each nostril until the redness was gone from his lips, and a subtle blue color cast over his face. His eyes rolled back into his head, and he fell back onto his pillow. Only then did his body resume breathing on its own again.

While he was regaining consciousness, his father ran out of the house and threw a sheepskin riding blanket over his strongest horse. He rode to the palace to tell the Legion the bad news.

It was sometime later when he rode back. He was followed by the Healer, Enoch, and several members of the Legion. Berc and the girls peeked from around the corner of a nearby house as others came out their doors or craned out their windows.

By the time the troupe of men and horses had arrived, Kahdi was out of the house and running behind his protec.

He stopped only briefly to stare at the assembled group before running behind the nearest refuse building and out of sight.

Hanging Face was the first to step down from his horse—a dark, moody stallion.

"Mister Kahdi," he snorted in a loud and condescending voice, "your presence is requested, and we expect you to comply with us forthwith."

No sound came from behind the building. Kahdi's mother was the closest to the side of the building. She looked around the corner, shrieked, and backed away.

Enoch looked at the Healer standing next to him and tried to determine what would be expected of a man—albeit a freshly minted man in Enoch's case—in a situation such as this. While this thought was still fermenting in Enoch's head, Kahdi-protec came out from behind the building.

He held, in his mouth, a giant piece of footwear. It had been on one of Kahdi's feet just moments before. Kahdi-protec stopped and wagged his short tail very slowly, once to the right and once to the left. All around him were silent, until Hanging Face announced that there had been exactly too much of this tomfoolery.

"We represent a great and mighty group of humans,"

he said while throwing his riding cloak onto the ground before him. "We are not going to stand here like a bunch of scared baby goats, bleating for their mothers. If this man…excuse me, if this man-child knows something about the forest, then we need to talk to him. If the Legion summons you, your choice is to face the Legion and you have no other choices. I, for one, refuse to stand here like a fool," he proclaimed while stomping forward, his jowls bouncing with each step, "while some ne'er-do-well keeps us waiting!"

He stormed off, right past Kahdi-protec and into the shadows behind the building. Just as all the witnesses were raising their eyebrows and craning their necks, they heard a crash. This was followed by a loud "oomph" as Hanging Face tried to reverse his direction and ran into the back of the refuse building. Somehow, he absorbed the impact and was able to keep himself upright, running back toward his horse. As he came around the corner, it became clear that Kahdi was chasing him…and Kahdi was naked.

Gasps went up from all around. Protecs barked as Hanging Face screamed. Enoch stole a glance back behind the building to make sure that Kahdi wasn't himself being chased. About this time, the running duo passed him close enough that he could see terror on the old man's face and the slightest hint of satisfaction—maybe even a little glee—on Kahdi's face.

Berc and the girls came out from behind their hiding place. Shouts and pleas trailed Kahdi and his prey. A couple of men tried to restrain Kahdi as he ran by. Once they were trampled, the rest of the crowd stood fast to the ground beneath them.

Hanging Face ran for his horse, but the horse whinnied and took off down the road. It was unclear at first whether the age of Hanging Face or the girth of Kahdi—albeit at least a little lighter without clothes—would fail first. Finally, Kahdi stopped and stood panting in the middle of the road.

A nice elderly lady looked for the closest object that could be commandeered to cover-up Kahdi. She retrieved a large cloak from the ground and was able to wrap it around Kahdi just as Kahdi-protec arrived and dropped his footwear before him.

Hanging Face looked up the road for a sign of his horse. He looked at his cloak and the giant mass of human that it now barely covered. He turned to the Apprentice and the Healer, who were attending to the two trampled men—now upright but still obviously shaken.

All others were staring at Kahdi or Hanging Face himself, who addressed the mayhem before him.

"As the leader of Verandale, many people look to me to provide leadership and guidance in toiled times such as these. It is clear, to all of us with brains, that the recent knowledge gained by our population may have come from Kahdi. It is also now abundantly clear this knowledge may have fallen upon him by pure happenstance, much as a single leaf may fall onto a man's head while thousands more are falling at his feet."

Enoch glanced over at Berc but realized quickly it was a bad idea. He stared back at the injured men, bit his lip, and tried not to laugh as Hanging Face continued on.

"…we often find ourselves responsible for those less gifted than ourselves. It is clear that our words may be unable to elicit helpful responses from Kahdi, to whom the world is certainly a playground. I therefore proclaim this meeting…adjourned."

With the word "meeting," many that were able to keep their snickers contained, by cupping hands over their mouths, now lost all control. Hanging Face was helped up onto the back of another Legion member's horse, failing to look regal as he wrapped his arms around the rider in front of him.

The kids and many others fell all over themselves laughing and reenacting some of the events they had just seen.

Of all the laughing people, some tended to the injured men, some gathered Kahdi's clothes, others were stilling anxious protecs, some discussed a trip home or to the tavern, but none were watching the forest.

29

He pressed the side of his head against the rough bark of the tree. This impaired his hearing on that side, but he reasoned that this amount of stealth was needed for an attack in the full light of the suns.

Nearby, his partner adopted the same stance and the same absolute silence. A short distance behind them, the Commander peered out from a thick copse of trees. He used a series of high-pitched staccato whistles that were barely audible to the two camouflaged attackers in front of him and the one behind.

The Commander's breathing quickened. He silently chastised himself for feeling as uneasy as a hatchling on its first hunt. But the amount of energy it had taken to fly and bound through the trees to this point had reinforced what he already knew—due to his advancing age, this would be the last mission under his command.

Along with the two in front of him, he edged forward to the ambush location. They maintained their vigil while waiting for their trailing partner to take up his pre-assigned flanking position.

Though they had decided that a diving attack from

the trees would be impossible in the light of midday, the sight in front of them gave hope for reconsideration. All the people and all of the protecting animals appeared to have abandoned their usual defensive postures and forgotten their proximity to the trees.

The One Who Sees had shed his covering fur and was chasing, or maybe even trying to harm, some of his fellow humans. Others were yelling and had apparently sent their cart-pulling animals running back to the village.

Ricit stood motionless behind a large mander tree which put him within two or three bounding leaps from the prey. The closest human was a female. He could easily take her down if he could get past her protecting animal. He was considering the possibility of attacking her first to enable the others to get to the target, when he heard a sound from the Commander.

Ricit rotated one eye backwards so as not to produce any unnecessary movement of his head. He saw the Commander motioning upwards and thought at first that this was a signal to abandon the mission—likely because there were so many more humans in the attack zone than had been expected. Then Ricit realized the Commander was motioning to the sturdier branches high up in the tree above him.

Surely, Ricit thought, he wasn't motioning because he was going to take flight this close to the humans. Attacking from above was always considered a better attacking angle, but few would dare a daytime ambush by taking flight this close to the edge of the forest. He had been taught from a young age that the hearing and seeing skills of the humans were less than their own. But now he understood—the humans were in such disarray they might not notice the Commander's flight up to an attacking perch.

The Commander braced his leg then pushed himself backward without making a sound. After another gaze at the mayhem taking place before them, the Commander crouched and leapt upwards. The sound and the rush of air from his beating wings enveloped Ricit's head. He dared a slight turn of his head back to the humans. Unbelievably, they had not heard or seen anything to distract them from their own chaos.

With everybody in place, Ricit focused on his target. The One was in the process of placing his covering furs back onto his body. Usually, this would be an exquisite opportunity to attack, but today he was surrounded by multiple other humans. He identified the most likely threat and waited for the diverting attack that was assigned to his partner, Ecron, a female that had recently returned from nesting on Egg Island. He had not seen her since she had helped with an attack in a field outside of Darnoc last winter.

Ricit caught himself holding his breath, then forced two long inhalations into his lungs. He started to calm himself, but this hunt was unlike all the other hunts in his lifetime. Today, they were not hunting for food; they were planning to kill The One that had revealed the secret of their Sabbath; The One who might lead all other humans through the forest.

The leaders of the horde stood silent in disbelief the day before, when the Commander had flown down during the rising of the first sun. He brought them proof that the humans had not only discovered the secret of their Sabbath, but also planned to traverse the forest. He had gone on to explain to the somber circle that this could result in human escape beyond the mountains and to the lands where no Cof dared to go. It would also likely cause a decline in—or even the disappearance of—the livestock that made up much of the Cofian diet. It was decreed that this would need to be dealt with immediately. They would attack whenever and wherever they had to: in the light of the suns, in the midst of the human village, even inside the human dwellings if needed. They would do whatever it took to eliminate The One Who Sees from the flock—stop the poison of his ideas from spreading to others in the human herd.

Ricit focused on his target who had finished recollecting his furs and was lying flat on the ground while many of the other humans surrounded him and continued the grunts that made up their type of communication.

Ricit knew that the time was now.

He watched the trees to his right. Ecron's beak was the only part of her that was visible behind the leaves of the trees and bushes. He watched the end of her beak slowly begin to turn and edge forward until her horn and part of her head came within his view. Though she had participated in few hunts over the past several seasons, Ricit could see why the Commander had picked her. She was good—so good that he could not see her move so much as he could detect more of her appearance with each passing moment.

Though her body was still perfectly camouflaged, it was now almost completely within view. She was ready. She rocked first backward and then forward. She transferred weight from her tail to her foot and sprang out of the forest.

Ecron bounded twice before the first human heads began to turn. The Commander launched himself into flight from his perch. Ecron was almost past the first protecting animal when a cutting rock whistled past her. The next one cut into her leg but she continued unhindered toward her target.

Ricit broke into the clearing. His assignment was to attack the protecting animal that guarded The One. Having overcome their initial surprise, all the humans were now up and fighting. One of the females had ducked beneath the attack coming from the left flank. She turned and wielded a scythe and was able to swing wildly at Ricit's foot. It missed but knocked him just enough off of his path that he skidded into the dirt short of his target. This gave the Commander a straight shot at his target.

The Commander's talons grasped at the enormous girth of The One, but only for a moment before the striped protecting animal leapt through the air and clamped down upon his throat. The Commander tried to turn but was dealt a thundering blow to his chest from one of the humans. Ricit righted himself just in time to see the Commander's body slumping, the protecting animal had pierced one tusk into the hide of his neck as its jaws clamped on for an even tighter hold.

Ricit charged to save his commander—his sense of mission now compromised by a blinding rage. He rammed his head into the side of the animal and felt the crunch of bone and tissue. While dazed from the impact, he saw the body of The One as it was dragged towards a building. All went silent in Ricit's ears. He heard no cutting rocks in flight, no piercing scream from the building up on the hill, no sounds of battle. He felt a pain pierce his side as one of the last humans ran past him.

He stumbled forward and nearly into two lifeless bodies. He gathered his bearings and looked toward the remaining humans. They had dragged The One back inside the doorway of his building and stood in protective stances in front of him.

Ricit knew he was too injured to attack anymore. He spread out his wings and felt a sharp pain under one of them but was able to take flight to save his own life. He aimed for the closest edge of the forest hoping to land safely within the trees and assess his wounds before he could be hurt further. He flew over the open area where he had often seen the humans learn to throw their cutting rocks. Though he still could not hear, he was able to see one of his fellow attackers enter the forest just behind him. Now safe, he collapsed beneath the trees.

One should always be in the safety of one's shadows during the day, the safety of one's hearth during the night.
—Unknown

30

Enoch leaned forward and labored for each breath. He was unable to lift his hands off his knees. He leaned against Sabri, who had landed on the ground beside him.

"Are you hurt?" he asked her.

"I don't think so, are you?"

"A little."

He looked behind him; Sasha and her protec were kneeling next to Kahdi in the doorway of his house. Blood oozed from talon lacerations covering his flank, and one finger pointed in an unnatural position. Otherwise, Kahdi appeared to be alive and breathing. Enoch turned to look for his brother and did not see him, but soon heard Berc and Falo's voices behind him.

Enoch let out a deep sigh then looked out over the area of the attack.

He saw bodies, but it took a moment for his mind to catch up to his eyes. There was a dead Cof in the distance, and an older man that he recognized from the house behind Falo's. Closer in, he saw another lifeless Cof that appeared older and more of a grayish blue than any he had ever seen before. Kahdi-protec still had jaws clamped around its neck. The jaws no longer held tightly though, and Enoch could see the protec's chest rise haltingly with each breath.

Enoch felt a hand on his shoulder and looked up to see the Healer. He said nothing as he motioned towards Hanging Face. Though Enoch had learned to despise the leader of the Legion, he now saw the natural ability that had led him to a position of leadership.

Hanging Face yelled out to several palace guards who had come sprinting or on horseback with the sounding of the tocsin. They spread out to cover both sides of the crowd while they loaded spikes and surveyed the sky and the trees. Others set out to check the areas behind nearby buildings.

With both flanks protected, Hanging Face motioned to the Healer, who grabbed Enoch by the arm. They walked forward to try and separate the injured from the dead.

The man and the two Cofs were clearly dead, but Kahdi-protec was still moving. The Healer grabbed the medicine bag. After one more look for other survivors, he and Enoch ran to Kahdi-protec.

The Healer knelt behind the protec who had now let go of the dead Cof. He dropped his bag and placed his ear against the chest of the animal. After listening for a moment, he motioned to Enoch to help him roll the animal onto its other side. Enoch gripped both back legs and rolled as gently as possible. The other side of Kahdi-protec's chest appeared sunken. It flailed inwards instead of expanding outwards with each tortured breath.

The Healer grabbed a container from the bag and

motioned to the Apprentice. Enoch recognized the poultice that looked like the one his father had made to soothe his mark. He had seen similar concoctions applied to a few painful wounds during his recent days as the Apprentice.

But the Healer did not apply it to any of Kahdi-protec's open wounds. Instead, he wiped dirt and other debris from the fur overlying the injured ribs and gently rubbed in the medicine. He pointed to a corner of the bag. Here, Enoch found an object that had been wrapped with great care. He unwrapped the layers of cloth to reveal a straight, desiccated mander tree sapling a little longer than his hand. He remembered a lesson, from school, describing how the core of young mander trees remained hollow for the first few years of growth.

The Healer took the wood and exerted gentle pressure at its midpoint until the hollow wood snapped in half. He sharpened the broken end with a knife. He handed it to Enoch who coated the entire implement with the poultice. Enoch handed it back careful not to let it touch the ground.

The Healer pressed a finger from his left hand into a space between two of the animals crushed ribs. With steady pressure from the sharpened tip of the wooden tube, he forced it through the skin. Air and blood rushed out of Kahdi-protec's chest, but he uttered no growl and no part of him moved.

Enoch remembered something the Healer had told him many days before—if a person doesn't complain or an animal doesn't flinch in response to pain, this is the surest sign they are extremely sick or injured.

The Healer nodded to Enoch to again listen to Kahdi-protec's lungs. He put his ear to an area that was somewhat clear of blood and marveled at lung sounds that had returned nearly back to normal. As he lifted his head, he saw Kahdi walking over and braced himself for Kahdi's response.

Kahdi knelt down in front of his protec. With his giant hand slowly moving back and forth, he stroked the fur behind his protec's ears and tusks.

"Proek," was all he said.

Enoch placed a hand on Kahdi's shoulder as the Healer fashioned bandages and wrapped them around the tube and the animal's chest.

Enoch tried to hide his tears in his sleeve as he heard the wailing that marked the arrival of the dead man's family to the scene of the battle. All around him, the survivors mixed relief of their continued existence with mourning for the injured and the dead.

Care for not just the body, but also for the soul.
—The Healer

31

Four days later, Enoch was exhausted. He leaned his head back against the wall of the shack that had been converted into Kahdi-protec's treatment area. He felt as if he had mastered the routine. This was good, because the Legion announced the Healer would be joining Berc, Falo, four palace guards, and three others in the journey up the eastern mountains that would begin on the next day of Cof rest—now just two days away.

The Healer had spent the first day after the announcement with his protégé but told Enoch he was now ready to hand over the reins. The Healer taught Enoch how to care for the tube in the animal's chest and told him they had done everything possible for the animal. It was now time to see if the protec's body could heal itself or if the body would shut down after so many injuries.

Enoch tried to keep the sadness out of his mind. He balanced his need for sleep with his duties for Kahdi-protec and his desire to spend as much time with his brother before the historic day of the breach. Egard and

Sune recognized the dilemma and helped Berc move his cot into the shack with Enoch so he could stay with his brother for a night before resuming his preparations.

Enoch spent much of each day cleaning and re-dressing the animal's wounds. He also learned he would need to unplug the wooden tube and draw air out at even intervals at least six times per day. When Enoch asked how he would know when it was time to clear the tube, the Healer told him to wake up at least once each night, then perform the procedure every time he had to relieve himself. Enoch thought this was a strange way to monitor an animal's health but found that by day two the system was quite reliable. By day three, Kahdi-protec had still barely moved, but he did occasionally open his eyes.

The Healer told him to remember that caring for the sick and the injured was often the easy part—it was relating to the family of the patient that could be the most difficult.

Of course, dealing with Kahdi could be difficult, if not downright dangerous, on any day. But to his surprise, Enoch found that Kahdi was sad, but also much more predictable during the days his protec was in Enoch's care.

Kahdi came to the shack at each mealtime and once each night before going to bed. Enoch made sure the animal's wounds were covered lest the site of the injuries would upset Kahdi. He also made sure to have a bowl of water freshly filled before each of Kahdi's visits. Enoch showed him how to dip a cloth into the bowl and then hold it over Kahdi-protec's mouth until drops fell onto the animal's tongue. Kahdi did this once but then dipped a finger into the bowl and placed it between the sharp teeth. He did this over and over. Each time, Kahdi spoke a single word— "food"—to his protec.

A couple of times, Enoch thought he saw the injured animal move his mouth. He hoped that this was a good sign, but worried he was hoping for too much.

Besides the visits from Kahdi, his family, and multiple Legion members, Enoch received occasional updates couriered from Ibrakrim. The old man had stayed sequestered in the library with the coded Runal note and was pouring over every old scroll and parchment he could find to decipher it. His assistants reported to Enoch that the librarian was now talking to the books—maybe even the walls at times—but still thought he would have the answer soon.

The day before the breach was to commence, Enoch's father brought him his best tunic. Sasha arrived in her best dress and brought a necklace of flowers she had woven to fit around Kahdi-protec's neck. The doors of the shack were propped open to look out over a grassy hill. Most all of Verandale began to assemble along the hill while Enoch continued to treat his patient.

Berc and Falo were the last to arrive. They walked through the crowd and approached Orgard—who had refused help travelling up the hill and had needed extra time to catch his breath.

Once his breathing was restored, he faced the assembled crowd and read from the document that had been reproduced and hung in almost every couple's house in the land. It was the Document of Betrothal. When the reading was done, Berc and Falo kissed and turned to face the people for their first moment as husband and wife.

It was the first applause and genuine joy Enoch had seen since the mortal Cof attack at Kahdi's house.

As the crowd began to file away, Sasha walked up to the doorway that had served as the impromptu backdrop for the marriage ceremony.

"So, my protec has a scratch on his ear, and I hear you are the best there is at healing protecs." Sasha tried to smile but Enoch could tell the strain was beginning to wear on her just as much as everyone else.

"Thanks for your faith in me, but…," Enoch paused to look down at his patient, "I wish I could tell if I was doing any good. According to the Healer, the next day or two will decide if his body will recover or if it will give up."

They leaned on each other and stood next to the animal, surrounded on the bed by bandages and other makeshift supplies.

"You know, Berc tells me he is ready," he continued. "He said it feels as if this is the moment that he and Falo were made for. Like this journey will be the thing that makes them legends to be read about, rather than just 'those kids that snuck around with each other while avoiding their chores.' But I can't help thinking that life was so much simpler the way it was before."

Sasha looked up at him and said, "I agree with you. Remember how we would just hang around with your brother and sister; throwing rocks, racing protecs, laughing at Kahdi stories. It seemed like all we had to do was keep one eye on the trees and get ourselves inside before dark, and everything would be just as happy when we woke up the next day."

It was a moment before Enoch spoke. "I know we are

doing the right thing and all, but right now a big part of me wishes that Runal had never happened."

Sasha leaned into Enoch. She stroked the fur of Kahdi-protec as her own protec reached up to lick the paw that dangled off the edge of the bed.

Silence filled the room.

They hoped the coming days would bring fewer tears.

You should reach higher than the some who reach halfway up.
—Herol

32

The official written plan—which had been distributed to every home, building, and market table—was to act as if their lives were unchanged and not approaching one of the most important days in the history of the land. This was done in order to hide their plans from any Cof scouts who might be observing from the mountainside.

Enoch's family had dinner together at the shack the night before. It was a somber experience, as expected, but they had managed to make it as happy as possible by talking about how much they would look back on the events and laugh when they were one day united on the other side of the mountains.

Enoch had actually managed to get the "last-time-I-will-ever-see-my-brother" thoughts out of his head for moments at a time. Berc had made everyone laugh when predicting the upcoming Cof reaction when Falo blasted them with one of her newly practiced yelling-wife lectures.

Sune and Sabri brought out every embarrassing story

they could think of from Berc's childhood and laughed when telling a few that Falo had not yet heard.

After a long meal and many hugs, Enoch said goodnight. But when he checked on Kahdi-protec, he found the animal's breathing more labored and his heart beating much faster. He quickly checked the tube and listened to the lungs. He could detect no other difference until he felt the heat coming off the animal.

The Healer had warned him that an excess of heat coming from the patient was a sign of a possible infection and was the most feared complication of any injury. Enoch tried to remember what the Healer had told him to do if this were to occur. He paced within the walls occupied by only him and the protec. His panic grew until it overwhelmed him. He asked a guard to summon the Healer.

Enoch's panic lessened when he saw the Healer had brought his entire pack, weapons bag, and torch for the next day's breach with him to the shack. Enoch was so relieved he could have hugged him, but the Healer could see Kahdi-protec's dire status from the doorway and rushed past Enoch.

He examined the animal. To Enoch's surprise, the Healer told him that he had done a remarkable job caring for the animal and the injuries.

"The only step you forgot is to cool the patient," he said as he reached past Enoch to grab a bowl of water.

The Healer carefully poured the water over the head, soaking down the fur while keeping water out of the nostrils. He then poured the rest of the water over Kahdi-protec's body.

"It is time to call the family."

"But...but he was starting to move his tongue and open his eyes," Enoch protested.

The Healer looked at Enoch and put a hand on his upper back.

"I believe that you have done very well, my distinguished Apprentice. We will continue to treat Kahdi-protec the best we possibly can. But he suffered serious injuries which have now led to serious infection. A body—even the stubborn and powerfully muscled body of a protec—cannot survive both. Our most important job now is to make sure he experiences no pain. It is time to call the family."

Enoch stood in the middle of the shack, frozen until the Healer motioned with an extra nod of his head toward the doorway. In the fading light of the day, Enoch ran the short distance to Kahdi's house. He was too overcome to even talk when Kahdi's parents answered the door, but when they looked at him, they understood. After bringing their son to the shack, it actually looked as if Kahdi also understood.

Enoch brought out an extra-large chair, and Kahdi spent the rest of the night leaning his head against his dying protec. The Healer offered to stay up with the animal—all pretense of not talking having ceased days ago with the announcement of the Healer's participation in the breach—but Kahdi's parents were able to convince him to sleep on the cot.

By dawn's approach, every person in the crowded shack was exhausted. Kahdi-protec was still alive but no longer moved or opened his eyes. The Healer had given Enoch a pouch just before he retired to the cot. Enoch used the contents—some of the strongest tlok-vine tea he had ever smelled—to replace Kahdi-protec's water. The Healer told him it would make his last moments of life comfortable and hopefully even pleasant.

Kahdi-protec died just before dawn.

Enoch summoned all the strength he could to tell Kahdi, but Kahdi had already looked up at the same moment Kahdi-protec stopped breathing. Enoch hugged Kahdi, embarrassed that he had ever been afraid to be in his presence.

Kahdi put his head down against the fur of his protec for a moment, then stood up and left, returning a few moments later with a stick. It was scored in the middle with teeth marks and looked like the same stick he had "fetched" the day they had all witnessed the two of them playing in front of Kahdi's house. Kahdi set the stick gently next to the nose of his protec.

"Play there," Kahdi whispered while sobbing. Enoch and the Healer stepped outside and closed the doors, so his parents could be alone with him. Enoch strained his eyes to see the first light of the new day.

As he did this, he saw Berc and Falo. They had their packs in place and were surrounded by all the other members of the expedition. Just before the first sun appeared over the mountains, he whispered an idea to Berc, who told it to the rest of the breach party.

They all agreed and dropped to their knees in a nearby patch of wildflowers. They walked in single file back to the shack. Each placed one flower over Kahdi-protec, then hugged Kahdi and his parents. No words were needed.

They regrouped into the formation Enoch had seen them practice in the palace a few days before. He went to his brother's side as Sabri went to the other. They both squeezed Berc.

"Come on you guys," Berc said grimacing and shaking them off. "Do you want to get my hair and clothes all messed up when they might use this pose someday for my giant statue carved into the largest rock of the Darnoc bridge?"

Berc told Enoch about a meeting he had with Ibrakrim the evening before. The old librarian had taken one of the burnt rocks and rubbed off part of the charred residue on one side. Berc demonstrated this on a rock removed from his pocket. A light shone outwards from the body of the rock just as had the one back on *The Indomitable*.

"You're not going to believe this, little brother." Berc turned Enoch around and positioned his head so that he could see the light, coming out of the rock and shining onto a large boulder nearby. "Now watch this."

Berc placed his thumb next to the light's exit point. He smudged the charred blackness across the spot—quickly to avoid being burned—and the light disappeared. Berc held the rock up and then tossed it upwards. Enoch caught it and looked more closely.

"Berc, that is amazing!"

"I thought so too. But you know what is even more amazing? Ibrakrim found some old-time scroll or something that talked about how to make these. It turns out, Runal gets all kinds of amazing lightning storms. So back in the day when they were excavating rocks for the palace, the miners would put Runal rocks up on the roof of the tallest building or even next to a piece of metal that made a lightning rod. If the lightning hit near the rocks, they would burn and make a 'charged rock.' And here is the best part; he told me that if we get attacked, I can take one of these rocks, scrape open a hole to let the light out and then throw it at a Cof. According to the legend, if a charged rock hits a Cof, it will make a giant explosion! What could be better than that?"

Berc wrapped Enoch's hands around the rock. "I want you to keep this one. You know those crazy lizards have only been getting meaner lately."

Enoch made Berc show him the rest of the stones one more time. Seeing them wrapped and carefully positioned at the top of Berc's weapons bag, he reluctantly let go of his brother. Goodbyes were exchanged along with hugs from his parents.

Berc and Falo started up the side of the mountain with the rest of the breach party.

Enoch looked up at the eastern mountains, quietly scratching behind Dew's ears as he stood with Sasha and his family. They watched for as long as they could until the breach party was swallowed by the shadowy layers of the forest.

A couple of hundred Verandalians started to disperse, leaving a small cadre of guards assigned at the forest's edge.

As Enoch talked with his family, Kahdi's parents opened the doors of the shack and came out. They told Enoch and his family that Kahdi had requested that his protec be buried next to the Healer's house.

Enoch had long ago stopped asking how they were able to get this kind of information from their son, but Kahdi's mother told him anyway. "We asked him if we could bury him on our property, but he said 'no, flood' and then drew a picture of the Healer's house in the dirt.

I have no idea what flood he is talking about, but we told him we would discuss this with you since you will one day move into the Healer's house."

Enoch hadn't thought this far ahead but told her he would be glad to help bury him there. His family also pledged their help. Though no one could resist a few more yearning looks up the mountain, they all knew that there was nothing they could do to help the travelers now. They also knew they would have no insight into the progress of the breach until dusk, when the breach party would light their torches to signal their progress back to Verandale, as well as help keep the Cofs at bay.

Enoch and about a dozen others stood in the front yard of the Healer's house. Everyone was covered in sweat and dirt, but they had dug a proper grave and everyone in attendance had paid their respects and said goodbye, except for Kahdi. He stared down at his protec, who was wrapped— along with sticks, flowers, food, and a few other items placed by his owner— in the blanket that had been on Kahdi's bed.

Enoch gently nudged Kahdi. "Alright big guy, your turn to tell him goodbye or say whatever special thing you would like."

Kahdi stared for a moment before he grasped the pickaxe that was near his feet and hoisted it up onto his shoulder. He then said, "Temple cry."

Everyone stayed silent and waited for either more words or at least words that made sense.

"Well, um, all right." Enoch stammered. "I think, Kahdi, that that is a very nice thing that you have told to your protec that always understands what you have always told him."

Enoch knew if Berc were here, he would be either biting his lip or simply turning away at this point—lest he start laughing at a funeral.

The pain of missing his brother hit Enoch for the first of many times and felt like a hard kick to his stomach.

Kahdi turned with his axe and began to walk toward the village. All those behind him struggled to think of something to say but stayed silent. One by one, they heaved shovels full of dirt back into the grave.

Enoch sat next to Sasha on the front stoop of the Healer's house as she held a piece of herky fish a little in front of her protec's nose. She pulled it sharply away and giggled as he snapped his teeth in mid-air, but then gave it quickly back to him.

"He doesn't like it too much if I do that more than once. Remember that time he knocked the whole plate out of my hands? I was lucky to get any of that meal back at all."

Enoch was staring up at the mountains, trying to see any movement and trying to guess how far they could have traveled. Despite her best efforts to cheer him up, it was clear Sasha would not get an answer from him.

"You know, they're going to come out of this all right." Sasha stood up and moved in front of Enoch. "They are going to have all day to hoof it up the mountain, and you know they are going to be going fast. Then tonight, they have like a thousand torches they are going to light to keep the Cofs away and to signal us. All they have to do after that is make it to the top in tomorrow's daylight."

Enoch broke his silence and his trance on the distant hills and stood up next to her.

"I guess you're right. Plus, he has the rocks, all the guards, and…"

"Falo!" They both yelled together and laughed.

"All we really have to do now is kill a whole lot of time until we can see the torches tonight," Enoch added. "What do you want to do?"

"Well, since the rumor around town is that this house is going to be yours one day, you could show me and S.P. around the place."

"You know, if half the rumors around here were true, it would be an even stranger place."

They started into the house, but shortly heard hoof beats and a wagon on the road behind them. They turned to see a tall man, reins in hand, with long hair and well-worn robes blowing in the wind.

The horses were barely reined to a stop when Ibrakrim stepped off and ambled over to Enoch and Sasha.

"Enoch…Oh, my apologies. I mean 'Apprentice.' And good evening to you, Miss Sasha," he said with a tip of his imaginary hat. "I have decoded the documents that you brought out of Runal. Quite the problematic deciphering, I would have to say." He undid a satchel at his side, removed a scroll, and unrolled it before Sasha and Enoch.

"It was a code the likes of which I had not seen before. I finally realized I was going about it all wrong. I had been pouring through the ancient documents trying to uncover any possible hints at codes, other languages, old drawings, anything I could get my hands on. Some people around me had even started to think I was losing my mind. Then, just a short while ago, it dawned on me. Some poor soul likely sat in that little guard house at the quarry, day after day. He could not even work off his nervousness like those around him. He would simply be incredibly bored, until there was an attack and he was supposed to sound the tocsin before anyone could get hurt. He would then be expected to shout orders and organize the defense of the whole camp. I have had some difficult jobs before, but that job…would challenge even the most vigilant."

Enoch stared back and forth between the code and the ranting librarian. He couldn't take the suspense any longer and did something he could have never imagined—he interrupted Ibrakrim.

"So, what does the code say?" Enoch covered his own mouth immediately after blurting out the words, as if this would excuse his outburst.

"What it tells us, Enoch, is something that is very unfortunate and something I never would have guessed even if I were to live twice as long. The small-brained Cofs that attack anything that moves are actually much smarter than we have ever given them credit for. You see, for at least the last eighty years—since the time of *The Chimera*— the Cofs have known our plans almost as soon as we have, for they have learned to read the words of man!"

Our greatest fear realized: Creatures learned to read!
—Ezrin

33

With Ibrakrim's words still hanging over him, Enoch stood amongst almost every remaining person in Verandale. Their shadows were long and the sky above them was a brilliant orange. They looked to the eastern mountains for any sign of the breach party.

Enoch's eyes were heavy, and his heart overburdened with all he had witnessed in the last few days. He felt guilty just standing near his neighbors and having the ability to go home to food and comfort, while Berc and the others faced unspeakable dangers...if they were even still alive.

As always, the red sun was the last to set—shooting out one last blade of light before it dropped behind the distant mountains west of Darnoc. The tension in the air grew as hundreds of people watched the invisible route the breach party was supposed to have traveled.

Enoch stood between Sasha and Sabri. He held Sasha close as his sister knelt down and put one arm around each protec. She looked into the dirt—too nervous to look up at the mountains.

Time dragged on. The only sounds were from the rivers tracing their continuous paths to the Sea.

As the wait continued, the silence was broken by a messenger who came running from the palace to say that Kahdi had climbed the ancient stairs at the back of the palace foyer. He was spotted standing above the waters and swinging his pickaxe into the back wall above the mouth of the Salt River.

Enoch and Sasha looked at each other and then at those around them. Everyone else heard the news, but no one knew how to process the latest Kahdi incident in the wake of all that was going on before them.

He tried to picture or predict what Kahdi could possibly be doing. He pushed it to the back of his mind when a man began shouting, "There they are," and pointing eagerly to a point far south of where the travelers were supposed to be.

Enoch and Sasha squinted. They saw nothing at first, but then a small flicker of light. It was about half-way up the mountain, and soon became bigger—doubling in size as it appeared a second torch was being lit.

All stared with anticipation as a third, small, shimmering light grew out of the darkness. A huge number of people began yelling and celebrating.

"They made it! They are alive and lighting their torches just as planned!" Enoch recognized his father's voice. He jumped up and down and then hoisted Sune up into the air. He was more excited than Enoch had ever seen.

Sasha threw herself into Enoch's arms. He briefly considered trying to throw her into the air like his father had done with his mother.

The yelling grew, and the celebrating continued as more tiny specks of light blossomed to life up on the mountain.

Enoch could see several of those around him trying to count the different lights. This became more difficult as the lights began to move uphill, and another round of joy erupted throughout the village. He knew they were impossibly far away but wondered nonetheless how awesome it would be if his brother could hear their celebration.

"Can you even imagine if we were there?" Sasha asked him.

"Well, no. We knew the day of Cof rest would be the easiest. That is, if you can call going farther up the mountain than anyone has ever gone before, easy. At the same time, I don't even want to think about what tonight and tomorrow might bring."

They stood in their same spots and remained mesmerized. They kept staring at the lights, but Enoch found that the harder he looked at the torches, the harder it was to tell if they were even moving. He tried to look away for a while but was unable to keep his eyes from the history changing and unfolding before him.

As the night wore on, and the torches continued their slow ascent, some villagers began to retire back to their homes. Others left but traveled toward the red glow of the palace, saying they would have to confirm the latest Kahdi rumor before trying to get some sleep. The darkness and the night continued as hope danced in all the minds of the land.

Enoch and Sasha experimented with ways to monitor the progress of the torches. They tried to close their eyes for a while and then open them to try to see if they had traveled higher; they tried to have one watch and the other look away for a time; and they tried to hold hands up before their faces to see if they could use them as marks to measure the advance of Berc, Falo, and the others.

The night felt as if it had passed the halfway point, and the remaining villagers hoped for any sign that the suns would soon gray the blackness of the eastern horizon.

It was near this time that someone gasped and any eyes that had been diverted quickly flashed back up to the mountain.

The torches had stopped climbing and seemed to grow brighter. Enoch tried to imagine a scenario in which the torches could suddenly grow brighter, but then realized they were simply moving closer to each other.

Some stayed stationary for a moment, others moved ever so slightly, but also apart from the other lights. A shiver ran from the bottom of Enoch's back to the back of his head. His heart began to race. Sasha squeezed his hand tight.

No one could talk, and no one needed to. They were all thinking the same thing—the breach party was being attacked!

The shimmering of the torches continued to become more erratic. One light darted noticeably away from the others and then…it was swallowed up by the darkness and ceased to exist.

Some of those around him averted their eyes, but Enoch could not. He stared at the chaos of lights. His hopes fell, and his anger grew as he helplessly watched.

Another small light dashed in the direction of the one that was extinguished. It grew dim or was extinguished entirely—Enoch couldn't tell.

What happened after this would be harder to recount with every retelling for years to come. From their distant vantage, the torches appeared to move together into one larger light. They stayed like this just long enough for the observers to pray that the party had weathered a Cof attack and would huddle together long enough to survive until daybreak.

At this moment, a large blinding light mushroomed from the same spot where the previous two torches had extinguished. Some in the crowd shrieked and some shielded their eyes. Though the flash persisted for just an instant, Enoch's eyes were temporarily unable to see anything except for one small circle of white.

He leaned over trying to regain his sight by looking into the dirt at his feet. He grabbed onto Sasha and asked her, "Do you know what that was?"

She knew, and so did he. The explosion of light could only mean one thing—Berc had hurled one of the charged Runal rocks and had struck a Cof! During the time that followed, Sasha and Enoch, as well as most of the rest of the crowd could not see anything but white light still flashing in their eyes.

They depended on others such as Sabri—who had been briefly distracted by Dew and Sasha-protec during the explosion—to now focus on the mountain and recite the events as she saw them.

"There was a moment where I could see no lights at all and maybe some haze that I bet would be smoke if we could see during daylight. But now there are some smaller flickers of light coming back to life and…," she paused for a moment to be sure of what she said. "I thought they might actually be moving down but they are definitely moving back up the mountain."

Sabri slowed as those around her were able to regain their vision. All were quiet at first but then gathered around Enoch when they discovered he could explain the explosion in the middle of the forest. He retold the theory—now proved to be more of a truth—of charged Runal rocks that Berc had told him.

One old codger from the back of the crowd wanted to know why they hadn't bothered to share this discovery with any of the rest of them until now. In his exhausted state, Enoch wanted to reply that he had been "just a little bit busy," but decided to let it go.

The moving torches of the breach party were visible until just after dawn. Enoch and the others continued to stare at the spot where they had been, even at the spot where he thought they might be now. But the fact was the torches were either extinguished or were just overtaken by the light of the suns. All in Verandale would have to wait until nightfall for their next possible hint of the progress of the most successful breach party ever witnessed in the land.

Sabri came over and rested her elbows on Enoch and Sasha's shoulders.

"I don't know about the two of you, but I don't think I can stay awake much longer. What do you think about getting some quick food out to the animals, then getting a morning's worth of sleep?"

Enoch was ready to whole-heartedly agree when Sasha interrupted his thoughts.

"You know we are going to have to go up to the palace and see what mischief Kahdi has gotten himself into, right?"

"Oh, no," Enoch started an animated protest, "you know that the instant we go over there, everybody is going to assume that since we are his friends, then we can be the ones responsible for him. You don't want us to be involved in another great big incident, do you? Besides, I swear I saw his parents milling around here someplace. Let's just wish them the best of luck so we can all go home and sleep peacefully on our own cots."

Sasha looked up at him and pouted out her bottom lip.

"Come on, you can't let a couple of defenseless girls go there all alone with only a couple of protecs to defend us. We need a big strong Enoch-Apprentice along as well."

Enoch looked at his sister. He thought she would have been on his side—having just mentioned sleep and all—but she simply shrugged her shoulders and looked at him.

Enoch gave in as Sasha bounced up and down and clapped, causing her protec to jump up and down and growl.

"I'm so glad you have picked the right thing to do," she boasted, while beginning to walk away from Enoch. "I'm sure we will find that Kahdi is just carving a great picture or something that will liven up that boring back wall of the palace a little. Besides, this is the only way you are going to get me to tell you the story of what happened a few days ago when a bee landed next to Kahdi's breakfast."

Enoch took one last look back up at the mountain. It looked just as it had every other day of Enoch's life, giving up no clues to the unfathomable events that were likely taking place beneath the canopy of the high forest.

He turned back to the girls and their protecs on the old road to the palace.

Respect all shadows.
—Olia

34

Kahdi was perched at the apex of the old steps carved into the back wall of the palace foyer. His clothes were soaked with a combination of sweat and saltwater spray. As was so often the case, there was chaos all around him.

He was dancing back and forth, directly above the gaping mouth of the Salt River. He swung his pickaxe in a giant arc—first striking the red wall behind him, and then twisting with the next swing to strike the steps next to his feet. Pieces of rock flew with each strike. Some were swallowed in the water rushing below him; some caused people in the astonished crowd to cower and duck; still others flew upwards to strike Kahdi himself— who seemed not to notice.

His father was yelling at him to come down immediately. Palace guards were on both ends of the river's steps trying to hatch a plan to get Kahdi down, but one was already nursing a large bruise from earlier in the morning when he had maneuvered too close and Kahdi had kicked him in the shin.

The person with the best chance of getting him down was his mother, who was holding up a piece of ham, but Kahdi ignored her also. She, and the rest of the crowd, were relegated to watching and wondering what he could possibly be up to.

"Any ideas?" Sasha asked the other two.

"I have none, but" Sabri paused to hold up a finger in the air, "I remember this one time I came across Kahdi sitting on an old stone right over there near the entrance. He was staring at the water at the river's origin. I could see him mumbling so I went and sat next to him.

"He was saying all these names, but he seemed to be saying some of them over and over. I tried to get him to explain to me what he was talking about. Of course, the conversation went nowhere."

"Kind of like this one is going now," her brother interrupted.

"No, but get this. A couple of days later, I saw his mother in the village square, so I ask her to explain this to me. Do you know what she told me?"

Enoch rolled his eyes at his sister, but neither he nor Sasha had a guess.

"She told me whenever Kahdi is thinking really hard he likes to recite the names of all the members to have served in the Legion since the year before his great aunt was born."

Enoch looked at her while he tried to sort through the many biting retorts running through his mind. He was about to respond when Sasha interrupted by tugging on his sleeve. She pointed an arm toward the back doorways that led to the library.

They looked over to see Ibrakrim marching in their

direction. He was obviously flustered, his robe and his long hair flying behind him. To their amazement, he didn't even look at the spectacle that Kahdi was creating. Instead, he stopped directly in front of them.

"Please don't ask me what he is up to." The booming voice of the librarian carried over the sounds of the river and the sound of metal striking stone. "I have no idea. What I do know is that he has created a low rumble and there is a shake in the stones back in the library. Please come with me."

And with that, he turned and ran toward the large doors on the right side of the back wall of the foyer. They ran after him, past the still pleading figure of Kahdi's mother.

As they ran through the giant doorway, Enoch thought back to the last time he had come this way—when his father had brought him here to see Ibrakrim's marks. He sprinted down the torch-lit hallway while thinking of that day that now seemed like a lifetime ago.

They reached the library and Ibrakrim hurried them past the tables and many shelves to a darkly lit back room. He was still muttering about "that beast with the axe" as he lifted some wool blankets containing the most delicate and treasured documents in the land, sandwiched in-between. He handed several layers to each of the girls, and then an even larger stack to Enoch. The librarian also grabbed all that he could, and they ran back in the direction of the foyer.

Enoch was struggling to keep his feet—obscured by the armful of documents and blankets—beneath him while running over the uneven stones of the great hallway. He slowed down long enough to feel, for the first time, the rumbles the librarian had described.

They came with sounds that were low, deep, and horrible. Enoch had never been so scared as he realized it was from the shifting of the giant stones, or even the land below.

They ran to the doors that separated the hallway from the foyer. Enoch pushed against the wood while trying to hold onto his documents. The doors didn't move until Enoch and the girls threw their shoulders against them. They wedged open only enough to let the four of them through in a harried single file. Once through the damaged doorway, Enoch heard the increased sounds of the river. All who remained in the foyer could now feel the rumbling and shaking of the palace.

People were running, carrying children, or pushing loved ones before them. All of them aiming for the palace entrance.

The mouth of the river had grown substantially in the short time since they had run back to the library. The river's mouth—along with help from Kahdi's axe—was tearing into the rock wall that made up the back of the foyer. One large crack extended from the gaping maw of the river over to the northern doors that led back to the Legion chambers. Kahdi threw the axe into the raging river and started down that side of the steps, but as he did this, the crack splintered and extended out in several directions until most of the steps below him simply fell away.

Kahdi scrambled to make the steps on the other side, leading to the doors that Enoch and the girls had just left.

Enoch ran to the palace entrance just as one complete, quarried Runal stone toppled out of the wall to his left. A smaller chunk of stone fell between him and Sasha, striking both their shoulders as they scampered to save their lives. They made it past the entrance in time to see Sabri and Dew scurry out just ahead of them.

Enoch turned as they descended from the hill upon which the palace stood. He saw the librarian back in the main entrance. He was frantically trying to pick up parchments and shreds of other ancient documents that were falling from his arms as he tried to carry them out of the collapsing palace.

Enoch yelled for him but could not be heard. He motioned for the girls to keep running down the hill without him.

"Enoch don't be stupid!" his sister screamed from behind him.

Sasha also yelled something which Enoch couldn't hear as he dodged falling debris.

He found Ibrakrim in the spray of the expanding river. He had been knocked to the ground but was still grasping at the wet papers around him.

"What are you doing? The books are lost. Save yourself!" Enoch yelled at him.

Ibrakrim struggled to gain his feet using one arm and clutching what remained of the prized possessions with the other.

Enoch could take it no more. He grabbed the back of the librarian's robes near his neck and used all his strength to drag him along the red, rupturing floors of the palace. He had gone a few paces when he felt his hands slipping. He stopped to see if he could right Ibrakrim, but a wave of water hit them and knocked them both to the ground.

Enoch struggled to get up just as his father's two large

hands grabbed him. Together they pulled Ibrakrim up, and the three of them were able to run toward the daylight just as the western spire of the palace crashed into buildings nearby.

The heaving rapids of the Salt River were now several times their normal size.

Thunderous cracks and rumbles boomed behind them as they caught up with the girls and ran. They ran to save their lives and did not chance any more looks back as the dome of the palace fell in upon itself. It was replaced by a mighty torrent of salt water that exploded from the side of the mountain, sending the native gray rock of Verandale blasting into the Salt River along with the red remains of the palace.

May your future have more life than death,
your life have more laughter than tears.
—From the Toast of Betrothal

35

Enoch and Sasha sat with their feet dangling in the waters of the Sea. They were sitting on the edge of a dock in the hottest part of the day. Enoch leaned against the wood of a large post and Sasha leaned against him. It had been three days since the destruction of the palace. Enoch figured he had had one night's worth of sleep in that time.

Runal rock was scattered along the edge of the eastern mountains and on either side of the expanse of water that dwarfed the previous size of the Salt River. The rumbling and quaking of the ground beneath them had mostly stopped by the second night after the eruption of the Salt River through the back of the palace. The sound of the water coming through the giant rent in the side of the mountain had lessened slightly, or perhaps just become more tolerable.

Enoch could not stop looking at the spot where the palace—easily the largest man-made structure ever constructed in the land—used to be. He had had little time over the last few days to see the aftereffects while he tended to the many injured.

The body of Kahdi was found floating face down in the Sea, just beyond the sands at the edge of the village square.

He was thought dead until the people retrieving him from the water felt a heartbeat. They summoned Enoch. He was able to compress the massive chest of Kahdi until water came out, and he sucked a breath back in. Kahdi remained unconscious, but his heart and lungs seemed strong after he was loaded onto a cart and delivered to his parents' house. Enoch also treated a large wound across Kahdi's forehead which, so far, had been healing without evidence of infection.

Enoch stayed by him day and night until Kahdi began to improve. He was finally persuaded to get out of the house for a few moments only when Sasha came by and joined the persistence of Kahdi's parents.

Enoch conceded on the condition that they stay within shouting distance of Kahdi's bedside. They had walked down to the dock as Sasha filled him in on the events of the days since the fall of the palace.

Two people were missing and presumed to have been caught in the palace's maze of tunnels and hallways when the building collapsed. Amazingly, everyone else was found alive. The Salt River Bridge had collapsed under the weight and force of the explosion as the torrent of the waters increased. The land behind the palace was felt to be too unstable and too forested to allow any human travel. So, the village side and the farm side of Verandale were effectively cut off from each other, though some family members had been able to yell or signal across the roar of the waters.

No one had been able to see any sign of the torches as

darkness fell on the second night of the breach attempt. Many had feared the worst until a family who lived near the school brought encouraging news.

A little girl had awakened her father in the middle of the night to trek to the refuse building. He leaned against a nearby building talking to the night guard when she came out and announced that "there was a new star out tonight."

They peered far up onto the eastern mountains and saw a faint light that appeared to be moving. It had disappeared by the time they had summoned the rest of the family, but the father had marked his footprints in the dirt and carefully noted the angle and height of the light in comparison to the side of their house. With the rise of the suns the next day, he declared that the light had disappeared because it had passed over the summit of the mountains.

Enoch and Sasha sat quietly for a moment trying to make sense of the events—or even some of the events—that had happened over the last three days.

They heard footsteps approaching the dock and looked up to see Ibrakrim. He was limping in their direction, now healing a large gash to the back of his leg.

They stood to greet him. He stared at the waters bursting out of the mountainside, surrounded by ruins.

"Our ancestors thought they were building not only the greatest structure ever, but a structure that would last forever. Little did they know the power of the old saying 'everything is temporary.'"

He paused to motion towards the remains of the palace and bridge.

"You know, they were some of the greatest builders

and hardest workers this land has ever known. Yet their great palace only lasted the blink of an eye in the great expanse of time."

Ibrakrim pointed to the barnacles on the side of the dock where the posts went into the Sea. "Look at those barnacles and tell me what this means for our future."

Both of them looked closely. Enoch thought they looked like the barnacles that had probably been there for decades, starting just a few days after the posts were forced into the shallow Sea bottom.

"I have to say, I just see barnacles attached to wood," Sasha volunteered, and Enoch quickly agreed with her.

"The two of you saved my life getting me out of the palace. It will take me a long time to repay you, but I will start today by helping with your powers of observation. The barnacles are normally found on the wood all the way up to the surface of the water. Today however, we find the water at least two fingerbreadths above the highest barnacles." Ibrakrim stopped until he saw a light in their eyes and knew they understood.

"The Sea is rising," Enoch said in an amazed whisper.

"Exactly my son, the Sea has risen a small amount every year. Now, however, there is enough water bursting forth from the side of the mountain to make the whole Sea go up this much in just three days. We will soon see a quite different land around us. It is possible the Sea will rise a significant amount. One day we may even see dolphins in the forest. Of course, this means we will have to admit that Kahdi knew his actions could bring the waters much closer to the top of the mountains where we can soon go and hopefully reunite you with your brother and the others."

Ibrakrim placed a hand on the top of each of their heads and turned them so he could look each straight in the eyes.

"I know your parents are immensely proud of the both of you, and so am I. Now don't do anything dangerous or ridiculous like you have done so many times in the past. We have a lot of work to do before we can join the others on the other side of the mountains."

Ibrakrim turned and walked off the dock, back toward the village.

Enoch and Sasha stood alone on the edge of the dock and looked out over the waves rolling along the rising Sea.

"You know," Enoch broke the silence, "I am pretty proud of me, too."

Sasha looked at him seriously at first, and then saw the familiar beginnings of a smile at the corners of his mouth. She pushed her hands into his chest.

Enoch almost lost his balance but was able to regain it long enough to kick his foot into the water and spray his giggling girlfriend.

This was too much for Sasha-protec. He lunged at Enoch, and they splashed down into the water. By the time they were done, all three were splashing in the Sea.

Enoch and Sasha were screaming and laughing. It was the first laugh they had shared in many days.

All the destruction of Verandale loomed down from above them, but here with Sasha, in this tiny spot and in this tiny moment, Enoch was happier than he ever thought possible.

Coming soon, the sequel to *Amongst*:

Dolphins in the Forest

Acknowledgements

As I puttered around, taking way too many years to write a book, I inflicted ideas, manuscript fragments, and strange drawings on scores of unsuspecting friends and family. My greatest fear (besides panel vans and being caught in the forest after dark) is that I will forget to thank someone!

With that in mind, my heartfelt thanks goes out to Jake and Judy Cain, Ginger Chase-Watkins, Chris Chittick, Michael Gonitzke, Celes Hall, Andrea Holt, Gretchen Kelley, Will Keller, Jeff and Jenny Laird, Joe Maestas, The Olsen family: Rick, Suzy, Emma, and Christian, Dana Rogge, John and Aaron Schafer, Ana and Katy Simon, Jeff Spicoli, Bytor N. Snodog, Ray and Marie Vanderleest, Rene Vecka, and Nick Watenpaugh.

Finally to my wonderful editors Joe and Jan McDaniel of BookCrafters and illustrator Julie Anne Franklin without whom *Amongst* would be just a finger-painted cover and a bunch of misspelled words!

For behind-the-scenes and other secret stuff, please visit
www.AmongstBook.com.

About the Author

Robert E. Vander Leest was born and raised in Littleton, Colorado. After almost graduating college, he navigated an atypical path through medical school. During a thirty-year career as an ER doc, working mostly nightshift, he found it essential to be able to completely get away to imaginary realms, his most favorite of which was Verandale.

He lives with his wife and kids in Colorado.

If he lived in Verandale, he would likely have zero Cof kills!